Binchy, Maeve

Silver wedding

SILVER WEDDING

SILVER
WEDDING

Maeve Binchy

Delacorte
Press

Published by
Delacorte Press
Bantam Doubleday Dell Publishing Group, Inc.
666 Fifth Avenue
New York, New York 10103

This work was first published in Great Britain by Century
Hutchinson Ltd.

Copyright © 1989 by Maeve Binchy

Designed by Richard Oriolo

Library of Congress Cataloging in Publication Data

Binchy, Maeve.
   Silver wedding / Maeve Binchy.
      p. cm.
   ISBN 0-385-29826-9
   I. Title.
PR6052.I7728S5   1989
823'.914—dc19   89-1276
                                                       CIP

Manufactured in the United States of America

First U.S.A. printing

September 1989

10 9 8 7 6 5 4 3 2 1

Fic.

For Gordon Snell,
my dear love and my best friend

Contents

SILVER WEDDING

Anna

Anna knew that he was doing his best to be interested. She could read his face so well. This was the same look she saw on his face when older actors would come up and join them in the club and tell old tales about people long gone. Joe tried to be interested then, too, it was a welcoming, courteous, earnest look. Hoping that it passed as genuine interest, hoping that the conversation wouldn't last too long.

"I'm sorry, I'm going on a bit," she apologized. She pulled a funny face at him as she sat at the other end of the bed dressed only in one of his shirts, the Sunday papers and a breakfast tray between them.

Joe smiled back, a real smile this time.

"No, it's nice that you're so worked up about it, it's good to care about families."

He meant it, she knew, in his heart he thought it was a Good Thing to care about families, like rescuing kittens from trees and beautiful sunsets and big collie dogs. In principle Joe was in favor of caring about families. But he didn't care at all about his own. He wouldn't have known how many years his parents were married. He probably didn't know how long he had been married himself. Something like a silver anniversary would not trouble Joe Ashe.

Anna looked at him with the familiar feeling of tenderness and fear. Tender and protective—he looked so lovely lying there against the big pillows, his fair hair falling over his face, his thin brown shoulders so relaxed and easy. Fearful in case she would lose him, in case he would move on gently, effortlessly, out of her life, as he had moved into it.

Joe Ashe never fought with people, he told Anna with his big boyish smile, life was much too short for fights. And it was true.

When he was passed over for a part, when he got a bad review, there was the shrug: "Well, so it could have been different but let's not make a production out of it."

Like his marriage to Janet. It was over, so why go on pretending? He just packed a small bag and left.

Anna feared that one day in this very room he would pack a small bag and leave again. She would rail and plead as Janet had done and it would be no use. Janet had even come around and offered Anna money to go away. She wept about how happy she had been with Joe. She showed pictures of the two small sons. It would all be fine again if only Anna would go away.

"But he didn't leave you to come to me, he had been in a flat by himself for a year before he even met me," Anna had explained.

"Yes, and all that time I thought he would come back."

Anna hated to remember Janet's tearstained face, and how she had made tea for her, and hated even more to think that her own face would be stained with tears like this one day, and as unexpectedly as it had all happened to Janet. She gave a little shiver as she looked at the handsome easy boy in her bed. Because even if he was twenty-eight years of age, he was still a boy. A gentle cruel boy.

"What are you thinking?" he asked.

She didn't tell him. She never told him how much she thought about him and dreaded the day he would leave.

"I was thinking it's about time they did another film version of *Romeo and Juliet.* You're so handsome it would be unfair to the world not to get a chance to look at you," she said laughingly.

He reached out and put the breakfast tray on the floor. The Sunday papers slid after it.

"Come here to me," said Joe. "My mind was running on the same lines entirely, entirely at all, 'at all' as you Irish say."

"What a superb imitation," Anna said dryly, but snuggling up to him all the same. "It's no wonder that you're the best actor in the whole wide world and renowned all over the globe for your great command of accents."

She lay in his arms and didn't tell him about how worried she was about this silver wedding. She had seen from his face that she had already been going on about it far too long.

In a million years Joe would not understand what it

meant in their family. Mother and Father's twenty-fifth anniversary. They celebrated everything in the Doyle household. There were albums of memories, boxes chronicling past celebrations. On the wall of the sitting room at home there was a gallery of Major Celebrations. The wedding day itself, the three christenings. There was Grannie O'Hagan's sixtieth birthday, there was Grandpa Doyle's visit to London with all of them standing beside a sentry outside Buckingham Palace, a solemn young sentry in a busby who seemed to realize the importance of Grandpa Doyle's visit.

There were the three first communions, and the three confirmations; there was a small sporting section, Brendan's school team the year he had been on the Seniors. There was an even smaller academic section, one graduation portrait of Anna herself, very studied and posed, holding her diploma as if it were a ton weight.

Mother and Father always joked about the wall and said it was the most valuable collection in the world. What did they want with Old Masters and famous paintings, hadn't they gotten something much more valuable, a living wall telling the world what their life was all about?

Anna had winced whenever they said that to people who came in. She winced now, lying in Joe's arms.

"Are you shuddering at me or is that passion?" he asked.

"Unbridled passion," she said, wondering, Was it normal to lie beside the most attractive man in London and think not of him but of the sitting-room wall back in the family home?

The family home would have to be decorated for the silver wedding. There would be a lot of cardboard bells and silver ribbon. There would be flowers sprayed with a silver paint. They would have a tape of "The Anniversary Waltz" on the player. There would be windowsills full of cards, there might indeed be so many that it would call for an arrangement of streamers with the cards attached as they had for Christmas. The cake would have traditional decorations, the invitations would have silver edges. Inviting people to what? That was what was buzzing around Anna's head. As a family this was something they should organize for their parents. Anna and her sister, Helen, and her brother, Brendan.

But it really meant Anna.

She would have to do it all.

Anna turned toward Joe and kissed him. She would not think about the anniversary anymore now. She would think about it tomorrow, when she was being paid to stand in a bookshop.

She wouldn't think of it at this moment when there were far better things to think about.

"That's more like it. I thought you'd gone to sleep on me," Joe Ashe said, and held her very close to him.

Anna Doyle worked in Books for People, a small bookshop much patronized by authors and publishers and all kinds of media. They never tired of saying that this was a bookshop with character, not like the big chains which were utterly without soul. Secretly Anna did not altogether agree.

Too many times during her working day she had to refuse people who came in with perfectly normal requests for the latest best-seller, for a train timetable, for a book on freezer cookery. Always she had to direct them to a different shop. Anna felt that a bookshop worthy of the name should in fact stock such things instead of relying for its custom on a heavy psychology section, a detailed travel list, and poetry, sociology, and contemporary satire.

It wasn't as if they were even proper specialists. She had intended to leave a year ago, but that was just when she met

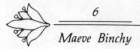

Joe. And when Joe had come to stay, it happened to coincide with Joe not having any work.

Joe did a little here and there, and he was never broke. There was always enough to buy Anna a lovely Indian scarf, or a beautiful paper flower, or find the most glorious wild mushrooms in a Soho delicatessen.

There was never any money for paying the rent or for the television, or the phone or the electricity. It would have been foolish of Anna to have left a steady job without having a better one lined up for herself. She stayed in Books for People, even though she hated the name, believing that most of the buyers of books *were* people anyway. The others who worked there were all perfectly pleasant, she never saw any of them outside work but there were occasional book signings, poetry evenings, and even a wine and cheese evening in aid of a small nearby theater. That was when she had met Joe Ashe.

Anna was at work early on Monday morning. If she wanted time to think or to write letters, then to be in before the others was the only hope. There were only four of them who worked there; they each had a key. She switched off the burglar alarm, picked up the carton of milk and the mail from the mat. It was all circulars and handbills. The postman had not arrived yet. As Anna put on the electric kettle to make coffee, she caught sight of herself in the small mirror that was stuck to the wall. Her eyes looked large and anxious, she thought. Anna stroked her face thoughtfully. She looked pale and there were definitely shadows under the big brown eyes. Her hair was tied up with a bright pink ribbon matching exactly her pink T-shirt. She must put on a little makeup, she thought, or she would frighten the others.

She wished she had gone ahead and gotten her hair cut that time. It had been so strange, she had made an appointment in a posh place where some of the Royal Family went to have their hair done. One of the girls who worked there as a stylist came into the bookshop and they had started talking. The girl said she would give Anna a discount. But the night she met Joe at the benefit evening for the theater, he had told her that her thick dark hair was beautiful the way it was.

He had asked her, as he so often did still, "What are you thinking?" And in those very early times she told him the truth. That she was thinking about having her hair cut the following day.

"Don't even consider it," Joe had said, and then suggested that they go to have a Greek meal and discuss this thing properly.

They had sat together in the warm spring night and he had told her about his acting and she had told him about her family. How she lived in a flat because she had thought she was becoming too dependent on her family, too drawn into everything they did. She went home, of course, on Sundays and one other evening in the week. Joe had looked at her, enthralled. He had never known a life where adults kept going back to the nest.

In days she was visiting his flat, days later he was visiting hers because it was more comfortable. He told Anna briefly and matter-of-factly about Janet and the two little boys. Anna told Joe about the college lecturer she had loved rather unwisely during her final years, resulting in a third-class degree and in a great sense of loss.

Joe was surprised that she had told him about the college lecturer. There was no hassle about shared property, shared children. He had only told her about Janet because he was still married to her. Anna had wanted to tell everything, Joe hadn't really wanted to hear.

It was only logical that he should come to live with her. He didn't suggest it, and for a while she wondered what she

would say if she were invited to take up residence in his flat. It would be so hard to tell Mother and Father. But after one long lovely weekend, she decided to ask Joe if he would move in properly to her small ground-floor flat in Shepherd's Bush.

"Well, I will, if that's what you'd like," Joe had said, pleased but not surprised, willing but not overly grateful. He had gone back to his own place, done a deal about the rent, and with two tote bags and a leather jacket over his arm he had come to live with Anna Doyle.

Anna Doyle, who had to keep his arrival very secret indeed from her mother and father, who lived in Pinner and in a world where daughters did not let married men come to spend an evening, let alone a lifetime.

He had been with her since that April Monday a year ago. And now it was May 1985, and by a series of complicated maneuvers Anna had managed to keep the worlds of Pinner and Shepherd's Bush satisfactorily apart while flitting from one to the other with an ever-increasing sense of guilt.

Joe's mother was fifty-six but looked years younger. She worked at the food counter of a bar where lots of actors gathered, and they saw her maybe two or three times a week. She was vague and friendly, giving them a wave as if they were just good customers. She hadn't known for about six months that they lived together. Joe simply hadn't bothered to tell her. When she heard, she said, "That's nice, dear," to Anna in exactly the same tone as she would have spoken to a total stranger who had asked for a slice of the veal and ham pie.

Anna had wanted her to come around to the flat.

"What for?" Joe had asked in honest surprise.

Next time she was in the pub, Anna went to the counter and asked Joe's mother herself.

"Would you like to come around and see us in the flat?"

"What for?" she had asked with interest.

Anna was determined. "I don't know, a drink maybe."

"Lord, dear, I never drink, seen enough of it in this place to turn you right against it, I tell you."

"Well, just to see your son," Anna went on.

"I see him in here, don't I? He's a grown-up now, love, he doesn't want to be looking at his old mum, day in day out."

Anna had watched them since with a fascination that was half horror and half envy. They were just two people who lived in the same city and who made easy casual conversation when they met.

They never talked of other members of the family. Nothing about Joe's sister, who had been in a rehabilitation center on account of drugs; or the eldest brother, who was a mercenary soldier of some sort in Africa; or the youngest brother, who worked in television as a cameraman.

She never asked about her grandchildren. Joe had told Anna that Janet did take them to see her sometimes, and occasionally he had taken the boys to a park nearby where his mother lived, and she had come along for a little while. He never took them to her home.

"I think she has a bloke there, a young fellow, she doesn't want a lot of grandchildren trailing around after her." To Joe it was simple and clear.

To Anna it was like something from another planet.

In Pinner, if there were grandchildren, they would have been the central pivot of the home, as the children had been for nearly a quarter of a century. Anna sighed again as she thought of the celebrations that lay ahead and how she would have to face up to them, as she had to face up to so many things on her own.

It was no use sitting in an empty bookshop with a coffee and a grievance that Joe wasn't as other men, supportive and willing to share these kinds of things with her. She had

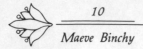

known there would be nothing like that from the first evening together.

What she had to do now was work out how the silver wedding could be organized in October in a way that wouldn't drive everyone mad.

Helen would be no use, that was for certain. She would send an illuminated card signed by all the sisters, she would invite Mother and Father to a special folk Mass with the community, she would get the day off and come out to Pinner in her drab gray sweater and skirt, her hair dull and lifeless and the big cross on a chain around her neck constantly in her hand. Helen didn't even look like a nun, she looked like someone a bit dopey and badly dressed retreating behind the big crucifix. And in many ways that's what she was. Helen would turn up, all right, if everything was organized, and in her canvas bag she would take back any uneaten food because one nun loved gingerbread and another had a weakness for anything with salmon in it.

With a sense of despair Anna could see months ahead into the future, with her younger sister Helen a member of a religious community in South London, picking her way through the food like a scavenger and filling a tin of biscuits with foil-wrapped tidbits.

But at least Helen would be there. Would Brendan come at all? That was the real worry, and the one she had been trying to avoid thinking about. If Brendan Doyle did not get the train and boat and then the train again and make it to Pinner for his parents' twenty-fifth wedding anniversary, they might as well call the whole thing off now. The disgrace would never be disguised, the emptiness would never be forgotten.

An incomplete family picture on the wall.

They would probably lie and say that he was in Ireland

and couldn't be spared from the farm, the harvest, or the shearing or whatever people did on farms in October.

But Anna knew with sickening clarity that it would be a paper-thin excuse. The best man and the maid of honor would know there had been a coldness, and the neighbors would know, and the priests would know.

And the shine would be taken off the silver.

How to get him back, that was the problem. Or was it? What to get him back for? Perhaps that was a bigger problem.

Brendan had always been so quiet when he was a school-boy. Who would have known that he felt this strange longing to go away from the family to such a remote place? Anna had been so shocked the day he told them. Utterly straightforward and with no care about what it would do to the rest of the family.

"I'm not going back to school in September, it's no use trying to persuade me. I'll never get any exams, and I don't need them. I'm going to Vincent. In Ireland. I'll go as soon as I can leave."

They had railed and beseeched. With no success. This is what he was going to do.

"But why are you doing this to us?" Mother had cried.

"I'm not doing anything to you." Brendan had been mild. "I'm doing it for me, it's not going to cost you any money. It's the farm where Father grew up, I thought you'd be pleased."

"Don't think he'll turn the farm over to you automati-cally," Father had spluttered. "That old recluse could just as well leave it to the missions. You could easily find you've put in all that hard work for nothing."

"Father, I'm not thinking of inheritances and wills and people dying, I'm thinking of how I'd like to spend my days. I was happy there, and Vincent could do with another pair of hands."

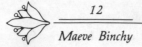

"Well, if he does, isn't it a wonder that he never married and provided himself with a few pairs of hands of his own around the place without asking strangers in to him?"

"Hardly a stranger, Father," Brendan had said. "I am his own flesh and blood, his brother's child."

It had been a nightmare.

And the communication since had been minimal, cards at Christmas and on birthdays. Perhaps anniversaries. Anna couldn't remember. Anniversaries. How was she going to assemble the cast for this one?

The maid of honor, as they always called her, was Maureen Barry. She was Mother's best friend. They had been at school together back in Ireland. Maureen had never married; she was the same age as Mother, forty-six, though she looked younger. She had two dress shops in Dublin—she refused to call them boutiques. Perhaps Anna could talk to Maureen and see what would be best. But a warning bell went off loudly in her head. Mother was a great one for not letting things go outside the family.

There had always been secrets from Maureen.

Like the time that Father had lost his job. It couldn't be told.

Like the time that Helen ran away when she was fourteen. That was never breathed to Maureen. Mother had said that nothing mattered in the end, everything could be sorted out just so long as family matters weren't aired abroad, and neighbors and friends weren't told all of the Doyle business. It seemed to be a very effective and soothing cure when things went wrong, so the family had always stuck to it.

You would think that Anna should phone Maureen Barry now and ask her as Mother's oldest friend what was best to do about Brendan and about the anniversary in general.

But Mother would curl up and die if she thought there

was the remotest possibility of any member of the family revealing a secret outside it. And the coldness with Brendan was a big secret.

There were no family members who could be asked to act as intermediaries.

So what kind of party? The day was a Saturday, it could be a lunch. There were a lot of hotels around Pinner, Harrow, Northwood, and restaurants and places used to doing functions like this. Perhaps a hotel would be best.

It would be formal, for one thing. The banqueting manager would advise about toasts and cakes and photographs.

There wouldn't have to be weeks of intensive cleaning of the family home and manicuring the front garden.

But a lifetime as the eldest of the Doyles had taught Anna that a hotel would not be right. There were all those dismissive remarks about hotels in the past, destructive and critical remarks about this family, which couldn't be bothered having the thing in their own home, or the other family, which would be quite glad to invite you to a common hotel, an impersonal place, but wouldn't let you over their own doorstep, thank you very much.

It would have to be home, the invitation would have to say in silver lettering that the guest was being invited to Salthill, 26 Rosemary Drive, Pinner. Salthill had been a seaside resort over in the West of Ireland where Mother and Maureen Barry used to go when they were young, it had been lovely, they said. Father had never been there, he said there was little time for long family holidays when he was a boy making his way in Ireland.

Wearily Anna made the list; it would be this size if there wasn't an Irish contingent, and that size if there were. It could be this size if there was to be a sit-down meal, that size if it

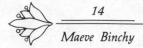

were a buffet. This size if it were just drinks and snacks, that size if it were a proper meal.

And who would pay for it?

Very often the children did, she knew that.

But Helen had taken a vow of poverty and had nothing. Brendan, even if he did come, which wasn't likely, was working for an agricultural worker's wages. Anna had very little money to spend on such a party.

She had very little money indeed. By dint of hard saving, no lunches, and a few wise buys at Oxfam, she had saved £132. It was in the building society hoping to become £200, and then, when Joe had £200, they were going to Greece together. Joe had £11 at the moment, so he had a longer way to go. But he was sure to get a part soon. His agent had said there were a lot of things coming up. He'd be working any day now.

Anna hoped that he would, she really and truly did.

If he got something good, something where they recognized him properly, something steady, then everything else could fall into place. Not just the Greek holiday but everything. He could arrange a settlement for his sons, give Janet something that would make her feel independent, begin the divorce proceedings. Then Anna could risk leaving Books for People and go to a bigger shop; she would easily get promotion in a large bookshop, a graduate, experienced in the trade already. They would love her.

The time had gone by in thought, and soon the keys were turning in the door and the others arriving. Soon the door was open to the public. Planning was over yet again.

At lunchtime Anna made up her mind that she would go out to Pinner that evening and ask her parents straight out how they would like to celebrate the day. It seemed less celebratory than telling them that it was all in hand. But to try to do that was nonsense, really, and she could still get it wrong. She would ask them straight out.

She phoned them to say she would be coming over. Her mother was pleased.

"That's good, Anna, we haven't seen you for ages and ages. I was just saying to Daddy I hope Anna's all right and there's nothing wrong."

Anna gritted her teeth.

"Why would there be anything wrong?"

"Well, it's just been so long, and we don't know what you do."

"Mother, it's been eight days. I was with you last week-end."

"Yes, but we don't know how you are getting on. . . ."

"I ring you almost every day, you *know* how I'm getting on and what I do, get up in Shepherd's Bush and get the tube in here, and then I go home again. That is what I do, Mother, like a great many million people in London do." Her voice rose in rage at her mother's attitude.

The reply was surprisingly mild. "Why are you shouting at me, Anna, my dear child? I only said I was delighted you were coming over this evening, your father will be overjoyed. Will we have a little steak and mushrooms? That's what we'll have as a celebration to welcome you back. Yes, I'll run down to the butcher's this afternoon, and get it. . . . That's simply great you're going to come back. I can't wait to tell your father, I'll give him a ring at work now and tell him."

"Don't . . . Mother, just . . . well, I mean . . ."

"Of course I'll tell him, give him pleasure, something to look forward to."

When she hung up, Anna stood motionless, hand on the receiver, and thought about the one time she had brought Joe to lunch at Salthill, 26 Rosemary Drive. She had invited him

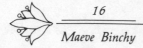

as "a friend" and had spent the entire journey making him promise not to reveal that he was (a) living with her and (b) married to someone else.

"Which is the more dangerous one to let slip?" Joe had asked, grinning.

"They're both equally dangerous," she had said with such seriousness that he had leaned over and kissed her on the nose in the train in front of everyone.

It had been all right as a visit, Anna had thought. Mother and Father had inquired politely about Joe's acting career and whether he knew famous actors and actresses.

In the kitchen Mother had asked if he was Anna's boyfriend.

"Just a friend," Anna had insisted.

On the way home she asked Joe what he had made of them.

"Very nice but very tense people," he had said.

Tense? Mother and Father. She had never thought of them as tense. But in a way it was true.

And Joe didn't know what they were like when there was no outsider there, Mother wondering why Helen hadn't been there on two occasions during the week when they had telephoned her convent. Father striding around the garden snapping the heads off flowers and saying that boy was so restless and idle that he could only end up with the job of village idiot sucking straws on a small farm, it was hard to know why he had to go back to the one village in Ireland where they were known, and live with the one man in Ireland who could be guaranteed to give the worst impression of the Doyles and all their activities, his own brother, Brendan's Uncle Vincent. Just to inherit that miserable farm.

Joe had seen none of this side of things and yet he still thought her parents tense.

She had pursued it. Why? How did it show itself?

But Joe didn't want to be drawn.

"It's like this," he had said to her, smiling to take any hurt out of his words. "Some people just live that kind of life where this can be said and that can't be said, and people think what can be told and what can't. It's a way of going on where everything is a pretense, an act. . . . Now that doesn't bother me if people want to live like that. It's not my way, but people make up a lot of rules and live by them. . . ."

"We're not like that!" She was stung.

"I'm not criticizing you, my love. I'm just telling you what I see. . . . I see Hare Krishnas shaving their heads and dancing and waving bells. I see you and your family acting things out just like they do. I don't let the Hare Krishnas get up my nose, I won't let your old man and old lady either. Right?" He had grinned at her winningly.

She had grinned back with a hollow empty feeling inside her and resolved not to go on about home anymore.

The day came to an end. One of the nicer publishing reps was there as the shop closed. He asked her to come and have a drink.

"I'm going to darkest Pinner," Anna said. "I'd better set out now."

"I'm driving that way, why don't we have a drink en route?" he said.

"Nobody's driving to Pinner." She laughed.

"Oh, how do you know I don't have a mistress out that way, or am hoping to acquire one?" he teased.

"We wouldn't discuss such things in Rosemary Drive," Anna said, mock primly.

"Come on, get in, the car's on a double yellow line." He laughed.

He was Ken Green, she had talked to him a lot at the

bookshop. They had both started work the same day, it had been a common bond.

He was going to leave his company and join a bigger one, so was she; neither of them had done it.

"Do you think we're just cowards?" she asked him as he negotiated the rush-hour traffic.

"No, there are always reasons. What's holding you back, these moral folk in Rosemary Drive?"

"How do you know they're moral folk?" she said, surprised.

"You just told me there'd be no talk of mistresses in your house," Ken said.

"Too true, they'd be very disappointed to know that I was one myself," Anna said.

"So would I." Ken seemed serious.

"Oh, stop that." She laughed at him. "It's always easy to pay compliments to someone you know is tied up, much safer. If I told you I was free and on the rampage, you'd run a hundred miles from me instead of offering me a drink."

"Absolutely wrong. I especially left your bookshop for last. I was thinking all day how nice it would be to see you. Don't you accuse me of being fainthearted."

She patted his knee companionably. "No. I misjudged you." She sighed deeply. It was easy to talk to Ken, she didn't have to watch what she said. Like she would when she got to Salthill in Rosemary Drive. Like she would when she got back to Joe later on.

"Was that a sigh of pleasure?" he asked.

With Joe or with Mother or Father she would have said yes.

"Weariness. I get tired of all the lies," she said. "Very tired."

"But you're a big girl now. Surely you don't have to tell lies about your life and the way you live it."

Anna nodded her head glumly. "I do, truly I do."

"Maybe you only think you do."

"No, I do. Like the telephone. I've told them at home that my phone has been taken out, so that they won't ring me. That's because there's a message on the answering machine saying, 'This is Joe Ashe's number.' He has to have it, you see, because he's an actor and they can't be out of touch."

"Of course," Ken said.

"So naturally I don't want my mother ringing and hearing a man's voice. And I don't want my father asking what's this young man doing in *my* flat."

"True, he might well ask that, and why he didn't have a machine of his own and number of his own," Ken said sternly.

"So I have to be careful about not mentioning things like paying the phone bill. I have to remember I'm not meant to *be* on the phone. That's just one of the nine million lies."

"Well, is it all right at the other end of the line? I mean, you don't have to lie to this actor chap?" Ken seemed anxious to know.

"Lie? No, not at all, what would I have to lie about?"

"I don't know, you said all the lies you had to tell everywhere. I thought maybe he was a jealous macho fellow, you couldn't tell him you went for a drink with me. That's if we ever get anywhere near a drink." Ken looked ruefully at the taillights.

"Oh, no, you don't understand. Joe would be glad to think I went for a drink with a friend. It's just . . ." Her voice trailed away. What was it just? It was just that there was an endless, utterly endless need to pretend. Pretend she was having a good time in the odd place where they went. Pretend she

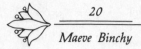

understood this casual relationship with his mother, his wife, his children. Pretend she liked these fringe theaters where he played small parts. Pretend she enjoyed lovemaking every time. Pretend she didn't care about this heavy family business ahead of her.

"I don't lie to Joe," she said, as if she were speaking to herself. "I just act a bit."

There was a silence in the car.

"Well, he *is* an actor, I suppose," Ken said, trying to revive the conversation a little.

That wasn't it. The actor didn't act at all, he never pretended to please anyone else. It was the actor's girlfriend who did all the acting. How odd that she had never thought of it that way before.

They sat and talked easily when they eventually found a pub.

"Do you want to ring your people to say you've been delayed?" Ken suggested.

She looked at him, surprised that he should be so thoughtful.

"Well, if they've bought steak and everything . . ." he said.

Mother was touched. "That was nice of you, dear. Father was beginning to look out for you. He said he'd walk down to the station."

"No, I'm getting a lift."

"Is it that Joe? Joe Ashe, the actor?"

"No, no, Mother, Ken Green, a friend from work."

"I don't think I got enough steak. . . ."

"He's not coming to supper, he's just driving me there."

"Well, ask him in, won't you? We love to meet your friends. Your father and I often wish you brought friends back here more often. That all of you did over the years." Her voice sounded wistful, as if she were looking at her wall of pictures and not getting a proper charge from them.

"I'll ask him in for a moment then," Anna said.

"Could you bear it?" she asked Ken.

"I'd like it. I can be a beard."

"What on earth is that?"

"Don't you read your gossip magazines? It's someone who distracts attention from your real love. If they get to meet upright fellows like me, they won't get the wind of evil, sensual actor lovers who have their answering machines tied to your phone."

"Oh, shut up!" She laughed. It was easy laughter, not forced.

They had another drink. She told Ken Green about the anniversary. She told him briefly that her sister was a nun, her brother had dropped out and gone to work on the farm of her father's eldest brother, Vincent, a small run-down place on Ireland's west coast. Feeling a little lighter and easier already, she told him that this was why she was having supper with her parents. For the first time in a long while she was going to come right out in the open, ask them what they wanted, tell them the limitations. Explain the problems.

"Don't go too heavily on the limitations and problems, if they're like you say. Dwell more on the celebratory side," he advised.

"Did your parents have a silver wedding?"

"Two years ago," Ken said.

"Was it great?" she asked.

"Not really."

"Oh."

"When I know you better, I'll tell you all about it," he said.

"I thought we knew each other well now." Anna was disappointed.

"No. I need more than one drink to tell the details of my whole life."

Anna felt unreasonably annoyed that she had told him all about Joe Ashe and about how he had to be kept a secret at home.

"I think I talk too much," she said contritely.

"No, you're just a nicer person. I'm rather buttoned up," Ken said. "Come on, drink that back and we'll head for the Saltmines."

"The what?"

"Isn't that what you said your house was called?"

Anna laughed and hit him with her handbag. He made her feel normal again. The way she had felt a long time ago when it was great to be part of the Doyle family, instead of walking through a mine field, which is what it was like these days.

Mother was waiting on the step.

"I came out in case you had any difficulty parking," she explained.

"Thanks, but it seemed to be quite clear . . . we were lucky." Ken spoke easily.

"We haven't heard much about you, so this is a nice surprise." Her mother's eyes were bright, too bright.

"Yes, it's a surprise for me too. I don't know Anna very well, we just talk when I go to the bookshop. I invited her for a drink this evening, and as it was one of her evenings for coming to Pinner, it seemed like a good chance of a drive and a chat."

Ken Green was a salesman, Anna remembered. He earned

his living selling books, getting bigger orders than booksellers wanted to give, forcing them to do window displays, encouraging them to take large cardboard presentation packs. Naturally he would be able to sell himself as well.

Her father liked him too.

Ken managed to ask the right questions, not the wrong ones. He asked easily what line of business Mr. Doyle was in. Her father's usual mulish, defensive look came on his face. His voice took on the familiar pitch he had when he spoke of work and rationalization.

Most people shuffled and sort of sympathized, mixed with coaxing Desmond Doyle along when he began the tale of woe, the company that had been going along very nicely thank you until in the cause of rationalization a lot of jobs, perfectly sound secure jobs, went. Desmond Doyle's job had gotten changed, he told Ken Green. Changed utterly. It wasn't the same breed of men in business these days.

Anna felt weary. It was always the same, Father's version of the story. The truth was that Father had been sacked over what Mother called a personality conflict. But it was a secret. A great secret nobody was to know. At school it was never to be mentioned. Anna's first great habits of secrecy must have begun then, she realized. Perhaps that was when the secrecy all began. Because a year later Father was employed again by the same firm. And that was never explained either.

Ken Green didn't mutter agreement about the world in general and the ways of businessmen in particular.

"How did you manage to survive the rationalization? Were you in some essential job?"

Anna's hand flew to her mouth. No one had been as direct as this before in this household. Anna's mother looked with alarmed glances from one face to another. There was a short pause.

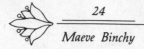

"I didn't survive it, as it happens," Desmond Doyle said. "I was out for a year. But they brought me back, when there was a change of personnel along the line, when some personality differences had been ironed out."

Anna's hand remained at her mouth. This was the first time that Father had *ever* acknowledged that he had been a year unemployed. She was almost afraid to see how her mother had taken it.

Ken was nodding in agreement. "That often happens. It's something like putting all the pieces into a paper bag and shaking a few of them back on to the board. Though the pieces aren't always put back in the right holes?" He smiled encouragingly.

Anna looked at Ken Green as if she had never seen him before. What was he doing, sitting in this room, interrogating her father about forbidden subjects? Was there the remotest possibility that Mother and Father would think she had discussed private business with him?

Mercifully Father hadn't taken it at all badly; he was busy explaining to Ken that people had indeed been relocated into the wrong positions. He himself, who should have been Operations Manager, was in fact Special Projects. Special Projects meant as little or as much as anyone wanted it to mean. It was a non-job.

"Still, that leaves it up to you to make what you will of it, that's the thing with non-jobs. I have one, Anna has one, and we try in our different ways to make something of them."

"I do *not* have a non-job!" Anna cried.

"It could be called that, couldn't it? There's no real ceiling, no proper ranking or way of getting recognition. You make it a good job because you're interested in publishing, you read the catalogs, you understand why books appear and

who buys them. You could stand filing your nails like that
colleague of yours with the purple hair."

Anna's mother giggled nervously.

"Of course you're right. When you're young, Ken, people
have chances to make something of their job, but not when
they're old. . . ."

"So you were all right, then." Ken was bland.

"Come now, don't be flattering me. . . ."

"I wasn't." Ken's face showed that nothing was further
from his intentions. "But you can't be more than forty-six,
can you, forty-six or forty-seven?"

Anna fumed at her own stupidity, inviting this lout
home.

"That's right, forty-seven next birthday," Father was
saying.

"Well, that's never old, is it? Not *old* like fifty-eight or
sixty-two."

"Deirdre, can we make that steak stretch to four pieces?
This young fellow's doing me good, he has to stay for supper."

Anna's face burned. If he said yes, she would never forgive him.

"No, thank you, Mr. Doyle. No, I mean it, Mrs. Doyle.
I'm sure it would be lovely but not tonight. Thanks again. I'll
just finish my drink and let you get on with your evening."

"But it would be no trouble and we'd like to—"

"Not tonight. Anna wants to talk to you, I know."

"Well, I'm sure if it's anything . . ." Anna's mother
looked wildly from her daughter to this personable young
man with the dark hair and dark brown eyes. Surely Anna
couldn't have come home with some announcement about
him. Was the message written in her face . . . ?

Ken put her out of her misery. "No, it has nothing to do

with me. It's a family thing. She wants to talk about your silver wedding anniversary and how you're going to celebrate it."

Desmond Doyle was disappointed that Ken was definitely leaving. "Oh, that's not for months," he said.

"Anyway, whenever it is, the main thing is that you discuss it and do what you both want, and I know that's what Anna came home to talk to you about, so I'll leave you to it."

He was gone. There had been handshakes all around and a quick grip of Anna's arm with his other hand.

They watched him pull out into the road, and he tooted his horn very gently, just an acknowledgment.

The three Doyles stood almost wordlessly on the doorstep of Salthill, 26 Rosemary Drive.

Anna faced them. "I just told him casually that we were going to make plans, I don't know why he made such a big thing out of it."

She got the feeling that neither of her parents was listening to her.

"That wasn't the only reason I came back. I came, anyway, to see you both."

Still a silence.

"And I know you won't believe it, but I just said that to him because . . . well, because I had to say something."

"He's a very pleasant young man," Desmond Doyle said.

"Good-looking, too. Smartly turned out," Deirdre Doyle added.

A wave of resentment washed over Anna. They were already comparing him favorably with Joe Ashe, Joe whom she loved with her body and soul.

"Yes," she said in a dull voice.

"You haven't talked much about him before," her mother said.

"I know, Mother, so you told him two seconds after you met him."

"Don't be insolent to your mother," Desmond Doyle said automatically.

"I'm twenty-three years of age, for chrissake. I'm not insolent like a child," Anna stormed.

"I can't think what you're so upset about," her mother said. "We have a lovely supper for you, we ask a civil question, pass a remark about how nice your friend is, and get our heads bitten off."

"I'm sorry." This was the old Anna.

"Well, that's all right, you're tired after a long day. Maybe the little drinks on top of all that driving didn't agree with you."

Anna clenched her fists silently.

They had walked back into the house and stood, an uneasy threesome, in the sitting room. They were beside the wall of family pictures.

"So what do you think we should do, eat now?" Mother looked from one to the other helplessly.

"Your mother went down to the shops especially when she heard you were coming tonight," Father said.

For a mad moment she wished that Ken Green hadn't left after all, that he was here to drive a wedge through this woolly mass of conversation, this circular kind of talk that went nowhere. It just rose and fell, causing guilt, creating tension, and then was finally patted down.

If Ken were still here, he might have said, "Let's leave the meal for half an hour and talk about what you would really like to do for your anniversary." Yes, those had been his very words. He hadn't said anything about what should be done or what might be expected, or what was the right way to go about it. He had said as he was leaving that Anna would want

to talk to her parents about what they would both like for this day.

Like. That was a breakthrough in this family.

On an impulse she used exactly the words she thought Ken Green would say.

Startled, they sat down and looked at her expectantly.

"It's your day, it's not ours. What would *you* like best?"

"Well, really . . ." her mother began, at a loss. "Well, it's not up to us."

"If you all want to mark it, that would be very gratifying, of course . . ." her father said.

Anna looked at them in disbelief. Did they really think that it wasn't up to them? Could they possibly live in a wonderland where they thought that life was a matter of all their children deciding to mark the occasion together? Did they not realize that in this family everything was acting . . . and that one by one the actors were slipping off the stage—Helen to her convent, Brendan to his remote rocky farm in the West of Ireland. Only Anna, who lived two rail journeys away, was even remotely around.

A great wave of despair came over her. She knew she must not lose her temper, that the whole visit would have been useless if it ended in a row. She could hear Joe asking her mildly why on earth she took such long, wearying journeys if it only ended up making them all tense and unhappy.

Joe had life worked out all right.

She felt an ache, a physical ache to be with him and to sit on the floor by his chair while he stroked her hair.

She hadn't known it was possible to love somebody so intensely, and as she looked at the troubled man and woman sitting obediently on the sofa in front of her, she wondered if they had ever known any fraction of this kind of love. You never could think of your parents expressing love, it was gross beyond imagining to think of them coupling and loving like real people did . . . like she and Joe did. But Anna knew that everyone felt that about parents.

"Listen," she said, "I have to make a phone call. I want you to stop worrying about dinner for a moment, and just talk to each other about what you'd really like, then I'll start organizing it. Right?" Her eyes felt suspiciously bright. Maybe the little drinks *hadn't* agreed with her.

She went to the phone. She would find an excuse to talk to Joe, nothing heavy; just to hear his voice would make her feel fine again. She would tell him that she'd be home a little earlier than she thought, would she get Chinese take-out or a pizza or just some ice cream? She wouldn't tell him now or later how bleakly depressing her old home was, how sad and low her parents made her feel, how frustrated and furious. Joe Ashe wanted to hear none of this.

She dialed her own number.

The phone was answered immediately; he must have been in the bedroom. It was a girl's voice.

Anna held the phone away from her ear like people often do in movies to show disbelief and confusion. She was aware she was doing this.

"Hello?" the girl said again.

"What number is that?" Anna asked.

"Hang on, the phone's on the floor, I can't read it. Wait a sec." The girl sounded good-natured. And young.

Anna stood there paralyzed. In the flat in Shepherd's Bush, the phone was indeed on the floor. To answer it you had to lean out of bed.

She didn't want the girl to struggle anymore; she knew the number.

"Is Joe there?" she asked. "Joe Ashe?"

"No, sorry, he went out for cigarettes, he'll be back in a few minutes."

Why hadn't he put the answering machine on? Anna asked herself. *Why* had he not automatically turned the switch, like he did always when leaving the flat? In case his agent rang. In case the call that would mean recognition came. Now the call that meant discovery had come instead.

She leaned against the wall of the house where she had grown up. She needed something to give her support.

The girl didn't like silences. "Are you still there? Do you want to ring him back or is he to ring you or what?"

"Um . . . I'm not sure." Anna fought for time.

If she got off the phone now, he would never know that she had found out. Things would be the same as they were; nothing would have changed. Suppose she said wrong number, or it doesn't matter, or I'll call again. The girl would shrug, hang up, and maybe might not even mention to Joe that someone had called and rung off. Anna would never ask, she wouldn't disturb what they had.

But what had they? They had a man who would bring a girl to her bed, to *her* bed, as soon as she was out of the house. Why try to preserve that? Because she loved him, and if she didn't preserve it, there would be a big screaming emptiness and she would miss him so much that she would die.

Suppose she said she'd hold on, and then confronted him? Would he be contrite? Would he explain that it was a fellow actress and they were just learning their lines?

Or would he say it was over? And then the emptiness and ache would begin.

The girl was anxious not to lose the call in case it might be a job for Joe.

"Hang on, I'll write down your name if you like, won't be a jiff, just let me get up, should be up anyway. . . . Let's see, there's some kind of a desk over here by the window. No, it's a dressing table . . . but there's an eyebrow pencil or something. Right, what's the name?"

Anna felt the bitter bile in her throat. In her bed, lying under the beautiful expensive bedspread she had bought last Christmas, was a naked girl who was now going to carry the phone across to the simple table where Anna's makeup stood.

"Does the phone stretch all right?" Anna heard herself asking.

The girl laughed. "Yes, it does, actually."

"Good. Well, put it down for a moment on the chair, the pink chair, and reach up onto the mantelpiece, good, and you'll find a spiral-backed pad with a pencil attached by a string."

"Hey?" The girl was surprised but not uneasy.

Anna continued. "Good, put back the eye pencil, it's kohl anyway, it wouldn't write well. Now just put down for Joe: 'Anna rang. Anna Doyle. No message.' "

"Sure he can't ring you back?" A hint of anxiety had crept into the voice of yet another woman who was going to spend weeks, months, even years of her life trying to please Joe Ashe, say the right thing, not risk losing him.

"No, no, I'm with my parents at the moment. In fact, I'll be staying here the night. Could you tell him that?"

"Does he know where to find you?"

"Yes, but there's no need to ring me. I'll catch up on him another time."

When she had hung up, she stood holding on to the table for support. She remembered telling them that the hall was the very worst place to have a telephone. It was cold, it was too public, it was uncomfortable. Now she blessed them for having taken no notice of her.

She stood for a few moments, but her thoughts would

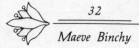

not be gathered, they ran and scurried like mice around in her head. Finally, when she thought she had at least recovered the power of speech, she went back into the room where her mother and father sat. They who had never known the kind of love she knew or the kind of hurt. She said that if it wouldn't put them out, she'd like to stay the night, then they'd have all the time in the world to discuss the plans.

"You don't have to ask can you stay the night in your own home," her mother said, pleased and fussing. "I'll put a hot-water bottle in the bed just in case, the rooms are all there for you, not that any of you ever come and stay in them."

"Well, I'd love to tonight." Anna's smile was nailed firmly on her face.

They had gotten to the actual numbers that should be invited when Joe rang. She went to the phone calmly.

"She's gone," he said.

"Has she?" Her voice was detached.

"Yes. It wasn't important."

"No. No."

"No need for you to stay over and make a big scene and meaning-of-life confrontation."

"Oh, no, none of that."

He was nonplussed.

"So what are you going to do?" he asked.

"Stay here, as I told your friend."

"But not forever?"

"Of course not, just tonight."

"Then tomorrow night after work . . . you'll be home?"

"Yes, indeed, and you'll be packed."

"Anna, don't be so dramatic."

"Absolutely not, calmness itself. Stay there tonight, of course. No, for heaven's sake there's no need to go immediately. Just tomorrow evening. Right?"

"Stop this, Anna, I love you, you love me, I'm not lying to you."

"And neither am I to you, Joe, about tomorrow night. Truly."

She hung up.

When he called back ten minutes later, she answered the phone herself.

"Please don't be tiresome, Joe. That's a great word of yours . . . tiresome. You hate when people press you on things and ask you about things that concern them, tiresome you call it. Maybe I'm learning from you."

"We have to talk. . . ."

"Tomorrow after work. After *my* work, that is, you don't have any work, do you? We can talk then for a bit like about where I'm to send your mail, and there won't be any answering machine messages, so you'd better set something else up."

"But . . ."

"I won't come to the phone again, you'll have to talk to my father, and you always said he was a nice bloke with nothing to say. . . ."

She went back to the discussion. She saw that her mother and father were wondering about the phone calls.

"Sorry for the interruptions, I've been having a row with Joe Ashe, my boyfriend. It's very antisocial to bring it into this house, if he rings again I won't talk to him."

"Is it serious, the row?" her mother asked hopefully.

"Yes, Mother, you'll be glad to know it's fairly serious as rows go. Possibly final. Now let's see what people should have to eat."

And as she told them about a very nice woman called Philippa who ran a catering business, Anna Doyle's mind was far away. Her mind was back in the days when things had

been new and exciting and when her life was filled to every corner by the presence of Joe.

It would be hard to fill up all those parts again.

She said that they could ask for sample menus and decide what they wanted. They would write to everyone in very good time, individual letters, personal letters with the invitation, that would mean it was special.

"It is special, isn't it? Twenty-five years married?" She looked from one to the other, hoping for reassurance. The cozy, claustrophobic sense of family that the Doyles had managed to create around them. To her surprise and regret it didn't seem to be there tonight. Mother and Father looked uncertain about whether a quarter of a century of marriage had been a good thing. This was the one time in her life that Anna needed some sense that things were permanent, that even if her own world was shifting, the rest of civilization was on fairly solid ground.

But maybe she was only reading her own situation into it all, like those poets who believed in the pathetic fallacy, who thought that nature changed to suit their moods, and that skies were gray when *they* were gray.

"We'll make it a marvelous occasion," she told her father and mother. "It's going to be even better than your wedding day, because we're all here to help celebrate it."

She was rewarded with two smiles and she realized it would at least be a project for the great, yawning, frighteningly empty summer that lay ahead of her.

2

Brendan

Brendan Doyle went to the calendar to look up the date that Christy Moore was coming to sing in the town twenty miles away. It was sometime next week, and he thought he'd go in to hear him.

He had written it down on the big kitchen calendar the day he had heard it advertised on the radio. To his surprise, he realized that today was his birthday. It came as a shock to

think it was already eleven o'clock in the morning and he hadn't realized that it was his birthday. In the olden days he would have known it was his birthday weeks in advance.

"Only three weeks to Brendan's birthday," his mother would chirrup to anyone who might listen.

He had hated it when he was very young, all the fuss about birthdays. The celebrations. The girls had loved it of course, wearing smart frocks. There were never any outsiders there; Brendan couldn't remember having a real party, one with other children and crackers and games, just the family all dressed up and crackers and Jell-O with whipped cream and nuts and cherries on it. There would be presents from all the others, wrapped properly, with little tags, and birthday cards as well, which would all be arranged on the mantelpiece. Then there would be a photograph of the birthday boy all on his own, maybe wearing a paper hat. And then one with the rest of the family. These would be kept in the album, and brought out triumphantly when any guests arrived. The first of the birthdays, Brendan, wasn't he getting so big? And then this was Helen's birthday, and then Anna's. Look. And people looked and praised Mother. She was marvelous, they said, marvelous to do all that for them, go to so much trouble.

His mother never knew how he hated it. How he had hated the singing, and seeing her clapping her hands and running for the camera during the "For He's a Jolly Good Fellow."

He wished they could just sit down and get on with it instead of all these antics and actions. As if they were all onstage.

And all the secrecy too. Don't tell Auntie Maureen about the new sofa. Why? We don't want her to think that it's new. Why don't we want her to think that? We just don't want them saying we put a lot of store by it, that's all. But it's gorgeous, isn't it? Yes, but we don't want them to say that we think it's something special; when Auntie Maureen asks about it just say, "Oh, the sofa, it's all right," as if you weren't impressed. *You* know.

Brendan didn't know, he had never known. They always seemed to be hiding something from somebody. From the neighbors, from people at school, from people in the parish, from Maureen Barry, Mother's great friend, from Frank Quigley, who worked with Father, who was meant to be the greatest friend of the family. And especially from everyone back in Ireland. Don't tell this to Grannie O'Hagan, and never let a word of that be said in front of Grandpa Doyle.

It was quite simple to live by Mother's and Father's rules if you understood that nothing was to be said outside the family.

Brendan thought that there was very little of importance said within the family either.

He remembered his birthday the year that Father had lost his job. There had been *huge* secrecy at that stage of their lives. Father used to leave the house in the mornings at the usual time and come back again as if things were normal. What was it all for? Brendan had wondered then, and wondered still.

And here in Vincent's farm, the small farm on the side of a hill where his father had grown up, he felt even more remote from the man than he had when he lived in Rosemary Drive pretending that he was bright at school, pretending that he was going to get A's and go to university. When all the time he knew he was going to come back here to this stony place where nothing was expected and nothing claimed to be what it was not.

He had never been *Uncle* Vincent; even though he was the oldest of Father's brothers, he was Vincent from the start. A tall, stooped man, much lined and weather-beaten. He never spoke until he had something to speak about. There was no.

small talk in the small house on the side of the hill, the house where Father had grown up one of six children. They must have been very poor then. Father didn't speak of it or those times. Vincent didn't speak of any times. Although a television antenna waved from almost every small farm in the countryside hereabouts, Vincent Doyle saw no need of one. And the radio he had was small and crackly. He listened to the six-thirty news every evening, and the farm report that went before it. He sometimes came across some kind of documentary on the Irish in Australia, or some account of the armies of Napoleon coming to the West of Ireland. Brendan never knew how he tracked these features down. He didn't buy a daily newspaper or any guide to look up what was on. And he wasn't a regular enough listener to know what was being broadcast when.

He wasn't a hermit, a recluse, or an eccentric. Vincent always wore suits. He had never come to terms with a world of jackets and trousers. He bought a new suit every three years, and the current one was moved down a grade, so that one day it would have been the good suit for going to Mass and the day after a new purchase it would have been relegated to a different league. It could be worn when he went to tend the sheep, and even when lifting them in and out of his trailer.

Brendan Doyle had loved this place that strange summer when they had come for the visit. Everyone had been very tense all the way over on the boat and train, and there were so many things to remember. Remember not to talk about sitting up all night on the way to Holyhead. Remember not to talk about the crowds sitting on their luggage, or people would know they had gone steerage. Remember not to say that they had waited for ages on a cold platform. There were to be no complaints, it was all to have been fun. That was the message that Mother kept repeating over and over during the endless journey. Father had said almost the opposite, he had told them not to go blowing and boasting to their Uncle Vincent about all the comforts they had in London. Brendan remembered asking a direct question; he had felt slightly sick before he asked it, as if he knew it wasn't the thing to say.

"Well—which are we? Are we rich like we're pretending to Grannie O'Hagan, or are we poor like we're pretending to Uncle Vincent and Grandpa Doyle?"

There had been a great pause.

Horrified, his parents had looked at each other.

"Pretend!" they had cried almost with one voice. There was no pretending, they protested. They had been advising the children not to gabble off things that would irritate their elders or bore them. That was all.

And Brendan remembered the first time he saw the farm. They had spent three days with Grannie O'Hagan in Dublin and then a long, tiring train journey. Mother and Father seemed upset by the way things had gone in Dublin. At least the children had behaved properly, there had been no unnecessary blabbering. Brendan remembered looking out the window at the small fields of Ireland. Helen had been in disgrace for some horseplay at the station, the main evil of it was that it had been done in the presence of Grannie O'Hagan. Anna was very quiet and stuck in a book. Mother and Father talked in low voices over and over.

Nothing had prepared him for the sight of the small stone house and the yard with the bits of broken machinery in it. At the door stood his grandfather, old and stooped, and wearing shabby old clothes, a torn jacket and no collar on his shirt. Beside him was Uncle Vincent, a taller and younger version but wearing a suit that looked as if it were respectable.

"You're welcome to your own place," Grandpa Doyle had

said. "This is the land you children came from, it's a grand thing to have you back from all those red buses and crowds of people to walk your own soil again."

Grandpa Doyle had been to London once on a visit. Brendan knew that because of the pictures, the one on the wall taken outside Buckingham Palace, and the many in the albums. He couldn't really remember the visit. Now, as he looked at these two men standing in front of the house, he felt an odd sense of having come home. Like those children's stories he used to read when an adventure was coming to an end and they were coming out of the forest. He was afraid to speak in case it would ruin it.

They had stayed a week there that time. Grandpa Doyle had been frail and hadn't walked very much farther than his front door. But Vincent had taken them all over the place. Sometimes in the old car with its rickety trailer; the trailer had not changed since that first visit. Sometimes Vincent couldn't be bothered to untackle it from the car even though there might be no need to transport a sheep, and it rattled along comfortingly behind them.

Vincent used to go off to see his sheep twice a day. Sheep had a bad habit of falling over on their backs and lying there, legs heaving in the air; you have to right them, put them the right way up.

Anna had asked was it only Uncle Vincent's sheep that did this or was it all sheep. She didn't want to speak about it when she got back to London in case it was just a habit of the Doyles' sheep. Vincent had given her a funny look but had said quite agreeably that no harm could come from admitting that sheep fell over, it was a fairly common occurrence in the breed, even in England.

Then Vincent would stop and mend walls; sheep were forever crashing through the little stone walls and dislodging bits of them, he explained. Yes, he confirmed to Anna before she had to ask, this, too, was a general failing in them as a species.

In the town he brought them into a bar with high stools and bought them lemonade. None of them had ever been in a public house before. Helen asked for a pint of stout but didn't get it. Vincent hadn't minded. It was the barman who had said she was too young.

Even way back then, Brendan had noticed that Vincent had never bothered to explain to people who they were; he didn't fuss and introduce them as his brother's children, explain that they were over here for a week's visit, that in real life they lived in a lovely, leafy suburb of North London called Pinner, and that they played tennis on summer weekends. Mother and Father would have managed to tell all that to almost anyone. Vincent just went on the way he always did, talking little, replying slowly and effortlessly when he was asked a question.

Brendan got the feeling that he'd prefer *not* to be asked too many questions. Sometimes, even on that holiday, he and Vincent had walked miles together with hardly a word exchanged. It was extraordinarily restful.

He hated it when the week was over.

"Maybe we'll come back again," he had said to Vincent as they left.

"Maybe." Vincent hadn't sounded sure.

"Why do you think we might not?" They were leaning on a gate to the small vegetable garden. There were a few rows of potatoes there and easy things like cabbage and carrots and parsnips. Things that wouldn't kill you looking after them, Vincent had explained.

"Ah, there was a lot of talk about you all coming back

here, but I think it came to nothing. Not after they saw the place."

Brendan's heart skipped.

"Coming back . . . for more than a holiday, you mean?"

"Wasn't that what it was all about?"

"Was it?"

He had seen his uncle's eyes looking at him kindly.

"Don't worry yourself, Brendan boy, just live your life the best you can, and then one day you can go off and be where people won't be getting at you."

"When would that day be?"

"You'll know when it arrives," Vincent had said without taking his eyes away from the few rows of potatoes.

And indeed Brendan *had* known when the day arrived.

Things changed when they went back home to London after that visit. For one thing Father got his job back, and they didn't have to pretend anymore that he had a job when he didn't. And there had been all kinds of terrible rows with Helen. She kept saying that she didn't want to be left in the house alone. She would interrogate them all each day about what time they were going out and coming back, and even if there seemed to be five minutes of unaccounted-for time, she would arrange to go and meet Brendan when school finished.

He had tried to ask her what it was all about, but she had shrugged and said she just hated being by herself.

Not that there was ever much fear of that on Rosemary Drive. Brendan would have loved some time on his own instead of all the chitchat at mealtimes, and getting the table ready and discussing what they ate and what they would eat at the next meal. He couldn't understand why Helen didn't welcome any chance of peace with open arms.

Perhaps that was why she had gone to be a nun in the end. For peace. Or was it because she still felt the need to be with people, and she thought the numbers were dropping at Rosemary Drive, with Anna moving out to her flat and Brendan a permanent resident in Ireland?

It was strange to have lived for so long with this family, and lived so closely during weeks, months, years of endless conversation and still to know them so little.

Brendan had decided to go back to that stone cottage on the day that his school ran a careers exhibition. There were stands and stalls giving information about careers in computing, in retailing, in the telephone service, in London Transport, in banking, in the armed forces. He wandered disconsolately from one to another.

Grandpa Doyle had died since that family visit when he welcomed them to the soil they came from. They had not gone home for the funeral. It wasn't really *home,* Mother had said, and Grandpa would have been the first to have agreed. Uncle Vincent wouldn't expect it, and there were no neighbors who would think it peculiar and talk poorly of them for not going. There had been a special Mass said for the repose of his soul in their parish church, and everyone they knew from the parish sympathized.

The headmaster said that a decision about how to spend the years of one's life was a very major decision; it wasn't like choosing what movie to go to or what football team to support. And suddenly, like a vision, Brendan realized that he had to get away from this, he had to escape the constant discussions and whether this was the right decision or the wrong one, and how he must tell people he was a management trainee rather than a store clerk or whatever new set of pretenses would appear. He knew with the greatest clarity that he had ever possessed that he would go back to Vincent's place and work there.

Salthill, 26 Rosemary Drive, was not a house that you

walked out of without explanations. But Brendan realized that these would be the very last explanations he would ever have to give. He would regard it as an ordeal by fire and water, he would grit his teeth and get through it.

It had been worse than he ever could have imagined. Anna and Helen had wept and pleaded and begged him not to go away. His mother had wept, too, and asked what she had done to deserve this; his father had wanted to know whether Vincent had put him up to this.

"Vincent doesn't even know," Brendan had said.

Nothing would dissuade him. Brendan hadn't known that he possessed such strength. For four days the battle went on.

His mother would come and sit on his bed with cups of hot chocolate. "All boys go through a period like this, a time of wanting to be on their own, to be away from the family apron strings. I've suggested to your father that you go on a little holiday over at Vincent's; maybe that will get it all out of your system."

Brendan had refused. It would have been dishonest. Because once he went he would not come back.

His father made overtures, too. "Listen, boy, perhaps I was a bit harsh the other night saying you were only going to try to inherit that heap of old stones, I didn't mean that to sound so blunt. But you know the way it will look. You can see how people will look at it."

Brendan couldn't, not then, not now.

But he would never forget the look on Vincent's face when he'd come up the road.

He had walked all the way from town. Vincent was standing with the old dog, Shep, at the kitchen door. He shaded his eyes from the evening light as Brendan got nearer, and he could make out the shape in the sunset.

"Well, now," he said.

Brendan had said nothing. He had carried a small tote bag with him, all his possessions for a new life.

"It's yourself," Vincent had said. "Come on in."

At no time that evening did he ask why Brendan had come or how long he was staying. He never inquired whether they knew his whereabouts back in London or if the visit had official approval.

Vincent's view was that all this would emerge as time went by, and slowly over the weeks and months it did.

Days came and went. There was never a harsh word between the two Doyles, uncle and nephew. In fact, there were very few words at all. When Brendan thought he might go to a dance nearby, Vincent said he thought that would be a great thing altogether. He had never been great shakes at the dancing himself but he heard that it was great exercise. He went to the tin on the dresser where the money was and handed Brendan forty pounds to buy some new clothes.

From time to time Brendan helped himself from the can. He had asked in the beginning, but Vincent had put a stop to that, saying the money was there for the both of them and to take what he needed.

Things had been getting expensive, and from time to time Brendan went and did an evening's work in a bar for an extra few pounds to add to the till. If Vincent knew about it, he never acknowledged it, either to protest or to praise.

Brendan grinned to himself, thinking how differently things would have been run back in Rosemary Drive.

He didn't miss them; he wondered if he ever could have loved them, even a little bit. And if he hadn't loved them, did that make him unnatural? Everything he read had love in it, and all the films were about love, and anything you heard of in the papers seemed to be done for love or because someone

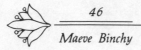

loved and that love wasn't returned. Maybe he was an odd man out, not loving.

Vincent must have been like that, too, that's why he never wrote letters or talked to people intensely. That's why he liked this life here in the hills and among the stony roads and peaceful skies.

It was a bit unnatural, Brendan told himself, to become twenty-two all by yourself, without acknowledging it to another soul. If he told Vincent, his uncle would look at him thoughtfully and say, "Is that a fact?" He would offer no congratulations nor suggest a celebratory pint.

Vincent was out walking the land. He would be back in by lunch. They would have that bacon cold, and plenty of tomatoes. They would eat hot potatoes with it because a dinner in the middle of the day without a few big, floury potatoes would be no use to anyone. They never ate mutton or lamb. It wasn't out of a sense of delicacy to the sheep that were their living; it was that they had no big freezer like some of their neighbors, who would kill a sheep each season. And they couldn't bear to pay the prices in the butcher's shop for animals that they had sold for a greatly smaller sum than would warrant such a cost by the time they got to the butcher's cold store.

Johnny Riordan, the mailman, drove up in his little van.

"There's a bunch of letters for you, Brendan, it must be your birthday," he said cheerfully.

"Yes, it is." Brendan had grown as taciturn as his uncle.

"Good man, will you buy us a pint later?"

"I might do that."

The card from his father was one with a funny cat on it. Quite unsuitable from an estranged father. The word *Father* was written neatly. No love, no best wishes. Well, that was all right. He sent an automatic card to Father with just "Brendan" on it each year, too.

Mother's was more flowery, and said she could hardly believe she had such a grown-up son, and wondered whether he had any girlfriends and if they would ever see him married.

Helen's card was full of peace and blessings. She wrote a note about the sisters and the hostel they were going to open and the funds that were needed and how two of the sisters were going to play the guitar for money at Piccadilly station and how the community was very divided about this and whether it was the right way to go. Helen always wrote about a cast of thousands, assuming he knew all these people and remembered their names and cared about their doings. At the end she wrote, "Please take Anna's letter seriously."

He had opened them in the right order. He opened Anna's slowly. Perhaps it was going to tell him some bad news; Father had cancer or Mother was going to have an operation. His face curled into a look of scorn when he saw all the business about the anniversary. Nothing had changed, simply nothing, they had gotten trapped in a time warp, stuck in a world of tinsel-covered cards, meaningless rituals. He felt even more annoyed about the whole thing because of Sister Helen's pious instruction to take Anna's letter seriously. Talk about passing the buck.

He felt edgy and restless, as he always did when drawn into family affairs. He got up and went outside. He would walk up the hills a bit. There was a wall he wanted to look at. It might need a bit more work than just rearranging the stones like they did so often.

He came across Vincent with a sheep that had gotten stuck in the gate. The animal was frightened and kicking and pulling so that it was almost impossible to release her.

"You came at a good time," Vincent said, and together they eased the anxious sheep out. She bleated frantically and looked at them with her silly face.

"What's wrong with her, is she hurt?" Brendan asked.

"No. Not a scratch on her."

"Then what's all that caterwauling out of her?"

Vincent looked for a long time at the distressed sheep. "That's the one that lay on its lamb. Crushed the little thing to death," he said.

"Stupid sheep," Brendan said. "Sits on her own perfectly good lamb, then gets stuck in a gate, that's what gives sheep a bad name."

The ewe looked at him trustingly and gave a great baaa into the air.

"She doesn't know I'm insulting her," Brendan said.

"Devil a bit she'd care. She's looking for the lamb."

"Doesn't she know she suffocated it?"

"Not at all. How would she know that?" Vincent said.

Companionably the two men walked back toward the house to make their lunch.

Vincent's eyes fell on the envelopes and cards.

"Well, now, it's your birthday," he said. "Imagine that."

"Yes." Brendan sounded grumpy.

His uncle looked at him for a while.

"It's good of them to remember you, it would be scant remembering you'd get if you had to rely on me."

"I don't worry about remembering . . . not that sort." He was still bad-tempered as he washed the potatoes at the sink and put them into the big saucepan of water.

"Should I put them up on the mantelpiece for you?"

Vincent had never said anything like that.

"No, no. I wouldn't like that."

"All right." His uncle collected them neatly and left them

in a little pile. He saw Anna's long typed letter but made no comment. During the meal he waited for the boy to speak.

"Anna has this notion I should go over to England and play games for some silver wedding celebrations. *Silver!*" He scoffed at the word.

"That's how many?" Vincent asked.

"Twenty-five glorious years."

"Are they married that long? Lord, Lord."

"You weren't at the wedding yourself?"

"God, Brendan, what would take me to a wedding, I ask you?"

"They want me to go over. I'm not going near it."

"Well, we all do what we want to do."

Brendan thought about that for a long time.

"I suppose we do in the end," he said.

They lit their cigarettes to smoke while they drank their big mugs of tea.

"And they don't want me there, I'd only be an embarrassment. Mother would have to be explaining me to people, and why I didn't do this or look like that, and Father would be quizzing me, asking me questions."

"Well, you said you weren't going, so what's the worry about it?"

"It's not till October," Brendan said.

"October, is that a fact?" Vincent looked puzzled.

"I know, isn't it just like them to be setting it all up now?"

They left it for a while, but his face was troubled, and his uncle knew he would speak of it again.

"In a way, of course, once in a few years isn't much to go over. In a way of looking at it, it mightn't be much to give them."

"It's your own decision, lad."

"You wouldn't point me one way or the other, I suppose?"

"Indeed I would not."

"It might be too expensive for us to afford the fare." Brendan looked up at the biscuit tin, Maybe this was an out.

"There's always the money for the fare, you know that."

He did know it. He had just been hoping that they could use it as an excuse. Even to themselves.

"And I would only be one of a crowd. If I were to go, it would be better to go on my own sometime."

"Whatever you say."

Outside they heard a bleating. The sheep with the foolish face, the one that had suffocated her lamb, was still looking for it. She had come toward the house, hoping that it might have strayed in there. Vincent and Brendan looked out the kitchen window. The sheep still called out.

"She'd have been a hopeless mother to it even if it had lived," Brendan said.

"She doesn't know that, she's just living by some kind of instinct. She'd like to see it for a bit. To know that it's all right, sort of."

It was one of the longest speeches his uncle had ever made. He looked at his uncle and reached out to touch him. He put his arm gently around the older man's shoulder, feeling moved to the heart by his kindness and generosity of spirit.

"I'll go off into the town now, Vincent," he said, taking his arm away. "I'll write a couple of letters maybe and maybe work pulling a few pints tonight."

"There's enough in the biscuit tin," Vincent said gently.

"There is, I know. I know."

He went out into the yard and passed the lonely ewe still calling for her lost lamb and started up the old car to drive to town. He would go back for their silver anniversary. It was only a little time out of this life. The life he wanted. He could give a little time to show them he was all right and that he was part of the family.

3

Helen

The old man looked at Helen hopefully. He saw a girl in her twenties in a gray sweater and skirt. Her hair was tied back in a black ribbon but it looked as if any moment it might all escape and fall wild and curly around her shoulders. She had dark blue restless eyes and freckles on her nose. She carried a black plastic shopping bag, which she was swinging backward and forward.

"Miss," said the old drunk, "can you do me a favor?"

Helen stopped at once, as he had known she would. There were passersby who went on passing by and those who stopped. Years of observation had taught him to tell one sort from the other.

"Of course, what can I do?" she asked him.

He almost stepped back. Her smile was too ready, too willing. Usually people muttered that they didn't have change or that they were in a hurry. Even if they did seem about to help a wino, they didn't show such eagerness.

"I don't want any money," he said.

"Of course not," Helen said, as if it were the last thing that a man with a coat tied with string and an empty ginger wine bottle in his hand would want.

"I just want you to go in there and get me another bottle. The bastards say they won't serve me. They say I'm not to come into the shop. Now, if I were to give you two pounds, then you could go in and get it for me."

From his grizzled face, with its wild hair above and its stubble below, his small, sharp eyes shone with the brilliance of the plan.

Helen bit her lower lip and looked at him hard.

He was from Ireland, of course, they all were, or else Scotland. The Welsh drunks seemed to stay in their valleys, and the English didn't get drunk in such numbers or so publicly. It was a mystery.

"I think you've had enough."

"How would you know whether I've had enough or not? That's not what we were debating. That, as it happens, was not the point at issue."

Helen was moved, he spoke so well, he had such phrases . . . *the point at issue.* How could a man who spoke like that have let himself go so far and turn into an outcast?"

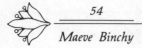

Immediately she felt guilty about the thought. That was the way Grandmother O'Hagan would talk. And Helen would immediately disagree with her. Here she was at twenty-one thinking almost the same thing.

"It's not good for you," she said, and added spiritedly, "I said I'd do you a favor, it's not a favor giving you more alcohol, it's a downright disservice."

The drunk liked such niceties and definitions, he was ready to parry with her.

"But there is no question of your *giving* me alcohol, my dear lady," he said triumphantly. "That was never part of our agreement. You are to act as my agent in purchasing the alcohol." He beamed at his victory.

"No, it's only going to kill you."

"I can easily get it elsewhere. I have two pounds and I will get it elsewhere. What we are now discussing is your word given and then broken. You said you would do me a favor, now you say you will not."

Helen stormed into the small store.

"A bottle of hard cider," she asked, eyes flashing.

"What kind?"

"I don't know. Any kind. That one." She pointed to a fancy bottle. Outside, the drunk knocked on the window and shook his head of shaggy hair, trying to point to a different brand.

"You're not buying it for that wino?" asked the young man.

"No, it's for myself," Helen said guiltily and obviously falsely. The drunk man was pointing feverishly at some brand.

"Listen, don't give it to him, lady . . . I beg you."

"Are you going to sell me this bottle of cider or are you not?" Helen could be authoritative in short bursts.

"Two pounds eighty," the man said. Helen slapped the money, *her* money, down on the counter, and in an equally bad temper the bottle was shoved into a plastic bag for her.

"Now," Helen said, "did I or did I not do what you asked me?"

"You did not, that's only rat's piss, that stuff, fancy bottles for the carriage trade. I'm not drinking that."

"Well, don't then." There were tears starting in her eyes.

"And what's more, I'm not spending my good money on it."

"Have it as a present." She was weary.

"Oh, high and mighty, Lady Muck," he said. He had a good quarter of it drunk from the neck by this stage. He was still holding it in its plastic bag.

Helen didn't like the look on his face, the man was working himself up into some kind of temper or even a fit. She looked at him, alarmed, and saw a huge amount of the despised cider vanishing down his throat.

"The urine of rodents," he shouted. "Bottled by these creeps of shopkeepers and dignified with the name of alcohol."

He banged on the window again loudly. "Come out, you cheat and rogue, come out here and justify this garbage."

There were fruit and vegetable boxes piled neatly with apples and oranges, with potatoes loose and mushrooms in baskets. The man with the nearly empty cider bottle began to turn them over onto the street systematically.

The staff ran from the shop; two of them held him, another went for the law.

"Thank you very much," said the boy who had served Helen. "That was a very nice day's work."

"You wouldn't bloody listen to me," shouted the man, who had foam flecks at the side of his mouth by now.

"Her sort don't listen to anyone, mate," said the irate shopkeeper, who was trying to immobilize him.

Helen moved from the scene awkwardly. She walked away almost sideways, as if she were trying not to turn her back on the chaos and distress she had created. But then, this happened so often.

It was always happening, Helen found, everywhere she went.

Back in the convent she wouldn't say anything to Sister Brigid about it. It would be so easily misunderstood. The sisters wouldn't grasp that it would all have happened anyway. The man might have gotten even more violent and upset if nobody had bought him the drink. He might have broken the window or hurt someone. But Helen wouldn't tell the upsetting tale. Brigid would be bound to look at her sadly and wonder why trouble seemed to follow Helen Doyle wherever she went.

It might even put further away the day when they would allow Helen to take her vows and become a member of the community rather than just a hanger-on. How much did she have to prove? Why did Sister Brigid keep putting off the time when Helen should be considered seriously as one of their community? She worked as hard as any of them; she had been with them for three years, and still, there was this feeling that it was somehow a passing whim.

Even the most minor and accidental events made them see Helen as unstable in some way. It was terribly unfair and she wouldn't add to the long list by telling them about the confusion she was walking away from. Somehow it would be seen as her fault.

Instead she would think about the silver wedding celebrations and what she could do best to help.

Well, obviously she hadn't any money or anything, so

there could be nothing expected from her on that score. And as well as the vow of poverty that she had taken—or to be more honest, was trying to take—she was a bit unworldly these days, she had left the mainstream of everyday life. And even if she did go out to work each day, as all the sisters did, she didn't see the side of life that Mother and Anna would be concentrating on, the more material end of things. And she wouldn't be any good rounding up neighbors and friends. Perhaps she could see whether they might have a special Mass or liturgy. But Helen was doubtful whether the old priest in the parish church where the Doyles went was going to be well up on the modern liturgy of renewal.

Better leave it to Anna, who had plenty of time for all that sort of thing. Anna got so touchy when Helen did things to help; it was often better to do nothing, to say in a calm voice, Yes, Anna, No, Anna. Three bags full, Anna. This is what Brigid would suggest. Brigid was very big on the calm voice. Or on Helen's developing it. It often sounded like blandness and even hypocrisy to Helen, but Brigid said that it was what the world in general seemed to want. And there were times when Helen thought gloomily that she might be right.

Certainly Mother always wanted things underplayed and understated, and in most cases not mentioned at all. Mother would like not calm so much as silence. Perhaps Mother might be pleased if Helen had been born deaf and mute.

By this stage she had arrived at St. Martin's, the house where the sisters lived. Brigid never called it the convent, even though that is what it was. Brigid called it just St. Martin's, or home. She didn't criticize Helen Doyle for using a more formal and official word to describe the redbrick house where eleven women lived and went about their daily business as social workers in various London agencies.

Nessa was working with young mothers, most of them under sixteen, and trying to teach them some kind of mothering skills. Nessa had had a child herself a long time ago; she had brought the baby up on her own, but the child had died when it was three. Helen couldn't remember whether it was a boy or a girl. The other sisters didn't talk about it much. But it did give Nessa the edge when it came to looking after children. Brigid usually worked in the day center for vagrants. Serving them lunches, trying to organize baths and delousing. Sister Maureen worked with the group that was rehabilitating ex-prisoners. The days were gone when these kinds of nuns just polished the big tables in the parlor in the hopes of a visit from a bishop. They went out to do God's work and found plenty of opportunity to do it in the streets of London.

Helen had moved from one area to another since she had come to join St. Martin's. She would like to have worked with Sister Brigid running the day center. What she really would have liked was if Brigid would let her run it on her own and just call in from time to time to see how things were getting along. This way Helen felt she would be really useful and special, and that once seen in a position of calm control over the well-being of so many people, she would have no difficulty in proving her readiness to be a full member of the community.

She realized that obedience was very much part of it, and like poverty and chastity, this was no problem to her, Helen believed. She didn't want to be laying down the law and making rules; she would obey any rule. She didn't want money for jewels or yachts, she laughed at the very notion of such things. And chastity. Yes, she was very sure she wanted that, in a highly positive way. Her one experience of the reverse side of that coin was quite enough to reassure her on this particular score.

She had worked in the kitchen, done her turn as a skivvy. She was never sure why Brigid hadn't liked her using that term. *Skivvy.* She had not been able to understand that people used that word quite respectably nowadays, as a sort of a joke. Debs said they were skivvying for a while before going skiing, it meant minding someone's house. Australians over here for a year often got jobs in bars, in restaurants, or as skivvies. It wasn't an insulting term.

Helen sighed, thinking of all the gulfs in understanding there were everywhere. She let herself in the door of St. Martin's. It was Sister Joan's month for running the house, as Brigid liked it called. Joan called out from the kitchen as she heard her come in.

"Just in time, Helen, I'll take the stuff from you now. You couldn't have timed it better, as it happened."

With a lurch Helen remembered the reason she had taken the large black plastic bag that had been swinging emptily beside her on her journey home. She had meant to come by the market and buy cheaply what the sellers hadn't gotten rid of during the day. She had forgotten it once, and that was why she had been heading toward the grocery store where she had assisted her compatriot in destroying his liver even faster than he was already doing. She had been given three pounds to buy the vegetables. She had spent it on hard cider for an alcoholic.

"Sit down, Helen. It's not the end of the world," said Joan, who didn't know the details of the story but recognized the substance and knew there would be no vegetables for the casserole.

"Sit down, Helen, stop crying. I'll put on a cup of tea for you just as soon as I've scrubbed some of those potatoes. We'll have baked potatoes with a little bit of cheese. It will be just as nice."

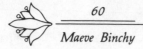

Nessa was tired; it had been a particularly bad day.

An eighteen-year-old mother had sat whimpering in a corner while her fate was being discussed by social workers and a woman police officer. Her baby would live, thanks to Nessa, but what kind of life?

The mother had not turned up at the center for two days running, and Nessa became worried. The door to the block of flats always swung open, and as Nessa went in, she almost fell over Simon crawling along the filthy corridor. Beer cans and bottles were strewn everywhere, the place smelled of urine, there were dangers every few feet, broken bicycles, crates with sharp corners. Simon was crawling earnestly toward the open door. In a minute he would have been on the street where no car or motorcycle would have expected a child to crawl. He would have been dead.

As it was, he was alive, the sores from his stinking diapers being treated. Antitetanus injections were being given against the germs he must have encountered, and his bruised eye was pronounced mercifully intact.

His mother hadn't beaten him, of this Nessa was sure, but she was too feebleminded to look after him. He would be in care when he came out of hospital. A lifetime of care lay ahead of him. But care with a capital C.

Nessa was not in the mood for Helen's tears and explanations. She cut her very short.

"So you forgot the vegetables again. So what, Helen? Let's have a little peace. That's what would be really nice."

Helen broke off in mid-sentence. "I was only taking it all on myself. I didn't want you to blame Sister Joan."

"Oh, for God's sake, Helen, who in their right mind would blame Sister Joan or any sister? Cut it out, will you?"

It was the sharpest remark that had ever been made in St. Martin's House, a place of peace and consideration.

Sister Joan and Sister Maureen looked shocked at Nessa, with her white, tired face, going up the stairs.

Helen looked at all three of them and burst into tears again.

Sister Brigid never seemed to be aware of any little atmosphere. It was one of her characteristics. Sometimes Helen thought it was a weakness, a rare insensitivity in an otherwise remarkable character. Other times she wondered whether it might in fact be a blessing and something that Sister Brigid cultivated purposely.

There was no mention made of Helen's red eyes and blotchy face as they sat, heads bent, waiting for Sister Brigid to say the simple blessing over their food. Nobody acknowledged that Nessa looked white and drawn, though they were solicitous about passing her things and smiling at her a little more often than they smiled at the rest of the table. Eleven women, including Brigid, the quiet Mother Superior, who never used that title. She had been very stern with Helen for calling her Reverend Mother.

"But isn't that what you are?" Helen had been startled.

"We are sisters here, it's a community, this is our home, it's not an institution with ranks and rules and pecking orders."

It had been hard to grasp at first, but after three years Helen felt that she had surely earned her place. Biting her lip, she looked at the ten women chattering around the simple meal, made more simple still by the fact that she had forgotten the vegetables.

They talked easily about the work they had done during

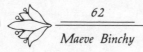

the day, the practicalities, the funny things, the optimisms, the chance of more help here, of fighting the cuts there. Brigid had said that they must not bring their problems to the supper table or even home to the house, otherwise St. Martin's would be weighed down by the collective grief and anxiety of these workers in the sad end of society. They would become so depressed if they were to dwell every night on the amount of misery and pain they had seen in their different worlds that it would be counterproductive. People needed escape, time out, retreat. They didn't have the luxury of going *on* retreat like the nuns of a previous generation, but neither did they have the demands and responsibilities that many trained social workers who were married women or men had. There were no children needing time, love, and attention; there were no social demands nor the intensity of one-to-one relationships. Brigid told them often that small communities of nuns like theirs were ideally situated to serve the many and apparently increasing needs around them in London. The only thing they had to fear was too great an introspection or a depth of worry which might render their help less effective because it was becoming self-important.

Helen looked around at their faces. Apart from Nessa, who was still looking frail, the others were like women who had few cares. You would not know from listening to them that some of them had spent the day in magistrates' courts, in police stations, in welfare centers, or in squatters' houses and run-down housing projects, or, like herself, in a clothing center.

She was pleased that they laughed when she told them about the bag lady who had come in to get a coat that morning. Helen's job was to arrange the sorting, the dry-cleaning, and the mending of clothes that came into the bureau. A generous dry-cleaning firm let them use the big machine free at off-peak hours if they ensured that paying customers didn't realize they were sharing them with hand-me-downs for tramps.

The woman had been very insistent. "Nothing in green. I've always found green an unlucky color, Sister. No, red's a bit flashy. In my day only a certain kind of woman wore red. A nice mauve, a lilac shade. No? Well, safer to settle for a brown, then. Not what you'd call cheerful for spring. But still." A heavy sigh. Helen Doyle was a good mimic, she caught the woman perfectly; all the others could see her as clearly as if they had been there.

"You should be on the stage, Helen," said Joan admiringly.

"Maybe she will one day," said Maureen innocently.

Helen's face clouded. "But how can I? I'll be here. Why don't any of you believe I'm going to stay? I've joined as much as you'll let me." The lip was trembling. Dangerously.

Sister Brigid intervened. "What did she look like in the brown coat, Helen?" she asked firmly. The warning was plain.

With an effort Helen pulled herself back to the story. The woman had asked for a scarf, too, something toning she said, as if she had been in the accessories department of a fashion store.

"I found her a hat in the end, a yellow hat with a brown feather in it, and I gave her a yellow brooch I was wearing myself. I said it sort of brought the whole color scheme together. She nodded like the Queen Mother and was very gracious about it, then she picked up her four bags of rubbish and went back to the Embankment."

"Good, Helen." Sister Brigid was approving. "If you can make it seem like a fashion store with a bit of choice, then you're doing it exactly right, that woman would never have taken what she thought was charity. Well done."

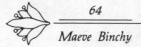

The others all smiled, too, and Nessa's smile was particularly broad.

"There's no one like Helen for these old misfits," Nessa said, as if to make up for her earlier outburst. "You always get onto the wavelength so well."

"It's probably that I'm there already," Helen said. "You know, about taking one to know one and all that."

"You'd never be a bag lady, Helen," Brigid said affectionately. "You'd lose the bags." The laughter around the supper table at St. Martin's was warm and good-natured.

Helen felt very much at peace and very much at home.

She thought she heard Nessa get up in the middle of the night and go downstairs. It was an old house full of creaks and sounds. They could each recognize the others' steps and coughs. Like a family.

Helen was about to get up and follow her down to the kitchen for cocoa and a chat. But she hesitated. Brigid had often said that when people were upset, the last thing they needed was someone to arrive in on top of them offering tea and sympathy. Helen had listened without agreeing. It was what she always wanted. There hadn't been any of it at home. Daddy too tired, Mother too anxious, Anna too busy, Brendan too withdrawn. It was why she had found this other family. They always had time to sympathize. It was what their work was all about. Listening.

Surely she should go down now and listen to Nessa, and maybe tell her all about the drunk today and how upsetting it had been. But maybe not. As Helen was deciding, she heard Sister Brigid's light step go down the stairs.

She crept to the landing to hear what they were talking about.

Strangely it was all about the garden and what they should plant. Shrubs would be nice to sit and look out on, Brigid said.

"When do you ever sit down?" Nessa spoke in a tone that was both scolding and admiring.

"I do sit down, lots of times. It's like that thing we got to charge the batteries for the radio, it puts new energy into me, into all of us."

"You never seem tired, Brigid."

"I feel it, I tell you. I'm getting old anyway. I'll be forty soon."

Nessa laughed aloud. "Don't be ridiculous, you're only thirty-four."

"Well, forty is the next milestone; I don't mind, it's just that I don't have as much energy as I used to. Who'll do the garden, Nessa? I'm too full of aches and pains. You can't be spared from the children."

"After today I think I could be spared only too easily. I don't have any judgment . . ."

"Shush, shush . . . Who will we ask to do it? It's hard work, you know, trying to make that little patch look like something restful and peaceful."

"Helen maybe?" Nessa sounded doubtful.

Helen, on the landing, felt a dull red come up her neck and to her face.

"Oh, she'd do it certainly, and she'd be full of imagination." Sister Brigid sounded doubtful, too. "The only thing is . . ."

Nessa came in immediately. "The only thing is she'd lose interest halfway through after we'd bought all the plants, and they'd die. Is that what you mean?"

Helen felt a wave of fury come over her.

"No, it's just that I don't like her to think that we're

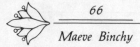

shunting her to do something that isn't really . . . our work, you know."

"But it's *all* our work, isn't it?" Nessa sounded surprised.

"Yes, you know that, I know that, Helen doesn't. Anyway, we'll see. Come on, Nessa, if us old ones are to be of any use to this community, we'd better get a few hours of sleep a night." She was laughing. Sister Brigid had a lovely warm laugh that included you and wrapped you up.

"Thank you, Brigid."

"I did nothing, said nothing."

"It's the way you do it, say it." Nessa was obviously feeling better now.

Helen slipped back into her room and stood for a long time with her back to the door.

So they thought she wouldn't finish things? She'd show them, by heavens she would show them.

She'd dig that garden single-handedly, she'd build a magic garden where they could all sit and think and be at peace and they would realize that Sister Helen, more than any of them, knew that anything done for the community was as important as any other thing. Then they would have to let her take her vows. And she would be completely part of their world. And safe. Safe from everything else.

Like everything Helen had touched, the building of the garden had its highs and lows. Helen found three boys who said they were anxious to help the sisters in their great work building a refuge and they'd be happy to join in with a bit of the heavy work. They brought spades and shovels and Sister Joan said it was beyond the mind's understanding how much tea they wanted, how they couldn't have this butter on their bread, or margarine, it had to be a particular spread. And they wondered if there was a little something going on at lunch-time. Sister Joan said nervously that the nuns all had their meal in the evening, but fearing that the volunteer work force would abandon everything, she ran out and bought provisions.

After three days Sister Brigid thanked them and said that there could be no further imposition on their kindness.

The lads had begun to enjoy the good food and overpowering gratitude of the nuns and didn't really want to leave at all.

They left the place in a possibly greater mess; earth had been turned over certainly, but no pattern or plan had emerged.

But Helen soldiered on, she dug until she had blisters, she spent her scant time off in bookshops reading the sections of gardening books that concentrated on "Starting Out."

She learned the differences between one kind of soil and another.

She told the sisters amazing things each evening about the sexuality of growing things.

"They never told us a word about this at school," she said indignantly. "It's the kind of thing you should know, about everything being male and female even in the garden, for heaven's sake, and going mad to propagate."

"Let's hope it all does propagate after your hard work," Brigid said. "You really are great, Helen, I don't know where you find the energy."

Helen flushed with pleasure. And she was able to remember those words of praise, too, a little later when the problem of bedding the plants came up. The nice woman who said she really admired the sisters even though she wasn't a Roman Catholic herself and disagreed with the Pope about everything, brought them some lovely plants as a gift. Red-faced

with exertion from planting them, Helen assured the others that evening they were very, very lucky. It would have cost a fortune if they had to buy all these, nobody knew how expensive things were in garden centers.

She had barely finished talking when the news came that the plants had all been dug up from a park and a nearby hotel. The repercussions were endless. The explanations from every side seemed unsatisfactory. Helen said she had to protect her sources and wouldn't give them the name of the benefactor. But in mid-conversation she mentioned to the young police-woman that Mrs. Harris couldn't possibly have taken them deliberately, she wasn't that kind of person, and that was enough for the two constables to identify exactly whom she was talking about. Mrs. Harris had been in trouble before. A latter-day Robin Hood was how she was known down at the station, taking clothes from one wash line, ironing them, and presenting them as gifts to another home.

Only Helen could have gotten herself involved with Mrs. Harris. The other nuns sighed. Only Helen could have gotten them all involved, was Brigid's view, but she didn't say anything at the time.

Helen realized that the garden couldn't be considered her full-time work. And even when she had reassured the community that she was taking on no further assistance from gargantuan eaters of meals or compulsive plant thiefs she felt she should take on more than just a horticultural role. She was determined to play her part as fully as possible. She said she would do half the skivvy work, leaving Sister Joan or Sister Maureen free for a half day to do something else.

It worked. Or it sort of worked.

They all got used to the fact that Helen might not have scrubbed the table or taken in their washing when it started to rain. They knew that she would never know when they were running out of soap or cornflakes. That she wouldn't really rinse out and hang up the dishcloths to dry. But she was there, eager and willing to help.

And she did answer the phone and more or less coped when people came to call.

Which is why she was there when Renata Quigley came to see the sister in charge.

Renata. Tall and dark, somewhere in her mid-thirties. Married for fifteen years to Frank Quigley.

What on earth could she want, and how had she tracked Helen down to St. Martin's? Helen felt her heart race and she could almost hear it thumping in her ears. At the same time there was a sense of ice-cold water in the base of her stomach.

She hadn't seen Renata since the wedding, but she had seen pictures of her, of course, in magazines and in the trade papers Daddy had brought home. Mrs. Frank Quigley, the former Miss Renata Palazzo, exchanging a joke or enjoying herself at the races or presenting a prize to the apprentice of the year or walking among the high and mighty at some charity function.

She was very much more beautiful than Helen had thought, she had skin that Mother would have called sallow but looked olivelike and beautiful with her huge dark eyes and her dark shiny hair with its expensive cut. She wore her scarf very artistically caught in a brooch and draped as if it were part of her green and gold dress. She carried a small leather handbag in green and gold squares.

Her face was troubled, and her long, thin hands with their dark red nails were twisting around the little patchwork bag.

"Can I please speak to the sister in charge?" she asked Helen.

Helen looked at her, openmouthed. Renata Quigley

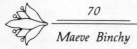

didn't recognize her. Suddenly the memory of an old movie came back to her, and some beautiful actress looking straight at the camera and saying, "Nobody looks at the face of a nun." It was the kind of thing that would drive Sister Brigid mad. Helen had never forgotten it. Until this moment she had never realized how true it was. There was Renata Quigley on her doorstep looking straight into her eyes, and she didn't recognize Helen, the daughter of Deirdre and Desmond Doyle, her husband's friends.

Helen, who had caused so much trouble that time.

But perhaps she had never known. With another shock Helen realized that Renata might have been told nothing at the time.

While all this was going through her mind, Helen stood at the door, a girl in a gray sweater and skirt, with a cross around her neck, her hair tied back with a black ribbon, her face perhaps covered in grime from the garden where she had been when she heard the doorbell.

Perhaps she didn't even look like a nun.

It was obvious that Renata didn't connect her with the child she had known in Rosemary Drive, Pinner, when she had come to call.

"I'm sorry, there's nobody here but me," Helen said, recovering slightly.

"Are you one of the community?" Renata looked doubtful.

"Yes. Well, yes. I'm here at St. Martin's, part of the house, one of the sisters." It was straining the truth but Helen was not going to let Renata Quigley go until she knew why she had come here in the first place.

"It's a little complicated, Sister," Renata said nervously.

Helen's smile nearly split her face in half.

"Well, come on in and sit down and tell me, that's what we're here for," she said.

And she stood back and held the door open while Frank Quigley's wife walked into St. Martin's. Into Helen's home.

That face, that dark, lean face with the high cheekbones. Helen Doyle knew it so well. She remembered well her mother saying with some satisfaction that it would run to fat all the same in the end, mark her words, all the middle-aged Italian women you saw with several chins, they, too, had been lean girls with long, perfectly formed faces. It was in their diets, in their life-styles, in the amount of olive oil they managed to put away.

When she was a child, Helen had been irritated with her mother for all this kind of niggling. What did it matter? Why was Mother so anxious to criticize, to find fault?

But later, later Helen was to look at pictures of the face and wish that her own were like it, that she had hollows and soft golden skin instead of round cheeks and freckles. She would have killed to get that dark heavy hair she saw in the photographs, and wear those loop earrings, which made Helen look like a tinker running away from an encampment but made Renata Palazzo Quigley look as glamorous as an exotic princess from a far land.

"I came here because I heard that there is a Sister Brigid . . . I thought perhaps . . ." She faltered.

"I suppose you could say I'm Sister Brigid's deputy," Helen said. In ways it could be true. She *was* in charge of the house when they were all out; that could be considered being a deputy. "I'll be glad to do what I can."

Helen fought back the other thoughts in her mind. She simply closed a door on Renata's picture in a silver frame on a small table with a long white cloth reaching to the floor. She closed another door on Frank Quigley, her father's friend,

with tears in his eyes. She tried to think only of this moment. A woman had come to St. Martin's for help in some way, and Sister Brigid was out. Helen was in charge.

"It's just that you're very young . . ." Renata was doubtful.

Helen was reassuring. She had her hand on the kettle and paused to look at Renata.

"No, no, I'm much more experienced than you think."

She felt a little light-headed. Could she really be saying these words to Frank Quigley's wife?

It had been impossible in Rosemary Drive that time when Father had lost his job. Helen thought back on it, and it flashed in front of her as if she were watching a video on that machine that she had gotten for St. Martin's once because the company had *assured* her it was free for a month and there would be no obligation. It had all been very difficult, the business about the video, like everything.

But nothing was as frightening as the time her father had left Palazzo. There was a council of war every night and Mother had warned them that they must tell nobody.

"But why?" Helen had begged. She couldn't bear her sister and brother to accept that this was the way things should be from now on. "Why does it have to be a secret? It's not Daddy's fault that they changed the place. He can get another job. Daddy can get *any* job."

She remembered still how Mother had snapped at her. "Your father doesn't want *any* job, he wants his job at Palazzo back. And he will have it back soon, so in the meantime nothing is to be said. Do you hear me, Helen? Outside this house not one word is to be said. Everyone is to think that your father is going to work as usual in Palazzo."

"But how will he earn money?" Helen had asked.

It was a reasonable question. To this day she didn't regret it, as she sometimes regretted the things she had said, the offers she had made, the questions she had asked.

Anna had said nothing, for an easy life she had explained.

Brendan had said nothing because nothing was what Brendan always said.

But Helen couldn't say nothing.

She was sixteen years old, grown-up, in her last year at school. She would not stay on and get A's like Anna. Even though she felt she was twice as bright as Anna in many ways. No, Helen was going to see the world, try her hand at this and that, get on-the-job experience.

She was so full of life, at sixteen some people thought she was years younger, a big schoolgirl. Other people thought she was years older, a lively student going on twenty.

Frank Quigley had no idea how old she was the afternoon she went to see him in his office.

The dragon woman, Miss Clarke, had protected him as she always had. Helen wondered if she could possibly be there still. It was years ago. Surely she had given up hoping that Mr. Quigley was going to look into her eyes and say that she was beautiful without her glasses.

Helen had left her school blazer downstairs with the doorman and had opened the top buttons of her school shirt in order to look more grown-up. The dragon woman had eventually let her in. There were very few who could withstand Helen when she was in full flow. Explanation came hard upon explanation, and all the time she was moving toward his office. Before the dragon realized it, Helen was in.

She was flushed and excited.

Frank Quigley had looked up, surprised.

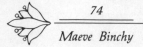

"Well, well, Helen Doyle. You're not meant to be here, I'm sure."

"I know." She laughed easily.

"You should be at school, not bursting into people's offices."

"I do a lot of things I shouldn't do."

She had sat on the corner of his desk swinging her legs, shoulders hunched up. He looked at her with interest. Helen knew she had been right to come here; the silence of Rosemary Drive was no way to handle things. There had to be confrontation.

"What can I do for you?" He had a mock gallantry. He was quite handsome in a way, dark with curly hair. Old, of course, as old as her father, even. But different.

"I suppose you could take me to lunch," she said. It was the kind of thing people said in films and on television. It worked for them, perhaps it would for her too. She gave him a smile much braver and more confident than she felt inside.

"Lunch?" He laughed in a short bark. "Lord, Helen, I don't know what kind of life-style you think we live down here—" He broke off, looking at her disappointed face.

"Aw, hell, I've not had lunch out for years."

"I never had," Helen said simply.

That did it.

They went to an Italian restaurant which was almost dark like night and there were candles on the table.

Every time Helen tried to bring up the subject of her father he skirted around it. She knew that in those television series about big business they always came to the point at the coffee stage.

There was no coffee. There was a Sambuca. A licorice-tasting liqueur. With a little coffee bean in it and the waiter set it alight. Helen had never seen anything so marvelous.

"It's like a grown-up's birthday cake," she said delight-edly.

"You're fairly grown-up for seventeen," Frank said. "Or is it older?"

This was to her advantage. If he thought she was older than sixteen, he would listen better. Take her more seriously.

"Almost eighteen," she lied.

"You've been around, despite the schoolgirl getup," he said.

"I've been around," Helen said.

The more traveled he thought she was, the more he would listen when the time came to talk.

The time didn't come to talk.

He had been affectionate and admiring and had patted her cheek and even held her face up to the candlelight to see if there was any telltale ring of red wine around her mouth be-fore she went back to school.

"I'm not going back to school," Helen said very defi-nitely. She looked Frank Quigley straight in the eye. "You know that, and I know that."

"I certainly hoped it," he said, and his voice sounded a bit throaty. Something about the way he stroked her cheek and lifted her hair made it difficult to talk about her father's job. Helen had felt it would somehow be wrong to bring the subject up when he was being so attentive. She was relieved when he suggested they go back to his place so that they could talk properly.

"Do you mean the office?" She was doubtful. The dragon woman would keep interrupting.

"I don't mean the office," he said very steadily, looking at her. "You know that and I know that."

"I certainly hoped it," she said, echoing his words.

The apartment building was very luxurious. Mother had

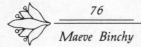

always said she could not understand why Frank Quigley hadn't bought himself a proper house now that he was a married man. But then he probably had expectations of the big white house with the wrought-iron gates and the large well-kept gardens. The house of the Palazzos.

But Mother couldn't have known how splendid the flat was. *Flat* wasn't the word for it, really. It was on two floors, there was a lovely staircase leading up to a floor which had a big balcony with chairs and a table outside, the balcony ran along the whole length of the place, past the sitting room and the bedroom.

They went out the sitting-room door to look at the view from the balcony. And Helen's heart lurched with a sudden realization as they left the balcony to return indoors through the bedroom.

Her hand went to her throat in an automatic gesture of fright. "Your wife . . . ?" she said.

Long, long afterward, when she played it back in her mind, she thought of all the things she could have said, should have said, might have said. How had it been that the only thing which *did* come to her to say was something that could obviously be taken to mean that she was willing and enthusiastic, but just afraid of discovery?

"Renata isn't here, Helen," Frank Quigley said softly. "You know that and I know that, just as we both knew you weren't going back to school."

She had heard that it wasn't healthy to try to blot something out of your memory, to try to pretend that it had never happened. Helen didn't care whether it was healthy or not; for a long time she tried to forget that afternoon.

The moment of no return, the look of bewilderment and anger when she had shied away from him first.

The urgency, and the pain, the sheer hurt and stabbing and fear that he was so out of control that he might do literally anything and kill her. The way he rolled away and groaned, not like that first groan but with shame and then with fury.

"You told me, you said you'd been around," he said with his head in his hands as he sat on one side of the bed, white, naked, and ridiculous-looking.

She lay on the other beside the silver-framed photograph of the lean, olive-faced Renata. Silent and disapproving-looking beside her marriage bed. As if she had always known what might happen there one day.

Helen had lain there and looked at the picture of Our Lady, it was the one you saw everywhere called Madonna of the Wayside. At least Our Lady hadn't had to go through all this to get Our Lord. It had been done miraculously. Helen looked at the picture because that meant she didn't have to look at her father's friend Frank Quigley, who was crying into his hands. And it meant she didn't have to look at the white sheets which were stained with blood and she didn't have to think about how badly he had injured her and if she would have to go to a doctor. Or if she might be pregnant.

She didn't know how long it was before she made a move to the bathroom and cleaned herself up. She didn't seem to have been very badly injured; the bleeding had stopped.

She dressed herself carefully and dusted herself with Renata's talcum powder, which wasn't in a tin like ordinary powder; it was in a big glass bowl with a pink swansdown puff.

When she came out, Frank was dressed. And white-faced.

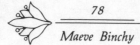

"The bed . . . ?" she began.

"Forget the bloody bed."

"I could—"

"You've done enough," he snapped.

Helen's eyes filled with tears. "I've done enough? What did I do, I came to talk to you about my father and why he'd been sacked, it was you, you who did all this. . . ." With her hand she waved in the direction of the bed.

His face was contrite. "Your father. You did this to try to get Desmond back his piffling little job. Jesus Christ, you'd whore around to get your father a penny-farthing nothing place in a supermarket."

"It is not a nothing job." Helen's face burned with anger. "He was a very important person there, and now, now he's been sacked and Mother says we are not to tell anyone, neighbors, relatives, anyone, and he goes off each morning pretending he's going to work. . . ."

Frank looked at her in disbelief.

"Yes, he does, and I just wanted to have lunch with you and tell you straight out how bad it was and you'd understand because you were Dad's friend way back at school in the brothers when you used to climb over stone walls . . . he told me . . . and you're doing so well there and married to the boss's daughter and everything . . . And *that's* all I wanted, I didn't whore around, I've never slept with anyone in my life and I didn't mean to sleep with you, I wasn't to know you'd fall in love with me and all this would happen, and now you say it's all my fault." She burst into tears.

He put his arms around her and held her close to him.

"Christ, you're only a child, what have I done? Christ Almighty, what did I do?"

She sobbed against his jacket for a bit.

He held her away from him and his eyes were full of tears.

"I'll never be able to make amends. Literally there's nothing I can do to tell you how sorry I am. I'd never . . . never if I hadn't thought . . . I was so sure that . . . but that doesn't matter now. What matters is you."

Helen wondered if he had always loved her, or was it only now? People could fall in love so easily.

"We'll have to forget this," she said. She knew that a woman had to take the lead in such matters. Men would dither and give in to temptation. Anyway, there was no temptation for Helen. If this was what it was like, then the rest of the world could have it, as far as she was concerned.

"It happened, it can't be forgotten. I'll do anything to make it up to you."

"Yes, but we can't keep on seeing each other, it wouldn't be fair." She looked over at the picture of Renata.

She thought he looked puzzled. "No, of course," he said.

"And we won't tell anyone, either of us." She was girlishly eager about this.

"Lord, no, nobody at all," he said, looking highly relieved.

"And my father?" She spoke without guile, she spoke as Helen always spoke, eager to get over the meaning and burden of what she wanted to say, heedless of timing or other people's feelings.

She saw a look of pain cross Frank Quigley's face.

"Your father will get a job. He told me that he didn't need one, that he was looking, that he had plenty of offers." Frank's voice was cold. "He will be reinstated in Palazzo. Not overnight, I have to talk to Carlo, these things have to be done tactfully. They can take a little time."

Helen nodded vigorously.

"And you, Helen. Will you be all right, will you forgive me?"

"Of course. It was a misunderstanding." Her voice sounded eager, as if she, too, wanted to be let off a hook.

"That's what it was, Helen, and Helen, listen to me, please. The only thing I can tell you is that it won't always be like this . . . it will be lovely and happy . . ." He was straining to try to tell her that this gross happening would not be the pattern for the rest of the lovemaking in her life.

He might as well have been talking to the wall.

"Are you sure I couldn't do anything about the sheets, like a Laundromat or anything?"

"No."

"But what will you say?"

"Please, Helen, please." His face was pained.

"Will I go now, Frank?"

He looked unable to cope.

"I'll drive you . . ." His voice trailed away. His face showed that he didn't know where he was to drive her.

"No, it's all right, I can get the bus. I know where I am, I'll just get the bus home and say . . . say I don't feel well." Helen gave a little giggle. "It's true in a way. But listen, Frank, I don't have the bus fare, could I ask you . . ."

She couldn't understand why Frank Quigley had tears pouring down his face when he handed her the coins and closed her hand over them.

"Will you be all right?" He was begging to be reassured. He was not ready for what she told him.

"Frank." Helen gave a little laugh. "I'm not a child, for heaven's sake, I was sixteen last week. I'm a grown-up. I'll find my way home on the bus."

She left then because she couldn't bear the look on his face.

Of course, he had to stay away from the house in case he wasn't able to control himself when he saw her. That's what she told herself.

She never remembered him coming to Rosemary Drive again after that. There had always been some excuse: he was on a conference, he was abroad, he and Renata were going to see some of her relations in Italy. He was terribly sorry, it was such bad timing. Mother said he was getting above himself; still, wasn't it great that they never had to go to him cap in hand to ask him to reinstate his old friend in Palazzo's? At least that idea had come straight from Mr. Palazzo himself, who had realized that this was no way to treat valued managerial staff.

Helen never knew whether her father realized that it was Frank. It was hard to talk to her father, he had built a little shell around himself almost for fear of being hurt, like Mother's shell for fear of letting themselves down somehow.

She had found those last school terms endless; the world had changed since that strange afternoon. She was always frightened of being misunderstood. She had started to scream one day when the singing master at school asked her to come into the storeroom and help him carry down the sheet music to the school hall. The man hadn't touched her, but she had this sudden claustrophobic fear that he would think she was encouraging him somehow and that he would begin this hurtful business and then blame her. As things turned out, he *did* blame her very much indeed and had said that she was a neurotic, hysterical fool, a troublemaker, and if she were the last female on earth, he wouldn't touch her with a ten-foot pole.

The principal of the school seemed to agree with him and

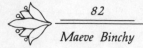

asked Helen sharply why she had begun to scream if she agreed that there had been no question of an attack or even an advance.

Helen had said glumly that she didn't know. She had felt that she was in some kind of situation she couldn't handle and that unless she *did* scream, something else would happen and it would all be too late and too complicated.

"Has anything of this sort happened to you before?" The principal was not entirely sympathetic. Helen Doyle had always been a difficult pupil, gushy, anxious to please, always creating waves of trouble around her.

Helen had said no, unconvincingly.

The principal had sighed. "Well, you can be certain that it will keep happening to you, Helen. It's your personality. This sort of thing will turn up in your life over and over again, situations that you can't handle. That is, unless you pull yourself together and take control of your own actions."

She sounded so final it was as if she were passing a life sentence.

Helen had been dazed at the unfairness of it all.

It was then that she decided to be a nun.

And now, years later, she was almost a nun. Well, she would be a nun if Sister Brigid had not been so adamant about telling her that she was only using the convent as a crutch, that she was using it as a place to hide and that those days were over in religious life.

Helen felt safe in St. Martin's. And even as she made a mug of coffee and sat down to join the beautiful Renata Palazzo Quigley, whose face had looked at her from a silver frame on that frightening day . . . she felt safe. Safe from the memories and the fear of that time.

"Tell me what you want and I'll see if there's anything

we can do," she said with the big smile that made everyone love Helen when they first met her.

"It's very simple," Renata said. "We want a baby."

It was very simple. And very sad. Helen hugged her mug of coffee to her and listened. Frank was too old at forty-six. Too old. How ridiculous, but adoption societies wouldn't consider him. Also, he had a poor medical history, some heart trouble, nothing very serious, because of stress at work, and all businessmen had this in today's world. Natural mothers and fathers were allowed to bring a child into the world into any kind of appalling conditions, tenements, places of vice, nobody stopped them and said that they couldn't have any children. But for adoption everything had to be perfect.

Renata had heard that sometimes, if she were only to meet the right person, there must be occasions where a child could be given to a good loving home, to a father and mother who would love the little boy or girl as their own. There surely were cases when this happened.

There was a look of longing in her eyes.

Helen patted the hand of the woman who had once looked at her from the silver frame.

She had told Renata that they would meet again in a week, when she would have made some inquiries. She thought it wiser not to consult Sister Brigid for the moment. Sister Brigid, being an authority figure, had to keep so well within the limits of the law . . . Better just let Helen inquire a little. All right? All right.

She told nobody. They said she looked feverish and excited, and Helen entertained the community with tales of how she made her garden grow.

"Anyone call?" Brigid asked.

"No. Not anyone really, you know, usual callers." Helen avoided her eye. It was the first time she had told a direct lie at St. Martin's. It didn't feel good, but it was for the best in the end.

If she could do this one thing, if she could do what she hoped she might be able to do, then even at the age of twenty-one her whole life would have been worth living.

It was Nessa's turn to do the kitchen for half a day. Nessa was the one woman at St. Martin's who found Helen almost impossible to get along with. Normally when they worked together, Helen stayed out of Nessa's way. But this time she positively hung around her neck.

"What happens when the children are born to really hopeless mothers, Nessa? Don't you wish you could give them to proper homes from the start?"

"What I wish isn't important, I don't rule the world." Nessa was short, she was scrubbing the kitchen floor, and Helen kept standing in her way.

"But wouldn't a child be much better off?"

"Mind, Helen, please. I've just washed there."

"And you always have to register the births, no matter what kind of mother?"

"What do you mean?"

"I mean, do you have to go to the town hall or the registry office or whatever and sort of say who the child is?"

"No, I don't always."

"Oh, why not?"

"Because I'm usually not the one who does it, it depends. It depends. Helen, do you think that if you're not going to do any work, you could move out of the kitchen so that I could clean it?"

"And no babies end up without being registered?"

"How could they?"

"I don't know." Helen was disappointed. She had thought there might be long twilight times when nobody knew who or what the baby was. She hadn't understood how the welfare system at least checked its citizens in and out of the world.

"And foundlings, babies in phone booths, in churches, where do they end up?"

Nessa looked up in alarm. "God, Helen, don't tell me you found one?"

"No, worse luck," Helen said. "But if I did, would I have to register it?"

"No, Helen, of course not, if *you* found a baby, you could keep the baby and dress him or her up when you remembered, and feed the child when it occurred to you, or when there was nothing else marginally more interesting to do."

"Why are you so horrible to me, Nessa?" Helen asked.

"Because I am basically pretty horrible."

"You can't be, you're a nun. And you're not horrible to the others."

"Ah, that's true. The real thing about being horrible is that it's selective."

"And why did you select me?" Helen didn't seem put out or hurt, she was interested. Actually interested.

Nessa was full of guilt.

"Oh, for heaven's sake, I'm just short-tempered, I hate doing this bloody floor, and you're so young and carefree and get everything you want. I'm sorry, Helen, forgive me, I'm always asking you to forgive me. Really I am."

"I know." Helen was thoughtful. "People often are. I seem to bring out the worst in them somehow."

Sister Nessa looked after her uneasily as Helen wandered back into the garden. There was something more than usual on her scattered brain and it was weighing very heavily.

Helen rang Renata Quigley. Same address, same apartment, same bed presumably. She said that she was still inquiring but that it wasn't as easy as people thought.

"I never thought it was easy." Renata sighed. "But somehow it does make all the going out to functions and to this celebration and that celebration a little easier if I think that somebody as kind as you, Sister, is looking out for me."

With a thrill of shock that went right through her body Helen Doyle realized that she would meet Frank and Renata Quigley at her parents' silver wedding party.

Frank Quigley had been the best man back in those days when he and Father were about equal.

Before everything had changed.

The garden was finished and more or less ran itself. Sister Joan loved being in the clothing center, and she was quick with a needle, so that she could do an alteration on the spot, move the buttons on a jacket for an old man, praise him, admire him, say that the fit made all the difference in the world. Let him think it was custom-tailored.

There was no real work for Helen, no real place.

Once more she asked Brigid about taking her vows.

"It's very harsh to keep me on the outside. Seriously, I have been here for so long, you *can't* say it's a passing fancy anymore now, can you?" She begged and implored.

"You're running, Helen," Brigid said. "I told you that from the word *go*. This is not like a convent in the films, a place in a forest where people went to find peace, it's a working house. You have to have found peace already to bring it here."

"But I've found it now," Helen implored.

"No, you're afraid of engaging with real people, that's why you're with us."

"You're all more real than anyone else. Honestly, I've never met any group I like so much."

"That's not the whole story. We shelter you from something. We can't go on doing that, it's not our role. If it's men, if it's sex, if it's the cut and thrust of the business world . . . we all have had to face it and cope with it. You're still hiding from something."

"I suppose it is sex a bit."

"Well, you don't have to keep indulging in it." Brigid laughed. "Go back out into the world, Helen, I beg you, for a couple of years. Stay in touch with us and then, if you still feel this is your home, come back and we'll look at it all again. I really do think you should go. For your own good."

"Are you asking me to leave? Truly?"

"I'm suggesting it, but do you see what I mean about this not being like the real world? If this was a real place, I'd be telling you to go or promoting you. It's too protective here for you, I feel it in my bones."

"Let me stay for a little while. Please."

"Stay until after your parents' twenty-fifth wedding anniversary," Brigid said unexpectedly. "That seems to be preying on your mind, for some reason. And then after that we'll see."

Helen went away from Sister Brigid's little workroom, more wretched than she had been for a long time.

She looked so sad that Sister Nessa asked if she wanted to come and help with the young mothers. This was the first time the invitation had ever been made.

Helen went along, for once silent and without prattle.

"Don't be disapproving or anything, will you, Helen?"

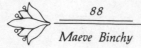

Nessa asked nervously. "We're not meant to be passing judgment, just helping them cope."

"Sure," Helen said.

She sat as listlessly as any of the girls who were on low-dose antidepressants or who lived in fear of a pimp who had wanted them to have an abortion. Nessa looked at her from time to time with concern. But Helen was quiet and obedient. She did everything she was asked to do. She was useful, too, in a way. She went out to the flats of those who had not turned up. Nessa had always been nervous since the incident of little Simon, who had crawled out of his flat almost into the mainstream of rush-hour traffic.

In the late afternoon Nessa asked Helen to go and find Yvonne, who was eight months pregnant with her second child. Her eldest—a beautiful girl with Jamaican eyes like her father, long gone, and a Scottish accent like her mother, who had given birth to her at sixteen—was waiting at the door.

"Mommy's gonna do wee-wee," she said helpfully.

"That's great," Helen said, and brought the toddler back into the house.

From the bathroom came the groans and the cries of Yvonne.

Suddenly Helen found courage.

"You're better in your bedroom," she said suddenly to the chubby child, and moved a chest of drawers to make sure the child couldn't get out.

Then she went to cope with what she thought was a miscarriage in the bathroom.

But in the middle of the blood, the screams, and the definite smell of rum all around the place, Helen heard a small cry.

The baby was alive.

Yvonne remembered nothing of it all. She had been so drunk that the day passed in a terrible blur.

They told her she had lost the child, that she had flushed it down the toilet.

The ambulance men had been tender and gentle as they lifted her on to the stretcher, they had looked around the place and even down the toilet bowl in confusion.

"They told us she was near to her time, she couldn't have gotten rid of a full-term fetus, surely."

But Helen, the cool-eyed girl who said she was a voluntary welfare worker at the mother and child center, and that she lived with the sisters at St. Martin's, assured them that she had not been able to get into the flat and had heard continuous flushing of the chain and then found the place covered in blood.

The small, round three-year-old seemed to back her up, saying that her mother had been a long time wee-weeing and that Helen had been a long time at the door.

Nessa, ashen-faced and trying not to let herself believe that this would never have happened if she had sent anyone else but Helen, agreed that Helen had been gone ages and ages and could get no reply. Helen had made a call to Nessa, saying that there were problems but that she knew she would get in if she could persuade the child to open the door. She had called from a nearby shop where she had stopped to buy a bottle of milk for herself because she felt faint thinking of what might be inside.

That night, with Yvonne in her hospital bed, with Yvonne's three-year-old lodged temporarily in a local orphanage until the care order could be signed, Helen told Brigid she felt restless and she would like to go out for a walk.

"You *are* restless tonight," Brigid said absently. "You've been out to the garden half a dozen times."

"I wanted to make sure it was all right," Helen said.

Carefully she picked up the little bundle, the boy who would inherit the Palazzo millions, and took him in her arms. She had him wrapped carefully in a towel and in one of her own nighties. She had a soft blue rug, which used to lie folded on the back of her chair, wrapped well around him.

She slipped out the back gate of St. Martin's and walked until her legs were tired. Then, in a shop where nobody would recognize her and mention to one of the sisters that they had seen one of the community carrying a baby, she found a phone and telephoned Renata.

"I have it," she said triumphantly into the phone.

"Who is this, you have what?"

"Renata, it's Sister Helen from St. Martin's. I have your baby."

"No, no, it's not possible."

"Yes, but I must give him to you now, tonight, this minute."

"It's a little boy, you got us a little boy?"

"Yes. He's very, very young, he's only one day old."

Renata's voice was a screech. "But no, one day. He will die, I cannot know what to do for a child of one day . . ."

"I don't know either, but I bought him a bottle of milk and he seems to be taking it off my finger," Helen said simply.

"Where are you?"

"I'm in London, of course, about two miles from the convent. Renata, have you any money?"

"What kind of money?" She sounded worried.

"Enough to pay for a taxi."

"Yes, yes."

"So will I come to your flat? And give him to you? No one must know."

"Yes, I don't know, perhaps I should wait till . . . I don't know what to do."

"I went to great trouble to get him for you." Helen sounded tired.

"Oh, I know, Sister, I'm so foolish, it's just that it's so quick and he is so very little."

"I'm sure you'll learn. You can always ring someone and ask them. Will I get a taxi now? It might cost a lot."

"Yes, come now."

"And Frank's not there, is he?"

"Frank, how did you know my husband is Frank?"

"You told me," Helen said, biting her lip.

"I suppose I must have. I don't know what to say."

The taxi driver said that this wasn't where he wanted to go. He was on his way home. South London is what he wanted. Not miles out to Wembley.

He saw the tears beginning to form.

"Get in before I change my mind," he said. "Anyway, at least you've had it. Let's look on the bright side, I could have ended up delivering it."

"That's true," Helen said, and the taxi driver looked at her anxiously, wondering if he would get his fare when he got to Wembley.

She recited the address of the apartment house as if by rote and asked the driver to wait. The lady of the house would be down in a moment and would pay him.

He told the other cabdrivers afterward that he had spotted her as trouble the very moment he saw her, the moment that her eyes had filled with tears when he said perfectly normally that in the evenings he wanted to go south of the river rather than up to this neck of the woods in Wembley. Any-

way, he said, it all seemed to have happened at once; the lady came down and was carrying a purse with money. Classy, she was, and foreign. She took one look at the baby and she started to scream.

"He's got blood on him, he's not properly formed, no, no, I didn't want this! This is a baby that still is not ready to be a baby. No, no."

She backed away from the girl in the gray skirt and sweater with her hand up to her mouth and at that moment a fellow in a Rover came along and leapt out. He took one look at what was happening and shook the foreign woman till her head nearly fell off, then he took the child and seemed to recognize the girl in the gray. He kept saying, "Oh, my God," too, as if she were something from outer space.

Then there was a bundle of notes stuffed in the taxi driver's window, four times the fare out to bloody Wembley. So he had to go, and he never knew what it was all about and how it ended.

It ended badly. As everything Helen Doyle had ever touched seemed to end.

She had refused to go into the flat, crying, too, now, louder than Renata, but neither of the women cried as much as the bewildered, hungry baby that had been born in a bathroom that morning.

Sister Brigid was eventually summoned, to make some sense out of the whole scene. She came with Nessa, white-faced but calm.

Nessa saw to the baby, and Brigid listened to the hysterical explanations.

The Italian woman was saying that she had intended only to inquire if any mother wanted to give her baby privately for adoption; she hadn't asked anyone to take one for her.

The tall Irish businessman was pleading for Helen, saying that she had done it for the best, as she had always done everything for the best, but the world was never able to perceive it that way. He sounded tender toward her and yet terrified of her as well.

He knew her parents, he explained. Desmond Doyle had been one of his oldest friends.

"She is the daughter of those Doyles?" Shock was being piled on shock for Renata.

"Yes, she can't have known it was us."

There was something in the way the man spoke. There was something that sounded a warning. Brigid looked from one stricken face to another to try to read the signals.

Helen was opening her mouth. "But I *did* know, I *did* know, it's only because it *was* Frank that I'd do this, I'd never have taken a baby and told all those lies. If it hadn't been Frank, I'd not have risked the baby's life. I felt I owed it to him, after all, after everything. . . ."

Brigid had worked with people for all her adult life. Mainly people who were in some kind of distress. She didn't know what was going to be said now, but she felt it was crucial that whatever it was, Helen should not say it. Helen was in mid-flight; through the tears and the gulps the story was coming out.

"I never meant it to be like this, but they could have given it such a good life, so much money, and Frank's too old to adopt a child, and she said he had been having heart attacks—"

"You told her that?" Frank snapped at his wife.

"I thought she was a nun miles away. How did I know she was bloody Doyle's daughter?"

Helen was oblivious. "I wanted to make amends, to make up for everything. To try to put things right. After all, my life

worked out all right and I got everything I wanted, but Frank didn't, he had no children and he had heart attacks, he was punished . . . I wanted to try to even it out."

Renata was looking from one to another now in confusion. Out in the other room Sister Nessa had quieted the baby, and Helen was gathering her breath again.

"You work with Mr. Doyle still?" Brigid asked quickly.

"Yes, and he helped my father when he was sacked, he asked Mr. Palazzo to give him back his job . . ."

Brigid saw an avenue of escape. She stood up as she spoke.

"So Helen with her usual impetuous nature decided to thank you for this by getting you a child when it was not going to be easy through the proper channels. Isn't that right?"

Frank Quigley looked into the gray eyes of Sister Brigid, competent, unemotional, strong. Irish perhaps a generation ago, but now with a London accent. She reminded him of bright men he met in business.

"That's it. Exactly, Sister."

Helen hadn't stopped crying. Brigid felt she might not have stopped speaking either. With what seemed like a deliberate effort she put her arm around the girl's shoulder.

"Let's take you home, Helen, back to St. Martin's. That's the best thing now."

"Will I drive you?" Frank asked.

"No, but if you could get us a taxi, Mr. Quigley."

At this moment Nessa came in; the baby was asleep. They would take him to the hospital, the one they knew, and where they were known. He would be looked after.

"It seems a pity in a way, Sister." Frank looked at Sister Brigid, and she looked back. The glance was a long one.

It was a pity in many ways. They could give the boy

everything, including more love than he would ever know from Yvonne.

"Yes, but if we do this, everything breaks down. Every single thing."

He felt she was tempted.

"Not everything, just a few forms to fill out. The mother thinks he is dead."

"Please," Renata said. "Please, Sister."

"I'm not God, I'm not even Solomon," said Brigid.

They knew it was hard for her, and they drew together, the handsome couple. Helen watched them with a look of pain in her face.

The doorman had been asked to hail a taxi, and the unlikely foursome walked to the lift, Helen tearful and supported by Sister Brigid, red-haired Sister Nessa carrying the tiny baby wrapped in its blue rug.

Renata stretched out her hand to touch Helen's arm.

"Thank you, Sister Helen, I know you meant kindly for me," she said.

"Sister Helen has a great big heart," Brigid said.

"Thank you," Frank said at the door. He did not look at Helen, he looked instead admiringly into the gray eyes of Brigid.

"There are countries where it is all legal. If you like, someday you can ask me and I will tell you what I know," she said.

"Good-bye, Frank," Helen said.

"Thank you, Helen. Sister Brigid is right, you have a great big heart." He touched her cheek.

In the taxi they were silent, until Helen said, "You called me Sister Helen, does this mean I can stay?"

"It means we won't ask you to go yet. But maybe now that you have faced some things you haven't faced before, it

mightn't be as necessary to hide as it once was. Perhaps you will be able to make your life somewhere else. Travel the world, even."

This time Helen didn't think that Sister Brigid was asking her to leave. She felt better than she had felt for a long time.

She looked at Sister Nessa, holding the tiny boy close to her breast.

"Isn't it sad that you can't keep the baby, Nessa?" Helen said with a rush of generous spirit. "To make up for the one you had that died. It could be a kind of substitute, couldn't it? A consolation."

She didn't even notice the two women glance at each other and then look out the windows on each side of the taxi.

4

Desmond

Of course the corner shop was more expensive than the supermarket, but then it *was* on the corner, that's what you were paying for. And the fact that it stayed open so late at night.

Desmond liked stopping in there. There was a mad, magical feel about the place and the way Suresh Patel was able to pack in so many goods on his shelves . . . and in such a way

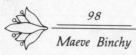

that they didn't all come tumbling down. Desmond often said that Mr. Patel must have a secret. Over in the big supermarket chain, Palazzo Foods, where Desmond worked, the principle was totally different. You had to give maximum space so that the customer could walk around and choose and, best of all, be persuaded by something that had not been on the original shopping list. Mr. Patel's business was at the other end of the market. They came in because they had run out of sugar or they hadn't bought anything for supper and the shop they intended to go to had been closed. They came for the evening paper and a tin of beans sometimes. Mr. Patel said that you'd be surprised how many people must be going home to a lonely evening. He often felt better off standing in his shop talking to whoever came and went.

Desmond's wife, Deirdre, said she had nothing against Mr. Patel personally, he was extremely polite and respectful always, but everything was that little bit dearer there. The place was a hodgepodge, a bit like those hucksters' shops you didn't go into years ago at home in case things mightn't be quite . . . well, fresh.

And she never knew why Desmond would stop and buy an earlier edition of the paper in the corner shop when he could have gotten one nearer work and had the pleasure of reading it on the way home.

Desmond found it hard to explain. There was something solid about the little place. It didn't depend on the fluctuations of faraway suppliers and huge multinationals. If Mr. Patel noticed a customer asking for something, he gave it a lot of thought. Like the time Desmond had asked for red-currant jelly.

"Is it a jam or a condiment?" Mr. Patel had asked with interest.

"I think it can be either." Desmond had been equally

interested in the definition. Between them they decided that once it had been bought, it would be placed on a shelf with the mustards, the chutneys, and the little green jars of mint sauce.

"Soon I will know exactly the tastes and temperaments of a fine British suburb. I will know enough to write a book, Mr. Doyle."

"I think you know that already, Mr. Patel."

"I am only starting, Mr. Doyle, but it is all so interesting. You know the saying they have in your country about all human life is here . . . that's what I feel."

"All human life is in my job, too, but I don't welcome it as much as you do." Desmond smiled ruefully.

"Ah, that's because your job is so much more important than mine."

Deirdre Doyle would have agreed with him. Mr. Patel was right to look with respect at a man like Desmond, who, though well under fifty, was Special Projects Manager at Palazzo. Palazzo was a name like Sainsbury's or Waitrose. Well, not quite like them, but in certain areas it was just as well thought of, and back home in Ireland, where nobody knew any of the others anyway, a Palazzo sounded much grander.

The Patels didn't live in Rosemary Drive, naturally they lived somewhere else, somewhere more suitable for Indian and Pakistani people, Deirdre said, when anyone brought the subject up.

Desmond knew that in fact Suresh Patel, his wife, his two children, and his brother lived in the tiny storerooms behind the small shop. Mrs. Patel could speak no English and the brother was fat and looked as if he had some illness. He used to sit there and smile perfectly pleasantly, but he spoke

little and did not seem to be any help in the running of the corner shop.

For some reason that he never totally understood, Desmond never mentioned that the Patel family lived there. That their two children, immaculate in school uniform and wearing blazers and spectacles, came out each morning from this tiny place. Desmond felt that somehow it demeaned the Patels to be thought to live in such a small place, and somewhere in his subconscious he felt that Deirdre might think it demeaned the neighborhood to have Pakistanis actually living there rather than just trading.

The shop was busy in the early morning, people buying papers, bars of chocolate, orange drinks, and plastic-wrapped sandwiches. The stuff that kept the commuters more or less alive on their journeys to work. The oil that ran the machinery of British industry.

Not that Desmond felt too cheerful about his own part in British industry. He was on his way to work at the big headquarters of Palazzo Foods, the supermarket chain which was now ninth largest in Britain. Desmond had begun to work for it back in 1959, when it was simply called Prince. That was the year he and Frank Quigley had left Mayo and come to London by train, boat, and train to make their fortune. They arrived during the heat wave that went on month after month; they thought they had come to paradise.

As Desmond took his regular morning journey down Rosemary Drive into Wood Road and on to the bus stop at the corner, he often looked back on those days when things were simpler and when he and Frank worked behind the counters in the two Prince Stores. One day they might be slicing bacon, another day dressing windows. Every day they met the customers and they knew everyone who worked in the shop.

It was Frank who had seen that this was a company

where they could rise and rise; it was no stopgap job. Prince Foods was breaking new ground, it was getting bigger, soon it would expand and Frank would be a manager in one branch and Desmond in another if they played their cards right. Frank played his cards magnificently. Desmond had always been slower to see the opportunities. But he saw how everything was changing and saw sadly that the higher he rose—dragged, pulled, and cajoled by his friend Frank—the farther he got from the people, which was what he had liked about it all in the first place.

Desmond Doyle had been a thin, wiry young man then, with a thick shock of fair brown hair. His children had often teased him about the old photograph, saying that he looked like a proper teddy boy, but their mother wouldn't allow that at all. That was the way all young men of style looked then, she would say firmly. He looked different now, combing his hair in a way in which it might look as if it were covering his head and wearing shirts that had a neck size far wider than he wore that first summer when he had only been able to buy two shirts as his entire wardrobe and there was always one hanging on the back of a chair drying.

He supposed that many people looked back on the old days as good days even though they had been practically penniless days. He certainly did.

He could never understand why people liked the Palazzo Building so much. It was a perfect example of Art Deco, they said, a thirties masterpiece. Desmond always thought it looked like one of those big brutalist buildings you saw in documentaries about Eastern Europe. It was a square, menacing-looking place, he thought. It was strange that there was a preservation order on it and articles in magazines talking about its perfect proportions.

Frank had been instrumental in getting that building for

Palazzo; it was then the disused headquarters of an automobile company that had gone bankrupt. Nobody else had seen its potential, but Frank Quigley, who knew everything, said that they had to have storage space for stock, they had to have a depot and maintenance center for their vans, and they had to have some kind of central offices. Why not combine them all behind this splendid facade?

A facade is what it was. Wonderful stairways and reception rooms on the ground floor. But upstairs a warren of prefabricated and jerry-built offices and partitions. Accounts had been modernized and gone on-line in computers, so that was housed in a modern extension at the back. But there was a strange limbo land on the third floor, a place where there were names on doors and people often bursting in saying, "Oh, sorry." There were vague storage areas where paneling that hadn't worked or plastic display units that hadn't fitted were left pending decisions.

There in the heart of this hidden chaos, the unacceptable face of Palazzo, lay Desmond Doyle's workplace. The Special Projects Department. Officially it was the nerve center of new ideas, plans, concepts, and illuminations that would wipe the competition off the map. In reality it was the place where Desmond worked and drew his month's salary and kept his managerial title because he was the boyhood friend of Frank Quigley. Because they went back a long way and because they had set out on the same day over a quarter of a century ago.

Frank Quigley, the quiet but powerful Managing Director, the man who had seen the way to jump and jumped with the Italians when it came to takeover time. The man who had married the boss's daughter. It was thanks to Frank that Desmond walked up to the third floor of Palazzo and opened the door of his office with a heavy heart.

The Special Projects Department was coming under scrutiny. There had been definite rumors that a big investigation was upcoming. Desmond Doyle felt the familiar knot of sour bile in his stomach and the panic beginning to grip his chest. What did it mean this time? An accusation that the section wasn't pulling its weight, a demand for exact quantifying of how much the last in-store presentations had realized, and the projected figures likely from the children's promotional exercises.

The antacid tablets seemed to do no good anymore, he was eating them like sweets. He was weary of the confrontations and the need to seem bright. Once that business of looking bright and being on top of things had been the be-all and end-all of his day. Not anymore. At an age which the rest of the world persisted in thinking of as young, Desmond Doyle felt like an old, old man. Forty-six going on ninety. That's what he would have answered truthfully if anyone had asked him caringly about his age.

His office, blessedly free from the photographs that covered the walls in his home, had a pale print of a Connemara countryside. It looked somehow more mauve, blue, and elegant than he remembered it, but Deirdre said it was the very spirit of the West of Ireland and he should hang it there so that it could be a conversation piece. He could talk about it to visitors, tell them this was the place he came from. Those were his roots.

Poor Deirdre, thinking that was the kind of conversation that took place in his boxlike cubicle of an office. He was lucky to have walls that were not that rough glass or Perspex; he was lucky to have a desk, a telephone, and two filing cabinets. The luxury of chats about roots based on overpastelized views of County Mayo was not anything he had known. Or would ever know.

He no longer felt that the words stuck with cardboard lettering on his door were important . . . there had been no Special Projects in the old days, it was only a made-up word. There had been real jobs like Stores Development Manager, Operations Manager, or Merchandising Manager. These were what the business was about. Special Projects meant nothing to Desmond Doyle because he knew that in his case it was nothing. In other countries it was a real job; he knew that from reading the retail magazines. In Palazzo Foods it meant only a pat on the back.

Desmond remembered way back reading an advertisement which said, "A title on the door means a Bigelow on the floor." A Bigelow was some kind of carpet. It was a lovely, innocent advertisement trying to drive young executives mad for status. He had told Deirdre about it once, but she had missed the point. Why shouldn't he have a carpet too? she had asked. Perhaps they could get an irregular carpet themselves and fit it over the weekend, then it would look important and nobody would have to go to war over it and risk a confrontation they might lose. Wearily at that time, he had settled for a small rug, which he kept under his desk so that nobody could see it but assured Deirdre that it gave the place class and superiority.

Desmond wouldn't lose his job in Palazzo even if the whole Special Projects Department was deemed to be useless, a criminal waste of time. It was hardly a department, anyway; he had that young pup who was meant to be a trainee and the very occasional services of Marigold, a big Australian girl with a mouthful of teeth and a mane of hair who was on what she called OE, Overseas Experience, and had worked in a funeral parlor, as a dentist's receptionist, and in the office of an amusement park, all to get an idea of what the world was like before she went home and married a millionaire from Perth, which was her goal.

She was a handsome, friendly girl who would sit on Desmond's desk companionably, asking if he had any correspondence or memos to type. She thought typing was the golden key to unlocking the world. "Tell your girls to learn to type, Dizzy," Marigold told him often. She never accepted that one of his girls had a B.A. and worked in a bookshop and the other was a sort of worker nun. Neither of them would take Marigold's golden key to the world.

If Special Projects was dissolved, Marigold would be sympathetic. She would tell Dizzy that Quigley was a sod and what's more, he always tried to pinch her rear. She'd offer to buy him a beer and tell him he was too good for Palazzo and should look around for something better. The young pup of a trainee would hardly notice; he would go and pick his nose in some other part of the store. The pup's father was an important supplier; he would be kept on no matter what happened.

As would Desmond himself. He had been let go once. Never again. Frank Quigley would see to that. His job or a form of it was his for life. He had almost fourteen years more with Palazzo. The company had a policy of retirement at sixty. In fact, it was less than fourteen years, it was now only thirteen and a bit. They would find something for him to do in that time.

Desmond Doyle would not find himself explaining his existence and justifying his role to his old friend Frank. No, if there was anything unpleasant like that ahead, you could be sure that Frank would have pressing business in the farthest part of the land or a meeting that was so important it could not be rearranged. Desmond would have to talk to Carlo Palazzo himself, the father-in-law, but in no way a godfather figure.

Carlo was a man who thought about his family and his soft leather jackets; he had always wanted to be in the fashion business, and now with the profit he was making from Palazzo he could have his showrooms and his life's dream. Carlo Palazzo, a mild-looking Italian whose accent seemed to become more pronounced with every year he spent in North London, made none of the day-to-day decisions about his supermarket empire. He left the running of all that to the bright Mr. Quigley, whom he was sharp enough to have spotted many years ago as the type of hungry young Irishman who could run it. And who could marry Carlo's daughter, too.

There were no children yet, and Desmond knew that this was a great sadness, but he kept hoping. Even though it seemed increasingly unlikely with every year that went by, fifteen years of marriage and Renata now well into her thirties.

Carlo was an optimist about his grandchildren. But he was a practical man about his profits, and if it were he who would conduct the investigation, Desmond sighed, there would be no emotional confidences today, only harsh facts and even harsher questions. What has Special Projects added to the sum of Palazzo's profit in the last six months? Just list the achievements, please, Desmond. Yes?

Desmond drew his pad nearer to him to get the sorry list together. It wasn't that he had no ideas—he was bursting with ideas—but somehow they got lost in this welter of departments and other pressures and needs.

Like the time he suggested they have a bakery on their own premises. That had been a long time ago and very much ahead of its time. Desmond had not been adventurous enough, he had suggested only that they make brown bread and scones. But his reasoning had been so sound it had been taken over on a larger scale than he had ever dreamed. He had said that the smell of freshly baked bread was very attractive when a customer came in the door; it was the living guarantee that it was absolutely made that day. The fact that they could see it being baked in hygienic conditions spoke volumes for the general hygiene of the rest of the store as well.

But somehow it had left him; it was never the Desmond Doyle idea, or the Special Projects suggestion, it had become part of Merchandising, and then a separate section called Bakery started and there were articles and photographs in all the papers about the unusual loaves and bread shapes and the yeast breads they made. Palazzo bread had become a legend.

Desmond didn't waste too many tears over it; an idea was only an idea, and once you gave it to other people, then it was no longer yours. In terms of seeing it through, it didn't really matter whether you got credit for it or not, it was out of your hands. But if you *had* gotten credit, of course, if you had the reputation of being Mr. Ideas in the company, then life would have a different color to it during the working day. There would be a bigger office, a proper name on the door, and even one of those carpets. Mr. Palazzo would ask him to call him Carlo and invite Desmond and Deirdre to their big summer parties in the large white house that had a swimming pool and a big barbecue. And he would beg Deirdre to try on a soft blue leather jacket that had just come in from Milan and exclaim that it looked so good on her, she must have it. As a gift, as a token of the esteem in which they held her husband. The ideas man in Palazzo.

The list was looking scrappy. Marigold came in saying she had a raging hangover, which had not been improved in the cafeteria, where she had gone to get some cold orange juice to dilute the miniature of vodka. In the cafeteria, Marigold had heard that Mr. Carlo was on the warpath. There had been a less than lovely session with his accountants, and he

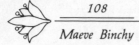

wasn't going to get enough pocket money to play with those dishcloth rags of leather jackets. So he was about to reorganize everyone. Stupid little wop greaseball, Marigold said. If he was back in Australia, he'd be man enough to get the hell out into whatever turned him on, like these pathetic frocks and coats, rather than pretend he knew how to run a business, which everyone knew was run by that gangster Frank Quigley.

Desmond was touched by the partisan nature of Marigold's response.

"Sit down there now and stop exciting yourself. You'll only make your head worse," he said sympathetically.

Marigold looked at him, her eyes pink and puffy but full of concern.

"Jesus, Dizzy, you're too good for this shower," she said.

"Shush, shush. I'm going past the freezer, shall I get you some ice for that? A cure's no good without ice."

"No wonder you'll never run the bloody place, you're a human being," said Marigold with her head in her hands.

Marigold had only been with Palazzo six months; she said it was nearly time for her to move on already. She had been thinking of a hotel next, or a job as receptionist in a Knightsbridge hairdressing salon where you might see members of the Royal Family coming in.

Greatly revived by her chilled vodka and orange, which she had tried to persuade Desmond to share without any success, she put her mind to dredging up some details of work done in the section during the period she had worked there.

"Jesus, we must have done *something*, Dizzy!" she said, her face frowning with concentration. "I mean, you were never coming in here every day and looking at that picture of the pale blue outback in Ireland all day, were you?"

"I wasn't . . . I don't think I was. There always seemed

to be things to do, but they were other people's things, you see." Desmond sounded apologetic. "So they don't count as being from here. It's not going to look very impressive."

"Where will they send you? If they wind it up?"

"This is one of the smallest offices. They might leave me here, reporting to someone else, you know. Same place, same job, different line of responsibility."

"They'd never give you the heave-ho?"

He reassured her. "No, no, Marigold, don't worry about that. No."

She smiled at him roguishly. "You mean, you know where the bodies are buried?"

"In a way," he said.

He spoke so softly and sadly Marigold let it go.

"I'll go out and see what I can gather from the letters I typed for you anyway," she said.

It was more or less as Desmond had thought it would be. Carlo sat in the small office, not even remotely impressed by the efforts Marigold made in calling him Mr. Doyle and talking about people on the telephone and saying he was in conference. Marigold had even been in to borrow two china cups and saucers for the coffee rather than use the two scarlet mugs with *D* and *?* on them that were usually brought into play.

Carlo Palazzo spoke about the need to redeploy, to continue to expand, to experiment, never to stand still. He spoke about the competition. He talked about inflation, recession, about industrial unrest, and about the difficulty of parking cars. In short, he brought in almost every common topic of gloom to support his reluctant decision that the department *as such* should be fused with other departments, and its work,

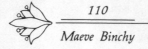
important and useful of course as it was, might best be served by being redeployed.

When he came around to using the word *redeployed* for the second time, Desmond felt that it was like going to the movies and recognizing the part where you had come in.

He felt a great weariness. A realization that this would happen again and again in the next thirteen and a half years. Until possibly the decision might be that he should work in the parking lots, that would be the best redeploying.

Desmond's head felt heavy, and he wondered how best to explain it to Deirdre that evening. He knew there would be no diminution of salary, he knew there would be no public announcement. Only the title would have gone. He was down to essentials now.

"And do you think I should continue in whatever new deployment is agreed from this room, this office?" he asked.

Carlo Palazzo spread out his big hands. If it were up to him, then, of course.

"But it's not, Mr. Palazzo?"

It wasn't, it appeared; it was reorganization and taking down some partitions and having an open flow, and a lot more light, and a change in some of the inventory-taking.

Desmond waited patiently. He knew that it would be told, and no amount of hurrying tactics would work.

He let his eyes wander to the picture with its unlikely blue skies and its soft grassy slopes. Mayo had never been like that. There had been very big white skies and stony walls and small brown fields. The picture was chocolate-box stuff.

Carlo Palazzo was coming to the point.

The point was definitely upcoming, Desmond thought to himself. He felt the familiar acid taste coming from his stomach to his mouth. Please let there be some kind of office. Something which need never have to be explained. Some part of the building where there would be a person, a person like Marigold who would answer the telephone to Deirdre. Someone who would say, "Hold on and I'll put you through," when his wife rang and asked, as she always did, to speak to Mr. Doyle, Special Projects Manager, please. With an upward inflection on the *please.*

Please let there be some word *manager* somewhere along the line, and let Deirdre not have to spend the rest of her life phoning a business that would not know who he was, let alone where he was.

"So we thought it best if your work was to be in a roving capacity," Carlo Palazzo said.

"Not roving, Mr. Palazzo," said Desmond Doyle. "Please, not roving."

The Italian looked at him with concern.

"I assure you, Desmond, that the work will be just as important, more important in many ways, and as you know, there is no question of changing the salary structure; that will remain, with the usual emoluments."

"Any kind of base. Anything at all." Desmond felt the sweat on his forehead. God Almighty, he was beginning to beg. Why could he not have talked it all the way through with Frank Quigley?

He and Frank, who had played on the stony hills of Mayo together, who had never seen a West of Ireland sky like the one in the picture, they knew the same language. Why had the barriers of years meant that he couldn't say to Frank straight out that he must have an office even if it was a doorway leading nowhere? It wasn't much after all these years to give Deirdre the belief that her husband was of managerial stuff in a large and important retailing organization.

There was a time when he and Frank had been able to talk about anything, anything at all. Like how Frank's father

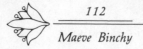
drank away a fortune of compensation in three weeks buying large measures for the whole town. Like how much Desmond wanted to escape from the farm and the silent brothers and sisters who seemed happy to stalk the barren land after the scrawny, difficult sheep.

They had told each other of their first conquests with girls when they had come here, two ignorant young paddies in the fifties; they had shared everything from the day they had gone to work for Prince Stores. But then a hunger had taken Frank over, and it must have been about that time that the close friendship died.

And Frank had gone forever up, forever and ever, he ran everything now. But the Palazzos had bought out Prince Stores and made it their own. It was known that Carlo Palazzo had never made a decision larger than what sauce he would have on his pasta without consulting Frank Quigley. So it was Frank who was dooming his old pal Desmond to be on a roving basis.

Did Frank not remember Deirdre? Did he not know how hard this was going to be for him?

Frank came so rarely to Rosemary Drive these days. But still, every time they met each other it was as if the old days were still the same. They banged each other on the shoulders and laughed, and since Desmond never made anything of being on such a low rung of a ladder they had joined so long ago, Frank equally never made any reference to his own high position. Only at the marriage to Renata Palazzo had the real gulf between them become apparent.

Nobody else from Desmond's level was at the wedding; everyone was many degrees above.

Deirdre had hated that wedding. She had been looking forward to it for months and even believed that she and Renata Palazzo would somehow become great friends. It had always been so unlikely that Desmond had never taken her seriously. Renata was years younger than they were, she was from a different world. Deirdre persisted in thinking of her as an Italian immigrant of her own age who would be shy and needing some kind of sisterly advice.

Desmond would never forget how Deirdre's smile had faded at the wedding when the bright yellow dress and coat made in matching man-made fiber came up against the pure silks and the furs of the other women. She who had left the house so cheerily that morning had been sinking into the background even during the church service when an Italian opera singer was getting through "Panis Angelicus" for the newlyweds. By the time they had arrived at the marquee and joined the line of guests waiting to be received, she was tugging at her dress and his arm.

It had been a black day for her, and her hurt had darkened the day for Desmond, too.

But none of it had been Frank Quigley's fault. Frank's smile never lessened, not ever in the years since then.

You could always go to Frank. You didn't have to say things in so many words. You could use code.

Where in the name of God was Frank today, this new black day when Carlo Palazzo was telling Desmond Doyle that he would have no office, no door, no telephone on a desk possibly?

Should he ask whether he could shortcut the whole thing for them by putting on one of the beige coats that the men who swept the shops put on, and getting down to work immediately with his bucket and pail and cleaning cloth, wiping the vegetable racks just after the doors closed? Would it perhaps be easier than waiting for half a dozen further slides? But then anger filled him, too; he wasn't a stupid man, he wasn't a fool who could be passed over like this. He could feel

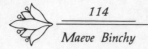

his face working in a way that was beyond his control. To his horror he saw something like pity in the older man's face.

"Desmond, my friend, please," Carlo began uncertainly.

"I'm all right." Desmond stood up behind his small desk. He would have strode across to the window so that the tell-tale tears in his eyes could subside. But his office wasn't one for striding, he would have had to squeeze past the filing cabinet and possibly knock over the small table or ask Mr. Palazzo to move his chair. It was too confined a place for grand gestures. Of course, come next week there would be no place for any gestures at all.

"I know that you are all right. I just don't want you to understand me wrongly. Sometimes, even after all these years in this country, I can't make myself clear . . . you know."

"No, you make yourself very clear, Mr. Palazzo, clearer than I do, and English is meant to be my native tongue."

"But perhaps I have offended you in something I said. Can I try to say it again? You are so valued here, you have been here so long and your experience is so necessary . . . it is just that circumstances change and there is an ebb and flow. Everything is being . . . what word will I use . . . ?"

"Redeployed," said Desmond flatly.

"Redeployed." Carlo Palazzo seized it and ran with it, not knowing he had already used it twice. His smile was broad. As if this word somehow rescued things.

He saw from Desmond's face that it didn't.

"Tell me, Desmond, what would you like best? No, it's not an insulting remark, not a trick question . . . I ask you what would you like best in work, what way would be the best way for things to work out for you today? Suppose it were possible for you to stay here, would that be your dream, your wish?"

The man was asking seriously, it wasn't a game of going forward and back. Carlo wanted to know.

"I don't suppose it would be my dream, no. Not to stay in this room as Special Projects Manager."

"So." Carlo looked for some silver lining desperately. "So why, then, is it so bad to leave it? What other place would have been your dream?"

Desmond leaned on the corner of the filing cabinet. Marigold had decorated the place a little with a few borrowed plants she must have grabbed from the carpeted offices. Desmond hoped she hadn't actually taken any of Carlo's own greenery. He smiled a little to himself at the thought, and his boss smiled back, looking up eagerly from the chair in front of the desk.

Carlo had a big, kind face. He didn't look shifty, he was the kind of Italian who always played the kind uncle or indeed the loving grandfather in a film.

It was Carlo's dream to be a grandfather many times over, to have a lot of little grandsons with half-Irish and half-Italian names running in and out of that huge white house. Children to leave his share of Palazzo to. Did Desmond dream of grandchildren, too? He didn't know. What a dull man he must be not to know his own dream when he was asked it by this big straightforward man.

"It's so long since I allowed myself to have a dream, I suppose I've forgotten what it was," he said truthfully.

"I never forgot mine, I wanted to go to Milano to work in fashion," said Carlo. "I want to have the finest craftsmen and stitchers and designers all together and to have my own factory with the name Carlo Palazzo."

"You have your own name over your work," Desmond said.

"Yes, but it is not what I wanted, not what I had hoped, I

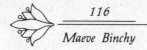
only have a little time in what I would have loved. My father he told me I must go into the food business, with my brothers, with my uncles, not playing with clothes like a ladies' dressmaker, he said."

"Fathers don't understand," Desmond said simply.

"Your father . . . did he not understand perhaps?"

"No, my father neither understood nor didn't understand, if you know what I mean. He was always an old man. When I was ten, he was old, and it wasn't just that I *thought* it, he looks it in every picture. He only understood sheep and hillsides and silence. But he never stopped me, he said I was right to go."

"Then how do you mean fathers never understand?"

"I didn't understand. I did all this for my son. I wanted him to have as good an education as possible, I didn't understand when he left."

"Where did he go?"

It had never been admitted outside Rosemary Drive. Never beyond the walls.

"He ran away, he ran back to the sheep and the stones and the silence."

"Well, you let him go." Carlo didn't seem shocked that Desmond's son had run off uneducated to the back of beyond.

"But not with a good grace." Desmond sighed.

Carlo was still puzzled. "So did you want a life of high education?"

For some reason the small, eager face of Suresh Patel flashed into Desmond's mind, his dark eyes feverish with the wish to heap degrees and diplomas on his family.

"No, not a high education. Just a place, I suppose, a place that was mine."

Carlo looked around the featureless office, which he

probably remembered as being even more featureless over the previous months without its injection of borrowed plants.

"This place? It feels so important?"

Desmond had somehow come to the end of the road.

"To be honest, Mr. Palazzo, I don't know. I'm not a man of very strong opinions. I never was. I have ideas, that's why I suppose Frank and you thought I'd be good here. But they are personal ideas, not corporate ones, and I'm inclined to get a bit lost whenever there's redeployment and the like. But I'll manage. I'll manage. I've always managed before."

He didn't sound frightened now or self-pitying. Just re- signed and practical. Carlo Palazzo was relieved that the mood, whatever it had been, had passed.

"It's not going to happen overnight, it will be in two to three weeks, and in many ways it will give you more freedom, more time to think about what you really want."

"Maybe it will."

"And there *will* be a title of manager, it hasn't been quite worked out yet, but when Frank gets back, I'm sure . . ."

"Oh, I'm sure he will," Desmond agreed readily.

"So . . ." Once more Carlo spread his hands out.

This time he was rewarded with a half-smile, and Des- mond stretched his own hand out as if to shake on something that had been agreed between two men of like mind.

Carlo paused as if something had struck him.

"Your wife? She is well?"

"Oh, yes, Deirdre's fine, thank you, Mr. Palazzo, bloom- ing."

"Perhaps she might care to come some evening to have . . . to have a meal in our house with us, the family, you know, Frank and Renata and everything. . . . You were all such friends in the old days . . . before any of this . . . that's true, yes."

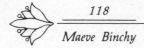
"That is very kind of you, Mr. Palazzo." Desmond Doyle spoke in the voice of a man who knew that no such invitation would be issued.

"That will be good, we will enjoy that." Carlo Palazzo spoke in exactly the same voice.

Marigold held the door open for the great chief Mr. Palazzo. He looked at her with a vague and pleasant smile.

"Thank you, thank you . . . um."

"I'm Marigold," she said, trying to iron out her Australian accent. "I'm lucky enough to work for Mr. Doyle. There have been several important calls, Mr. Doyle. I told them that you were in conference."

Desmond nodded gravely and waited until the footsteps were gone for Marigold to hiss at him, "Well, what happened?"

"Oh, Marigold," he said wearily.

"Don't 'Oh, Marigold' me, didn't I make you look good? Didn't you hear me? Bet he thinks a lot more of you now. Saying I was lucky to be working for you."

"I expect he thinks you're sleeping with me," Desmond said.

"I wouldn't half mind."

"You're possibly the nicest girl in the world."

"What about your wife?" Marigold asked.

"Oh, I don't think she'd like you to sleep with me, not at all."

"I mean, isn't she the nicest girl in the world, or wasn't she once or what?"

"She's very nice, very nice indeed." He spoke objectively.

"So no chance for me then." Marigold was trying to jolly him along.

"Palazzo's not the worst. That's a great Irish expression for you, to say a man is not the worst, it's grudging praise."

"He didn't give you the bum's rush then?" Marigold's face lit up.

"No, he gave me the bum's rush all right."

"Aw, shit. When? Where?"

"Soon, a week or two, when Frank gets back."

"Frank's not away," Marigold said furiously.

"No, but you know, we say he's away."

"And where are they sending you?"

"Here and there, roving apparently."

"Is there any good in it, any good at all?" Her eyes were tender, her big handsome face concerned, and she bit her lip at the unfairness of it all.

He couldn't bear her sympathy.

"Oh, it's all right, Marigold, there's plenty of good in it. I don't see this as anything we should fight them on the beaches for, do you . . . ?"

He looked around the office and made a theatrical gesture with his arms.

"But roving?" She seemed upset; he had to reassure her.

"It's more interesting than sitting here and seeing nothing at the end of it. I'll roam up and see you from time to time, you'd brighten my day."

"Did they say why?"

"Redeployment of resources."

"Redeployment of balls," Marigold said.

"Maybe, but what's the point?"

"You didn't *do* anything. They shouldn't take your job away."

"That could be it. Perhaps I really *didn't* do anything."

"No, you know what I mean, you're a manager, for God's sake, you've been here years."

"There's still going to be a manager's title, of whatever sort. . . . We don't know yet, we'll know later. . . ."

"Later, like when Frank gets back."

"Shush, shush."

"I thought you two were meant to be such friends."

"We were, we are. Now please, Marigold, don't *you* start."

She saw, sharp and quick, Marigold, and impulsively she said it.

"You mean you're going to have all this out with your wife tonight, is that it?"

"In a way, yes."

"Well, consider me a bit of a dry run."

"No. Thank you, I know you mean well."

She saw the tears in his eyes.

"I mean very well, and I'll tell you this: If your wife doesn't understand that you're one of the best . . ."

"She does, she does."

"Then I'll have to go around to your house and tell her she's got one beaut guy and I'll knock her head off if she doesn't know it."

"No, Deirdre will understand. I'll have had time to think about it, explain it properly, and put it in perspective."

If I were you, I wouldn't spend any time rehearsing. Ring her up, take her out to lunch, go on, find a nice place with tablecloths and buy a bottle of grog, tell her about it straight, there's no perspective."

"Everyone does things they want to in the end, Marigold," he said firmly.

"And some people, Dizzy, do nothing at all," she said.

He looked stricken.

Impulsively she flung her arms around him. He felt her sobbing in his arms.

"I'm such a loudmouth," she was saying.

"Hush, hush." Her hair smelled lovely, like apple blossom.

"I was trying to cheer you up, and look at what I ended up saying."

Her voice was becoming more normal. Gently he released her and held her from him, looking admiringly at the lovely Australian, the same age perhaps as his own Anna or a little older. The daughter of some man out on the other side of the world who had no idea of the kind of jobs this girl was doing and how she entered into them with all her heart. He said nothing, just looked at her until she sniffed herself to some kind of calm.

"Great if the old greaseball had come back and found us in a clinch, would have confirmed everything he suspected."

"He'd have been jealous," said Desmond gallantly.

"He would in a pig's eye, Dizzy," she said.

"I'm going out, I think," Desmond said.

"I'll tell them you're practicing roving if they ask," she said, almost grinning.

"Don't tell them anything," he said.

That was what he always said.

He phoned Frank from a call box near one of the entrance gates.

"I'm not sure if Mr. Quigley's available. Can I say who wants him?"

Long pause. Obviously a consultation.

"No, I'm very sorry, Mr. Doyle, Mr. Quigley's away on business. Was this not told to you? I believe Mr. Palazzo's secretary was to let you know. . . ."

"Sure, I just wondered if he was back." Desmond was mild.

"No, no." The voice was firm, as if speaking to a toddler who hadn't quite understood.

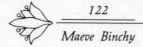
"If he calls in, tell him that . . . Tell him . . ."

"Yes, Mr. Doyle?"

"Tell him nothing. Say Desmond Doyle rang to say nothing, like he's been saying all his life."

"I don't think I quite—"

"You heard me. But I'll say it again." Desmond said the words again and felt some satisfaction at the sound of them. He wondered if perhaps he was going mad.

It was the middle of the morning and there was a strange sense of freedom about walking out through the big Palazzo gates. Like a child being sent home from school with some kind of sickness.

He remembered at the brothers years ago how he and Frank had played hooky for the day. Nobody knew that term over here, *skived* is what they called it. They had told the head brother that they had inhaled a bag of chemicals in the schoolyard and that their eyes were red and they were choking. They managed to persuade him that the cure would be fresh air.

Desmond could still recall thirty-five years later that freedom, as they ran and skipped over the hills, liberated in every way from the small classroom.

One of the things they had found lacking then was any way of finding people to play with. Everyone else was sitting resentfully in the classroom. They had felt the lack of a gang and had gone home earlier than they would have thought likely.

It was somehow the same today. There was nobody that Desmond could ask to come and play. Nobody to buy a bottle of grog for, as Marigold had suggested. Even if he were to take the train to Baker Street and go to Anna's bookshop, she might not be free. And she would be alarmed, it was so out of character. His only son, who had been lucky enough to recognize some kind of freedom and run for it, was far, far away. His other daughter, away in her convent, would not understand the need that he had to talk, the great urgency to define himself somehow.

It was a poor toting up of twenty-six years in this land that he could think of no other person in the whole of London that he could telephone and ask to meet him. Desmond Doyle had never thought of himself as a jet-setter but he had thought of Deirdre and himself as people with friends, people who had a circle. *Of course* they were. They were going to have a silver wedding anniversary shortly and their problem was not looking for people, it was trying to cut down on numbers.

What did he mean that he had no friends? They had dozens of friends. But that was it. *They* had friends. He and Deirdre had friends, and the problem had nothing to do with redeployment or managerial titles, the trouble was a promise made and a promise broken.

He had sworn to her that night so many years ago that he would rise in the business, he would be a name for the O'Hagan family in Ireland to take seriously. He had said that Deirdre would never go out to work. Her mother had never gone out to work, and none of Deirdre's friends who married back in 1960 would have expected to go and look for a job. Ireland had changed since then, had become more like England. Mrs. O'Hagan's nose, which seemed to turn up very easily, would not turn today if a young woman went on for further education or took any kind of work to help build a family home.

But those were black days long ago, and the O'Hagan scorn had been hard to bear. And Desmond knew that his promise was given under no duress. He had held Deirdre's small hand, and on the night they were about to tell her parents the news, he had begged her to trust him. He remembered his words.

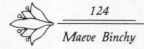

"I always wanted to be in buying and selling. I know it's not the thing to tell your family, but even when the tinkers came to town, I loved it, there was an excitement about it, about the way they put out their scarves and bright glittering combs on the ground. I knew what it was about."

Deirdre had smiled at him confidently, knowing he would never bring up anything as alien as tinkers in the O'Hagan household.

"I want *you*," he had said, "I want it more than anything in the world, and when a man has a dream, there's nothing he cannot conquer. I'll conquer the retail business in England. They'll be glad they didn't lose you to a doctor or a lawyer. The day will come when they'll be so glad they settled for a merchant prince."

And Deirdre had looked at him trustingly, as she had always looked ever since.

He supposed that she was still his dream, but why had she not come to his mind when Mr. Palazzo had asked him?

Desmond found himself walking the well-trodden path toward home. His feet had taken him on automatic pilot to the bus stop. At this time of day there were no crowds, no lines, how pleasant to be able to travel like this instead of during incessant rush hours.

Suppose he *did* ring Deirdre. He knew she was at home, she was working over that infernal silver silver wedding list again. Surely she would appreciate his honesty and directness.

She loved him in a sort of way, didn't she? Like he loved her. And he did love her. She had changed, of course, like everyone changed, but it would be ludicrous to expect her to be the fluffy, blond, desirable young Deirdre O'Hagan who had filled his thoughts and his heart so urgently. Why wasn't she the dream? She was connected with the dream in a way. The dream was to make good his promise. But he couldn't have told that to Carlo Palazzo in a million years, not even if he had been able to articulate it, which he hadn't. Not until this moment when the bus was approaching.

Desmond hesitated. Should he let the bus go, find a telephone, and invite his own wife out to lunch and tell her his own real thoughts? In the hope that they could somehow share them the way they had shared every little heartbeat during that time when they stood strong against the might of the O'Hagans about their marriage.

"Are you getting on or are you not?" the conductor asked him, not unreasonably. Desmond had been standing holding the rail. He remembered Marigold saying to him, "Some people, Dizzy, do nothing at all." But he was nearly on the bus.

"I'm getting on," he said. And his face was so mild and inoffensive that the tired young bus conductor, who also wanted a different and a better life, abused him no further.

He sorted it out for Deirdre as he walked toward Rosemary Drive, little phrases, little reasoning steps. There would be more scope in a roving managerial position, he would get to know the workings of the company at firsthand rather than being tucked away in his own little aerie. He would explain that Frank had been called away; he would mention that the exact wording was not firmed up but the magic word *manager* would be included. He would not mention the Palazzo invitation to supper, because he knew it would not materialize.

He felt no bitterness toward Frank for avoiding the confrontation. Nor, indeed, for initiating the move. Frank was probably right; the functions of Special Projects had indeed been taken over.

Frank might even be giving him a chance to find a better niche. He wished he could summon up more enthusiasm for this niche, whatever it might be.

It would confuse Deirdre to see him arriving home unex-

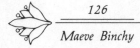

pectedly for lunch. She would fuss and say over and over that he should have warned her. The importance of his news would be lost in a welter of worries about there being nothing on hand.

Desmond decided that he would go into the corner shop, and tell Mr. Patel that yet again he had provided a service. They sold pizzas there, not very good ones, wrapped in rather too much plastic and with the wrong ratio of base and topping. Still, that might do. Or he might get a can of soup and some crusty French bread. He didn't remember whether Mr. Patel sold chicken pieces; that might be nice.

There were no customers in the shop, but more unusually there was nobody sitting at the cash register. On the few occasions when Suresh Patel did not sit there himself as if at a throne, still able to advise and direct his tiny empire, there was always another occupant. His silent wife, wordless in English but able to ring up the prices she read on the little labels. Sometimes it was the young, owlish son or the pert little daughter. Mr. Patel's brother didn't seem capable of manning the family business.

Desmond moved past the central aisle and saw with that lurching feeling of recognition that a raid was in progress.

There was that slow-motion sense of things not being real. Desmond felt as he looked at the two boys in their leather jackets beating the fat brother of Suresh Patel that this was like an action replay when watching a football match.

Desmond felt the old bile, but this time it was a sharper feeling. He thought he was going to choke.

He took two steps backward. He would run out and raise the alarm, he would run around the corner to the street where there would be more people passing by. *And,* if he was honest, where there would be less chance of the two muggers catching him calling for help.

But before he could go any farther, he heard the voice of Suresh Patel calling to the boys with the bars.

"I beg of you, I beg of you, he is simple in the head, he does not know anything about any safe. There *is* no safe. There is money in the night deposit. Please do not hit my brother again."

Desmond saw with another shock that he could feel physically in his own stomach that Mr. Patel's arm hung at an odd angle. As if it had already been beaten. And already broken.

Even if Marigold had not said to him sadly that there were some people who never did anything at all, he would have done what he did. Desmond Doyle, the man so mild that he had to be moved from an office lest he take root, so meek that he made a young Australian beauty cry over his future, knew suddenly what he had to do.

He lifted the stack of trays which had held the bread delivered that morning, and he brought it suddenly down on the neck of the first leather jacket. The boy, who could hardly have been as old as his own son, Brendan, fell with a thud to the floor. The other one looked at him wild-eyed. Desmond pushed him, jabbing him with the trays, and maneuvered him toward the back rooms, the living quarters of the whole family.

"Is your wife in there?" he shouted.

"No, Mr. Doyle." Suresh Patel looked up from the floor as people look up in films when rescuers arrive.

The brother who didn't know where the safe was smiled as if his heart were going to burst.

On and on Desmond pushed and prodded, his strength flooding to him. Behind him he heard voices come into the shop. Real customers.

"Get the police immediately, and an ambulance," called

Desmond Doyle. "There's been a raid. Go quickly, any private house will let you phone."

They ran, the two young men delighted to be on the safe end of a heroics job, and Desmond pushed a cabinet up against the door to the room where he had cornered the bewildered boy in the leather jacket.

"Can he get out that way?" he asked.

"No. We have had bars on the window and everything. You know, in case something like this . . ."

"Are you all right?" Desmond knelt on the floor.

"Yes. Yes. Did you kill him?" He nodded toward the boy on the floor, who was regaining consciousness and starting to groan.

Desmond had taken his iron bar away from him and stood prepared to deal another blow, but the boy was not able to move.

"No, he's not dead. But he'll go to jail. By God, he'll go to jail!" said Desmond.

"Perhaps not, but it doesn't matter." The shopkeeper tried to get himself to his feet. He looked weak and frightened.

"What matters then?" Desmond wanted to know.

"Well, I have to know who will run this shop for me—you see my brother, how he is, you know how my wife cannot speak, I must not ask the children to desist from school, they will miss their places and their examinations. . . ."

Far away Desmond heard a siren. The two heroes were bursting back in, saying the law was on the way.

"Don't worry about that," Desmond said gently to the man on the floor. "That will all be organized."

"But how, how?"

"Have you any relations, cousins, in businesses like this?"

"Yes, but they cannot leave their own places. Each place, it has to make its own way."

"Yes I know, but when we get you to hospital, will you be able to give me their names? I can get in touch with them."

"It is no use, Mr. Doyle, they will not have the time . . . they must work each in their own way."

His face was troubled and his big dark eyes filled with tears. "We are finished now. It's very simple to see," he said.

"No, Mr. Patel. I will run the shop for you. You must just tell them that you trust me and that it's not any kind of trick."

"You cannot do that, Mr. Doyle, you have a big position in Palazzo Foods; you only say this to make me feel good."

"No, it is the truth. I will look after your shop until you come back from hospital. We will have to close it today, of course, put up a sign, but by tomorrow lunchtime I will have it working again."

"I cannot thank you . . ."

Desmond's eyes also filled with tears. He saw that the man trusted him utterly. Suresh Patel saw Desmond Doyle as a great manager who could do what he willed.

The ambulance men were gentle. They said he had very likely broken a rib as well as an arm.

"It might be some time, Mr. Doyle," said Suresh Patel from the stretcher.

"There's all the time in the world."

"Let me tell you where the safe is."

"Not now, later, I'll come to see you in the hospital."

"But your wife, your family, they will not let you do this."

"They will understand."

"And afterward?"

"Afterward will be different. Don't think about it."

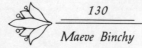

The policemen were getting younger, they looked younger than the villains. One of them was definitely younger than Desmond's son, Brendan.

"Who is in charge here?" the young policeman asked with a voice that had not yet gained the confidence it would have in a few short years.

"I am," said Desmond. "I'm Desmond Doyle of 26 Rosemary Drive and I'm going to look after these premises until Mr. Patel comes back from hospital."

5

*Father
Hurley*

*N*obody except his sister called Father James Hurley Jimbo; it would have been unthinkable. A man in his sixties with silver hair and a handsome head, he had the bearing of a bishop, and a lot of people thought he looked much more bishoplike than many of those who held the office. Tall and straight, he would have worn the robes well, and even better the cardinal's red. But Rome didn't go on appearances, and

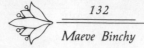

Father Hurley's name had never been brought to any corridors of power.

It was impossible to find anyone who would speak a word against him. His parishioners in several County Dublin districts had loved him. He was able, it seemed, to move just fast enough with the changes that came to the Church after the Vatican Council, but not too fast. He could murmur calming things that soothed the most conservative, and yet he seemed to go far along the road that allowed the laity to have a say. He wasn't exactly all things to all of his flock, but he certainly avoided irritating them.

And in a Dublin where anticlericalism among the younger liberals was becoming rife, this was no mean feat.

He was not a television priest, he had never been seen on the screen debating any issue. He was not the kind of man who would officiate at the marriage of known atheists having a church wedding just for the show, but neither was he the old-fashioned curate who went to Cheltenham in March with a pocket full of fivers, or cheered on the dogs at a dog race as they followed the hare. Father Hurley was a traveled, educated, soft-spoken man. People often said that he looked like an academic. This was high praise. And he was amused that it was sometimes regarded as even higher praise when he was described as looking not like a priest but more like a vicar!

James Hurley seemed to have moved quietly from parish to parish without either upward or downward movement. There did not seem to be the sense of advancement that such a well-spoken, thoughtful man might have been led to expect, but it was rumored that he never sought any promotion. You couldn't say he was unworldly—not Father Hurley, who liked fine wines and was known to enjoy pheasant and to relish lobster.

But he always seemed totally contented with his lot, even

when they had sent him to a working-class parish where he was in charge of fourteen youth clubs and eleven football teams instead of the drawing rooms and the visits to private nursing homes of his previous position.

He had been at school at one of the better Catholic schools in England, not that he ever talked about it. His family had been wealthy people, and it was rumored that he had been brought up on a big estate in the country. But none of this ever came from the man himself. He would laugh easily and say that nobody in Ireland should try to shake his family tree for fear of what might fall down. He had a sister who lived in the country with her husband, a country solicitor of substance, and their only son. Father Hurley did speak of this boy, his nephew, with great affection. Gregory was the only part of Father Hurley's private life about which he ever volunteered information.

Otherwise he was just a very good and interested listener to other people's stories. Which is why people thought he was such a good conversationalist. He talked only about them.

In the various presbyteries where Father Hurley's life had taken him there were pictures of his mother and father, now dead, in old-fashioned oval frames. There was a family picture taken at Gregory's first communion, and another one of Gregory's confirmation. A handsome boy with his hand lightly laid on his parchment scroll and his eyes smiling through the camera as if he knew much more than any other graduate who was posing for stiff formal photographs that day but took it all very casually.

For the people who told Father Hurley their own life stories, their worries and their tittle-tattle, Gregory was an ideal conversation piece. They could ask for him, and hear an enthusiastic response, enough to look polite, then they could return to their own tales again. They didn't notice that after a

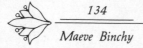

certain date the stories about Gregory never originated with Father Hurley and that his replies were vaguer and less informed than they had been once. He was far too diplomatic to let that be seen. That was another thing people said, he would have been very good at the Department of Foreign Affairs, or a consul or an ambassador even.

When James Hurley was a boy his mother had died, and he had always thought of Laura as being a combination of mother, sister, and best friend. Laura was five years older than he was, she had been seventeen when left in charge of a big crumbling house, a small crumbling brother, and a remote and withdrawn father who didn't give any of himself to his children any more than he had given of himself to his wife or the estate he had inherited.

Father James Hurley knew all that now, but then he had lived in a childlike fear of offending his stern, cold father still further. Laura could have gone away to a university, he always thought, if it had not been for her little brother. Instead she stayed at home and took a secretarial course in the nearby town.

She worked in the local grocery, which was eventually taken over by a bigger firm. Then she worked in the local bakery, which merged with three nearby bakeries, and her secretarial job there was over. She worked as the doctor's receptionist and during her time there he was taken off the medical register for professional misconduct. Laura used to tell her little brother, Jimbo, that she seemed to have a fairly unlucky effect and a dead hand on those she went to work for. Her little brother, Jimbo, used to suggest she come to work in his school in the hope that she would close it down.

She encouraged him in his vocation, she took long walks in the country roads with him, and together they sat on mossy banks and on the stile between the fields and talked about the love of God the way others might have talked about sports or the movies.

Laura Hurley had knelt with tears in her eyes to receive her brother's first blessing after he had said his first Mass.

Their father had died by this time, remote and uninvolved to the end. James had become a priest; he might have become a soldier or a jockey, it would have been on the same level of interest for his father.

While away at the seminary, James had often worried about Laura. She lived in the gate house of what had been their home. The big house was not really big in terms of the landed estates thereabouts, but it had been substantial. But Laura felt no sense of having come down in the world, living in the cottage where once people lived rent-free if they opened and closed the gates after the Hurley family. Laura had always said cheerfully that it was much easier to keep a small place than a big one, and since their father had gone first to a nursing home and then to his eternal reward, she was alone, so it didn't make sense to run the big house. When it was sold, there were so many debts that had gathered from James being a student, from Father being a patient in a private nursing home, that the place had been thoroughly mortgaged. There was little in the bank, there was no dowry for Miss Laura Hurley, faithful sister and dutiful daughter.

Laura never thought like that. She was happy, she walked her two big collie dogs, read her books in the evening by her small fire, and went to work by day for the local solicitors. She said laughingly that she hadn't managed to close them down as she had done to every other business she worked for, but she had managed to change them utterly.

Like changing the confirmed bachelor status of young Mr. Black. The Mr. Black who had once been the most eligible man in the county. At the age of forty he looked at Laura

Hurley, aged thirty-four, and a lot of his iron-hard resolve about staying single, uninvolved, and free began to chip away.

Then the letter arrived: "Dearest Jimbo, you'll never believe it but Alan Black and I are going to get married. We would very much like it if you could perform the ceremony for us. Since we're not in the first flush of youth, to put it mildly, we won't make an exhibition of ourselves here with everyone coming to stare. We would like to come to Dublin and be married in your parish if that's possible. Dearest Jimbo, I never knew I could feel so happy. And so safe and as if things were meant to turn out like this. I don't deserve it, I really don't."

Father Hurley always remembered that letter from his sister; he could see it, the words almost tumbling over each other on the small cream writing paper. He remembered the way his eyes had watered with a feeling of pleasure that things really did seem to have some point if this kind woman had found someone generous and good to share her life with her. He couldn't remember Alan Black except that he had been very handsome and rather dashing-looking in the past.

Father James Hurley felt that at twenty-nine he was a man of the world. And in a strange way he felt protective of his older sister as he joined her hand with Alan Black's at the wedding ceremony. He hoped this man with the dark eyes and dark hair just graying at the temples would be good to Laura and understand her generosity and how she had never sought anything for herself.

Several times he found himself looking at them and with a hope that was more than a wish. It was a silent prayer; he willed his sister to have a good relationship with this tall, handsome man. Laura's face was open and honest, but even on this, her wedding day, nobody could call her beautiful, her hair was pulled back and tied with a large cream-colored ribbon which matched the color of her suit. The ribbon was large enough to be considered a hat or head covering for church. She had a dusting of face powder and a smile that warmed the small congregation to the heart. But she was not a beautiful woman. Young Father Hurley hoped that the attentions of the handsome solicitor would not wander.

Years later he marveled at his own callow approach and wondered how he ever could have thought himself any use in advising men and women in their lives on their road to God. In a changing world there never was and never had been anything more strong and constant than the love Alan Black had shown to his bride. From the day that they had come to see him, back suntanned and laughing from their honeymoon in Spain, he should have realized that his own judgments based on appearances and vanity were superficial. Why should Alan Black, a bright, intelligent man, not be able to see the great worth, goodness, and love in Laura Hurley? After all, James Hurley had always seen it himself, why should he think it would pass Mr. Black, the solicitor, by?

And as the years went on, he used to go to stay with them. They had done up the little gate house and built on extra rooms. There was a new study out at one side of the house, filled with books from ceiling to floor. They lit a fire there in the evenings, and often the three of them sat in big chairs reading. It was the most peaceful, happy place he had ever been.

Sometimes Laura would look up from the chair where she lay curled up and smile at him.

"Isn't this the life, Jimbo?" she'd say.

Other days when he visited she might walk with him through the fields and over the stiles and hedges and ditches they had once owned.

"Did we ever think it would turn out so well, Jimbo?"
she said often, ruffling the hair of her young brother, who
would never be the great Father Hurley to her.

And then they told him they were building a similar
long, low room at the other side of the house. It was going to
be a nursery playroom. They would never call it the nursery,
they said, they would call it the child's room whatever his or
her name was. *Nursery* was only a baby word. The name was
Gregory. Father James held the baby in his arm for the bap-
tism. A beautiful child with the long, dark eyelashes of his
father. Gregory Black.

He was their only child; Laura said they would like to
have had a brother or sister for him, but it was not to be. They
made sure he had plenty of other children to play with. He
turned out to be the dream child that every doting uncle
hopes for.

Gregory would run from the window seat of his own big,
low room when he saw the car approaching.

"It's Uncle Jim," he would shout, and the old collie dogs
would bark and leap and Laura would rush from the kitchen.

When Alan got back from work, the smile was broad and
the delight obvious. They loved to see him come for a couple
of days mid-week. They loved the way he got on so well with
their son.

Gregory wanted to be a priest, of course, when he was
around ten. It was a far better life than working in his father's
office, he told them all seriously. As a priest you had to do
nothing at all, and people paid you money for saying Masses
that you'd be saying anyway, and you could get up on a pul-
pit and tell them all what to do or else they'd go to hell.
Sensing a delighted if half-shocked audience, Gregory went
on eagerly. It was the best job in the world. And you could

refuse to forgive anyone in confession if you didn't like them and then they'd go to hell, it would be great.

They came to Dublin to see him, too, and James Hurley never tired of talking about this warm, bright boy. Gregory wanted to know everything, to meet everyone. He could charm crabby old parish priests and difficult women parishioners who were always quick to fancy slights.

"I think you would be good as a priest actually," his uncle said to him laughingly one day when Gregory was fifteen. "An awful lot of it is public relations and getting along with people. You're very good at that."

"It makes sense," Gregory said.

Father Hurley looked at him sharply. Yes, of course, it made sense to present an amiable face toward people rather than a pompous one; of course, it was the wise thing to do to take the path that would not bring the wrath of authority around your ears. But fancy knowing that at fifteen. They were growing up a lot faster these days.

When Gregory got his place in UCD, he was studying law; that made sense too, he said. He had to study something, and law was as good a training as anything else. Meanwhile it kept his father, grandfather, and uncle happy to think another Black was going to come into the business.

"And is that what you are going to do?" Father Hurley was surprised. Gregory seemed to him to be too bright, too lively to settle in the small town. There wouldn't be enough to hold his sharp eyes, which moved restlessly from face to face, from scene to scene.

"I haven't really thought it out, Uncle Jim. It's what my mother and father would like, certainly, and since I don't know yet, it makes sense to let them assume that it's what I'll do."

Again there was a slight chill in the words. The boy had

not said he was lying to his family; he had said that since nothing in this world was definite, why cross your bridges before you came to them? Father James Hurley told himself that once or twice when he was saying his evening office and when the memory of Gregory's words troubled him. He began to think that he was becoming a foolish fusspot. It was ridiculous to read danger into the practical plans of a modern young man.

Gregory graduated well and was photographed on his own and with his father, mother, and uncle.

His father was now white-haired, still a handsome man. He was sixty-three now, forty-two years older than his boy. Alan Black had always said that it didn't matter whether you were eighteen years older than your son or forty-eight years older, you were still a different generation. But that in his case it had been everything and more than he had hoped, the boy had never wanted a motorbike, hadn't taken drugs or brought hordes of undesirables back to the home. He had been a model son.

His mother, Laura, looked well on his graduation day. She didn't twitter like other mothers did about having produced a son who could write "Bachelor of Civil Law" after his name and who would shortly be admitted to the Incorporated Law Society as a solicitor as well. Laura wore a bright pink scarf at the neck of her smart navy suit. She had spent what she considered a great deal of money on a haircut, and her gray hair looked elegant and well shaped. She did not look fifty-six years of age, but she did look the picture of happiness. As the crowds milled around the university campus, she grasped her brother by the arm.

"I almost feel that I've been too lucky, Jimbo," she said, her face serious. "Why should God have given me all this happiness when He doesn't give it to everyone else?"

Father Hurley, who certainly did not look his fifty-one years, either, begged her to believe that God's love was there for everyone, it was a matter of how they received it. Laura had always been an angel to everyone, it was just and good that she should be given happiness in this life as well as in the next.

He meant it, every single word. His eye fell on a woman with a tired face and a son in a wheelchair. They had come to watch a daughter graduate. There was no man with them.

Perhaps she, too, had been an angel, Father James Hurley thought. But it was too complicated to work out why God hadn't dealt her a better hand in this life. He would not think about it now.

They had lunch in one of the best hotels. People at several tables seemed to know Father Hurley. He introduced his family with pride, the well-dressed sister and brother-in-law. The bright, handsome young man.

A Mrs. O'Hagan and a Mrs. Barry, two ladies treating themselves to a little outing, seemed very pleased to meet the nephew of whom they had heard so much. Father Hurley wished they wouldn't go on about how often and how glowingly he had mentioned the young man. It made him feel somehow that he had no other topic of conversation.

Gregory was able to take it utterly in his stride. As they sat down at their own table, he grinned conspiratorially at his uncle.

"Talk about me being good at public relations, you're the genius, just feed them a little bit of harmless family information from time to time and they think they know all about you. You're cute as a fox, Uncle Jim."

It was a rescue from being thought to be the gossipy overfond uncle, certainly, but it did seem to classify him as something else. Something a bit shallow.

Gregory Black decided that he would practice law in Dublin for a few years in order to get experience. Make all his mistakes on strangers rather than his father's clients, he said. Even his old grandfather, now in his late eighties and long retired from the firm, thought this was a good idea, and his uncle, who had no children of his own. His parents accepted it with a good grace.

"It would be ridiculous to keep him down in a backwater after he's been so long on his own in Dublin," Laura told her brother. "And anyway, he says he'll come down and see us a lot."

"Does he just think that or will he really?" Father Hurley asked.

"Oh, he will. The only thing that made it difficult for him when he was a student was all the train and bus travel. Now that he'll have a car, it will be different."

"A car of his own?"

"Yes, it's Alan's promise. If he got a good degree, a car of his own!" She was bursting with pride.

And Gregory's gratitude was enormous. He embraced them all with pleasure. His father, gruff with delight, said that of course, in time Gregory would change this model and trade it in for another smarter kind. But for the moment . . . perhaps . . .

Gregory said he would drive it until it was worn-out. Father James Hurley felt his heart fill up with relief and pleasure that this dark, eager young man should know how much love and need encircled him and respond to it so well.

His parents went back happily to the country, his uncle went happily back to the presbytery, and the boy was free to do what he wanted with his life, with a brand-new car to help him on the way.

And Gregory did indeed visit home. He drove smartly in

the entrance of the gate house and fondled the ears of the collie dogs, children, and even grandchildren of the original collies that his mother had loved so much. He would talk to his father about the law and to his mother about his social life in Dublin.

He seemed to have lots of friends—men and women, Laura told her brother eagerly—and they went to each other's houses and even cooked meals for each other. Sometimes she baked a steak and kidney pie for him to take up to his flat. She always gave him bread and slices of good country ham, and bacon, and pounds of butter. Once or twice James Hurley wondered what she thought they sold in shops around the area where so many single people lived, where his nephew lived, but he didn't ever say anything. His sister loved the feeling that she was still looking after the big, handsome son she had produced. Why disturb that good, warm feeling? To use his nephew's own words, "It wouldn't make sense."

He hardly ever coincided with Gregory back home because the priest was never free on weekends, Saturdays were busy with confessions and house calls, Sundays with the parish Masses, the sick calls, and the evening benediction. But when he did get back himself mid-week for an overnight now and then, he was pleased to see that the pleasure of the visits totally outweighed what might be considered the selfish attitudes of their only son.

Laura talked delightedly of how Gregory had this big red laundry bag she had made him, and often he just ran into the kitchen and stuffed all the contents into her washing machine.

She said this proudly as if it had taken some effort. She mentioned not at all that it was she who took them out and hung them up to dry, she who ironed and folded the shirts and had all his laundry clean and packed on the backseat of his car for his return journey.

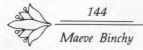
Alan talked about how Gregory loved coming to have Saturday dinner with them in the golfing club, how he appreciated the good wines and nice food that were served there.

Father Hurley wondered why Gregory hadn't on some occasions at least put his mother and father into the car they had bought him and driven them to one of the hotels nearby to treat them to dinner.

But as usual it made no sense to bring up something so negative. And he remembered with some guilt that he had never thought of treating his sister in the old days. He had a vow of poverty perhaps on his side, but there were things he hadn't thought of then. Maybe it was the same in all young men.

And Gregory was great company. He could talk a lot without saying anything, something that could be a compliment or an insult. In Gregory's case it was something to be admired, praised, and enjoyed.

Sometimes Gregory went swimming with his uncle out in Sandycove at the Forty-Foot, the men's swimming place. Sometimes he called in to have a drink in the presbytery, where he would raise the nice crystal Waterford glass to the evening light and admire the golden whiskey reflecting in the midst of all the little twinkling shapes of glass.

"Great thing, this ascetic life," Gregory would say, laughing.

You couldn't take offense at him, and it would only be a very churlish person who would notice that he never brought a bottle of whiskey with him to add to the store, ascetic or not.

Father Hurley was totally unprepared for a visit from Gregory in the middle of the night.

"I'm in a bit of trouble, Jim," he said right away.

No "Uncle," no "sorry for getting you out of bed at three A.M."

Father Hurley managed to shoo the elderly parish priest and the equally elderly housekeeper back to their respective quarters. "It's an emergency, I'll deal with it," he said soothingly. By the time he got into the sitting room, he saw that Gregory had helped himself to a large drink. The boy's eyes were too bright, he had sweat on his brow, and he looked as if he already had had plenty to drink.

"What happened?"

"A bloody bicycle swerved out at me, no proper light, no reflecting clothes, nothing. Bloody fools, they should be prosecuted, they should have special lanes for them like they do on the Continent."

"What happened?" The priest repeated the words.

"I don't know." Gregory looked very young.

"Well, is he all right, was he hurt?"

"I didn't stop."

Father Hurley stood up. His legs weren't steady enough to hold him. He sat down again.

"But was he injured, did he fall? Mother of God, Gregory, you didn't leave him there on the side of the road?"

"I had to, Uncle Jim. I was over the speed limit. Way over it."

"Where is he, where did it happen?"

Gregory told him, a stretch of dark road on the outskirts of Dublin.

"What took you up there?" the priest asked. It was irrelevant, but he didn't feel he yet had the strength to stand up and go to the phone to let the police and the ambulance know there had been an accident.

"I thought it was safer to come back that way, less chance

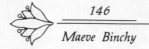
of being stopped. You know, breathalyzed." Gregory looked up, like the way he had looked up when he had forgotten to take one of the dogs for a walk or hadn't closed a gate in a far field.

But this time a bicyclist lay on the road in the dark.

"Please tell me, Gregory. Tell me what you think happened."

"I don't know. Jesus, I don't know. I felt the bike." He stopped. His face was blank.

"And then . . ."

"I don't know, Uncle Jim. I'm frightened."

"So am I," said James Hurley.

He picked up the phone.

"Don't, don't!" screamed his nephew. "For God's sake, you'll ruin me."

James Hurley had dialed the police.

"Shut up, Gregory," he said. "I'm not giving them your name, I'm sending them to the accident. Then I'll go myself."

"You can't . . . you can't . . ."

"Good evening, Sergeant, it's Father Hurley from the presbytery here. I've had a message, a very urgent one. There's been an accident . . ." He gave the road and the area. He thought the time was in the last half hour or so. He looked over at Gregory; the boy nodded miserably.

"Yes, it seems it was a hit-and-run."

The words had a disgusting finality about them. This time Gregory didn't even lift his head.

"No, Sergeant, I can't tell you any more. I'm sorry, it was reported to me in the nature of confession. That's all I can say. I'm going out there now to see what happened to the unfortunate— No, it was just confessed to me. I know nothing about any car or who the person was."

Father Hurley went for his coat. He caught a sight of his nephew's face and the relief that flooded it.

Gregory looked up at him gratefully.

"I never thought of that, but of course it makes sense. You *can't* really tell, because of the seal of confession."

"It wasn't confession. I could tell but I'm not going to."

"You couldn't break the sacred—"

"Shut your face!"

This was a different uncle from the one he had ever seen before.

He took a small bag with him in case he would have to administer the last sacrament to a seriously injured victim on the side of a dark road outside Dublin.

"What will I do?"

"You will walk home. And you will go to bed."

"And the car?"

"I will deal with the car. Get home and out of my sight."

The bicyclist had been a young woman. She was, according to the student card in her wallet, a Ms. Jane Morrissey. She was nineteen. She was dead.

The police said that it was always the same no matter how often they saw it, a dead body on the side of the road when some bastard had not stopped; it was terrible. One of them took off his hat and wiped his forehead, the other lit a cigarette. They exchanged glances over the priest, a pleasant, soft-spoken man in his fifties. He prayed over the dead girl and he sobbed as if he were a child.

He did it all for Laura, he told himself afterward on sleepless nights, because he couldn't drop off and be in a deep,

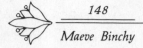

dreamless, unconscious state for seven and eight hours a night anymore. He had changed it to confession because if it hadn't been, then he would have had to report his sister's only boy as a hit-and-run driver. Even within the sacrament of confession he should still have urged the boy to confess and admit.

In real life things weren't like an old black-and-white movie with Montgomery Clift playing the tortured priest in an agony of indecision. Today a priest would insist that if a penitent wanted absolution, he must face up to the responsibility of his actions, he must make his restitution.

But James Hurley had thought of Laura.

This was a way to save her. It was a way to tell that weak son of hers that he was regarding the matter as one between sinner and confessor. There wasn't a leg to stand on in civil or canon law.

He lied to the police sergeant. He said it had been a hysterical call from someone trying to confess, that he had no idea who the driver was. He lied to the parish priest about the caller in the night; he said it was a man looking for alms.

He lied to his sister when she asked him why he couldn't come down soon and see them again. He said there was a lot going on in the parish. The truth was that he couldn't look them in the eyes. He couldn't listen while they told him some new tale of Gregory's excellence.

He had driven Gregory's car to a service station on the other side of Dublin in a place where nobody had known him. He had lied to the garage owner, said that he had driven the parish priest's car and hit a gate. The garageman loved to hear that a priest could do wrong too. He knocked out the dent and gave it a thorough going-over.

"The parish priest will think you kept it in great condition now," he said, glad to be in on some kind of a game.

"How much do I owe you?"

"Ah, go on, Father, there's nothing in it, say a few Masses for me, and my old mother, she's not been well."

"I don't say Masses in exchange for repairs." The priest had turned white with fury. "In God's name, man, will you tell me how much it cost?"

Frightened, the garage owner stumbled out an amount.

Father Hurley recovered and put his hand on the man's arm. "Please forgive me, I'm desperately sorry for losing control and shouting at you like that. I've been under a bit of strain, but that's no excuse. Can you know how sorry I am?"

Relief flooded the man's face. "Sure, Father, there's nothing like giving a car a bit of a tip against an old gate for putting the heart across you, and especially in the case of a respectable clergyman like yourself. Think nothing of it, it wasn't even as if there were any harm done."

Father Hurley remembered the white face of Jane Morrissey, nineteen, student of sociology, with the side of her head covered in rapidly drying blood. He felt faint for a moment.

He knew his life would never be the same again. He knew he had entered a different kind of world now, a world of lies.

He had placed the keys of the car in an envelope and left them in the mailbox of Gregory's flat. He had parked the car in the car port and walked back to the presbytery.

He read in the evening papers about the accident and listened to the appeal for witnesses on Radio Eireann.

He played a game of checkers with the old parish priest with his mind a million miles away.

"You're a good man, James," said the old priest. "You don't let me win like the others do. You're a very good man."

Father Hurley's eyes filled with tears. "No, I'm not, Canon, I'm a very weak man. A foolish, vain, and weak man."

"Ah, we're all foolish, weak, and vain," said the parish

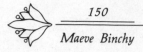

priest. "But given all that, there's goodness in some of us as well, and there certainly is in you."

But those frightening days were long over now, and still sleep didn't come. He had established an uneasy and formal relationship again with his nephew.

Gregory had phoned at once to thank him for the car.

Father James Hurley had said calmly into the phone, "I'm afraid he isn't here."

"But that *is* you speaking, Uncle Jim." Gregory was puzzled.

"I've told so many lies, Gregory, what's one more?" His voice sounded tired.

"Please. Please, Uncle Jim, don't talk like that. Is there anyone there listening to you, you know?"

"I've no idea."

"Can I come and see you?"

"No."

"Tomorrow?"

"No. Stay away from me, Gregory. Far, far away."

"But I can't do that, not forever. I don't want to, for one thing, and what about Mother and Father, for another? It would look . . . well, you know how it would look."

"I don't think they'd guess in a million years. I think you're safe. They would believe better of you. To them it will be just a small paragraph in the papers, another sad thing that happened in Dublin."

"No, I mean about us . . . if we're not going to be speaking."

"I suppose we'll speak again. Give me time. Give me time."

Gregory couldn't get through to him, not for weeks. If he turned up at the presbytery, his uncle apologized but said he was rushing out on a sick call. If he telephoned, it was the same.

Eventually he chose the one place where he knew he could get the undivided attention of the man who was running away from him.

In the confession box the little partition slid back. Father Hurley's handsome head could be seen leaning on his hand, not looking straight at the penitent but looking forward and slightly down. In a listening position.

"Yes, my child?" he began comfortingly.

"Bless me, Father, for I have sinned," Gregory said, beginning the ritual. His voice was too familiar not to be recognized. The priest looked up suddenly in alarm.

"Good God, have you decided to make a mockery of the sacraments as well?" he whispered in a low voice.

"You won't listen to me anywhere else, so I have to come here to tell you how sorry I am."

"It's not me you have to tell."

"But it is. I've told God already through another priest. I have decided to give a certain amount each month out of my salary to a charity to try to make up for it, even though I know it won't. I've given up drink. God, Uncle Jim, what more can I do? Please tell me. I can't bring her back to life. I couldn't have even then."

"Gregory, Gregory." There were tears in Father Hurley's eyes.

"But what is the use, Uncle Jim? What good will be served if you don't speak to me, and you don't come back home because you don't want to speak about me? I mean, if I

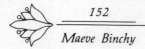

had been killed that night, too, it would all have been different. You'd have been locked in with my mother and father. So shouldn't we be glad I'm alive, anyway, even if that poor girl was killed in an accident?"

"By a hit-and-run drunken driver."

"I know, I've accepted it."

"But not the punishment for it."

"But what *good* would it do? Really and truly. It would break Mother's heart and disgrace Father, and humiliate you, and suppose it all came out now, weeks later, it would look so much worse. We can't relive that whole night. I would if I could . . ."

"Very well."

"What?"

"Just very well. We will be friends."

"Ah, I knew you'd find it in your heart."

"Good. Well, you were right, I've found it in my heart. Now can you allow someone else in to make their peace with God?"

"Thank you, Uncle Jim. And, Uncle Jim . . ."

The priest said nothing.

"Will you come and have lunch in my flat sometime? Maybe Saturday. No liquor but a couple of my friends. Please?"

"Yes."

"Thank you again."

He went to the boy's flat. He met two young men and a girl. They were pleasant, easygoing company. They drank wine with their lunch and argued genially about whether the Church still ruled everything in Ireland. Father Hurley was practiced in this kind of conversation; most of his friends' children took this line. He was bland and unfailingly courteous, he saw the point of view on this hand, on the other hand,

and on yet further hands. He had a soothing murmur, an ability to appear to lose a point in order to let the opposition concede a point too.

He watched Gregory carefully. Only mineral water went into his glass. Perhaps the boy was shaken and was trying to start a new life. Perhaps James Hurley really should find it in his heart to try to forgive the boy even if he couldn't forgive himself. He smiled at his nephew and got a warm smile back.

They all helped to clear the table out to the small, smart kitchen.

"Hey, Greg, what's this bottle of vodka doing here if you've given it up?" asked one of his friends.

"Oh, that's from the days before; take it with you." Gregory spoke easily.

Father Hurley wondered whether his own soul had become somehow poisoned, because he had a suspicion that his nephew's eyes were somehow too bright for a boy on plain water; perhaps he had been topping it up with vodka out in the kitchen. The other drink was kept on a sideboard.

But if this was the way he was going to think all the time, then there was no point in having any relationship with his nephew at all. He put it firmly from his mind. Into that store of other things he was simply refusing to think about these days.

He went to see Laura and Alan during the week. They were delighted to hear about the presence of the girl at the Saturday lunch party; they thought she might be a current girlfriend.

"She didn't seem to be relating to him especially." Father Hurley felt like an old lady gossiping at a tea party.

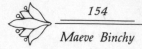

"She's been around for a while," Laura said happily. "I think this may be the one all right."

It had been a strange visit. Everything his sister and his brother-in-law said seemed to grate on him.

They told him he was lucky to have certainties. Sometimes in the law there were gray areas.

He smiled grimly. As if there were no gray areas in his line of work!

They said how lucky they were with Gregory. The son of a friend of theirs had joined Sinn Fein, first as a legal adviser, then as an active campaigner, and then as a fully fledged member of the Provisional IRA.

"At least he had some ideals, however misplaced and mad," Father Hurley said.

"Jimbo, you must be mad, there're no ideals in that lot," Laura cried.

And as always he smiled self-deprecatingly. There was no way he was going to explain to them that he thought any cause was better than the weak-minded cause of saving your own skin, which their son had done. With his connivance.

He looked uneasy and unhappy; Alan Black, in his diplomatic way, changed the subject.

"Tell us, are you officiating at any nice society weddings these days? We love to feel near the high and mighty of the land through you, Jim."

No, Father Hurley told them. Young people always had some friend of their own to marry them nowadays; they didn't go for old family friends of the parents. No, not a posh wedding coming up. A silver wedding, though, he said brightly, and in England no less.

They were interested, as they always were, in everything he did. He explained he had married this couple way back in 1960—it didn't seem like a quarter of a century ago but apparently that was what it was! The daughters and son of this couple wanted him to attend. They had said it would be meaningless if he didn't have some kind of ceremony for them all.

Laura and Alan thought that it was only right that this couple, whoever they were, would want Father Hurley again.

"I didn't know them very well," he said, almost as if talking to himself. "I know Deirdre's mother, Mrs. O'Hagan, slightly, and I knew Mrs. Barry, the mother of the maid of honor, Maureen Barry. But I didn't know the young man at all."

"You never mentioned them." Laura was drawing him out.

"Well, no, I suppose I marry a lot of people. Some I never see again. I always get a Christmas card from Deirdre, mind you. I used not to remember exactly who they were, Desmond and Deirdre Doyle and family . . ." He sighed heavily.

"Did you not like them?" Laura asked. "It doesn't matter telling us, we don't know them, we won't ever meet them."

"No, they were perfectly nice. I *did* like them, as it happened. I suppose I didn't think they were well suited, that they'd stay together . . ." He gave a little laugh to lighten the mood. "But there you go, I was wrong. They've been together now for twenty-five years and it doesn't seem a day too much."

"They must like each other." Laura was thoughtful. "Otherwise they wouldn't want you around and have a big do and everything. Will there be a renewing of vows?"

"I don't know. It was their daughter who wrote to me."

He relapsed into silence, but silence in the big book-lined room of Alan and Laura Black was never anything to worry about.

He thought about that wedding, the year that Gregory

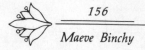

was born. He remembered how Deirdre O'Hagan had come into his sacristy saying that she had heard from her mother that he was going on a six-month temporary assignment to London. It was partly a study assignment and partly in case he might want to join the Irish chaplaincy scheme in Britain. There were so few English vocations, and so many of the Catholic flock were Irish or second-generation Irish who preferred a priest from their own tribe.

Deirdre O'Hagan had seemed distressed and tense. She wanted to know if he could organize a marriage for her in the next month or so.

It had all the hallmarks of a shotgun marriage, but she would not be drawn into any conversation about the reasons for the speed.

He had asked mildly that she should consider having the ceremony in Dublin, but she had been adamant. Her fiancé's people were from the West.

But surely Dublin was nearer to the West of Ireland than London was.

Deirdre O'Hagan—whom he had remembered as the pretty, giggling university student daughter of Kevin and Eileen O'Hagan, who were supportive and well-off parishioners —seemed to have developed a will of steel. She was marrying in London and said it would be a kindness to her family to involve a curate whom they knew and liked, but of course if he wasn't able to, she would make other arrangements.

Father Hurley had tried at the time, he thought looking back on it, to involve the girl in some questioning of the suddenness of her decision. He had said that one shouldn't go into matrimony too hastily and for all the wrong reasons.

He had obviously sounded stuffy and inquisitive, for he remembered her voice—clear as a bell and cold, very cold.

"Well, Father, if one was to take your own attitude to

matrimony, one would never marry at all and one would suddenly find that the whole human race had died out."

Despite this poor start, the wedding had been perfectly pleasant. The boy's people were simple, small farmers from the West, they didn't field a very large contingent. The O'Hagans were there in force. A nice man, Kevin, quiet and thoughtful. He had died some years back, but Eileen was still going strong.

The maid of honor had been that handsome young woman Maureen Barry, who ran the smart dress shops nowadays. He had seen her only the other day when he had said the requiem Mass for her mother. He wondered if she would go across to London for this ceremony. He wondered if he would. He sighed again.

"You're not in good form, Jimbo." Laura was concerned.

"I'd love to be an old settled priest, you know, totally certain about everything, no doubts at all."

"You'd be unbearable if you were," she said affectionately.

Alan looked up from his book. "I know what you mean. It would be easier if there was just one law and you had to administer it, abide by it. It's all this awful business of trying to judge each case on its merits that confuses things."

James Hurley looked at his brother-in-law sharply, but the solicitor had no hidden meaning, no insight about his son and the trouble he had caused. He was thinking in terms of the district court and a justice being lenient here and strict there, according to what he knew of the person before him.

"You'd end up like the Nazis if you couldn't make your own decisions," Laura consoled him.

"Sometimes they're not right, though." His face was still troubled.

"You'd never do anything unless you thought it was right at the time."

"And afterward? What happens afterward?"

Laura and Alan exchanged glances. Jim was never like this.

Alan spoke eventually. "Well, at least it's not like a hanging judge in the old days. You didn't actually sentence anyone to death." It was meant to be reassuring. It didn't really work.

"No. No, not to death."

"Shall we take the dogs for a walk?" Laura said.

They walked, the brother and sister, sprightly and strong, through the fields that they had walked since they were children.

"If I could help?" she said tentatively.

"No, Laura, I'm a weak man to be letting you see my black side."

"You're my younger brother, for all that you're a grand important priest."

"I'm not grand and important. I never got a parish, I never wanted one. I don't want to take charge."

"Why should you, then? People don't have to."

"There are some things they have to take charge of."

She knew he would talk no more about it, and his brow seemed to clear as they walked home in the fading light.

He knew after that afternoon that if the whole terrible business was to have any value whatsoever, he must cease these self-indulgent moods. What was the point of saving them worry on one score only to cause it on another? So, they had been spared from knowing that their son had killed a bicyclist while drunk and had failed to stop; that had been peace of mind. Why take that peace away from them again by letting them think that he was cracking up and heading for serious nervous trouble?

In the months that followed, he hardened his heart to the doubts and he fought the sense of betrayal when he sat with the only family he ever had or would ever know. He began to laugh easily at his nephew's jokes and managed not to wince at some of Gregory's more insensitive remarks. The priest told himself over and over that to expect a fallible human being to be perfect was to go against the revealed word of God.

He took pleasure in the simple joy that Gregory Black's parents got from their son. He reminded himself that in all his years of parish work he had never come across a family where there was such peace and genuine accord. Perhaps the price for this might never have to be paid in their lifetime.

He forced his smile not to falter when he saw Gregory helping himself liberally to the gins before dinner, the wines with, and the whiskeys after. The non-drinking resolution had not lasted very long. Neither had the girlfriend.

"She's too determined, Uncle Jim." He had laughed as he drove Father Hurley across the country rather too fast for the priest's liking. "You know everything is an absolute with her. No gray area."

"It's admirable in its way," Father Hurley said.

"It's intolerable. Nobody can be that sure, that definite."

"Did you love her, do you think?"

"I could have, I suppose, but not with all this black and white, honesty or dishonesty, you're either a saint or a devil. That's not the way it is in the real world."

Father Hurley looked at the handsome profile of his sister's son. The boy had forgotten the girl he had killed. The ambiguity and hypocrisy of that night literally had been put out of his mind. He was driving his uncle because Father Hurley's car was out of action, and Gregory had wanted to

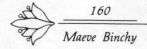
come down mid-week, wanted to talk to his father about a
loan. There was something coming up, he had heard a piece of
information, the kind of chance that comes only once in a
lifetime. Something he really shouldn't know, but if he in-
vested now. Boy!

Father Hurley felt sick that he should be allowed to receive this confidence. But then, what was he except another
gray-area person? Someone prepared to lie when it made
sense. It was a strange visit. Gregory's father seemed apologetic about not being able to raise the money that Gregory
needed and a little mystified that he wasn't being told exactly
what it was needed for.

Gregory's smile didn't falter, but he said he would drive
out to be on his own for a while near the lake.

Laura said after he had left that it was very sensible of
him to go and work out his annoyance while sitting looking at
the lake. She said that she wished Alan had just given him the
damn money, it would all be his after their time, why couldn't
he have it now?

By ten-thirty he hadn't come back.

Father Hurley knew he was in the pub, the roadhouse out
on the lake drive. He said he'd fancy a walk himself, it was a
nice night. It was a three-mile walk. He found his nephew in
the bar being refused a drink.

"Come on, I'll drive you home," he said in what he hoped
didn't sound a tone likely to anger his very drunk young
nephew.

When they got to the car, Gregory pushed him away.

"I'm perfectly able to drive." His voice was steely.

James Hurley had a choice once the boy was behind the
wheel—go with him or let him go on his own.

He opened the passenger door.

The corners were legion and the surfaces were not good.

"I beg you, take it slowly, you don't know what's coming around the corner, there's no way we can see the lights."

"Don't beg me," Gregory said, his eyes on the road. "I hate people who whine and beg."

"Then I ask you . . ."

They were on top of the donkey and cart before they saw it. The frightened animal ahead reared and was emptying the two old men and their belongings onto the road.

"Jesus Christ."

Helpless, they watched as the donkey, roaring in pain, dragged the cart over the body of one old man and started to slip down the bank toward the lake.

Father Hurley was running toward the cart where two children were screaming.

"You're all right. We're here, we're here," he called.

Behind him, he felt the breath of his nephew.

"You were driving, Uncle Jim. In the name of Christ, I beg you."

The priest didn't stop. He had caught the first little tinker child in his arms and pulled her to safety, then the second, and with all the strength in his body he pulled at the braying donkey too.

"Listen, I beseech you. Think about it, it makes sense. They'll hit me with everything, but they can't put a finger on you."

It was as if Father Hurley hadn't heard him; he had children and cart up to the road where the two dazed old men sat. One was holding his head in his hands and blood was coming through his fingers.

In the moonlight Gregory's face was white with terror.

"They're tinkers, Uncle Jim. They're not meant to be out here without any signs or warning or lights . . . nobody

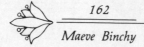

could blame you . . . they heard you saying you were driving me home."

Father James Hurley knelt beside the old man and forced him to take his hands away so that he could see the wound.

"It's all right my friend, it's all right. When somebody comes, we'll get you to the hospital, it'll only be a stitch or two."

"What are you going to do, Uncle Jim?"

"Oh, Gregory."

The priest looked up with tears in his eyes at the only son of the two people who would realize tonight that perhaps life wasn't meant to be all that good on this earth and that some people had been too lucky.

6

Maureen

The one thing Maureen's mother would have insisted on had she been alive was that the funeral be done right. Maureen knew exactly what that meant. It meant that there be sufficient notice in the paper for everyone to attend, that there be a judicious invitation back to the house, not everyone but the right people. Both on the day she was brought to the church and on the following day after the burial itself.

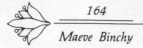
Maureen arranged it meticulously, a last homage to the mother who had given her everything and had made her what she was.

She wore a magnificently cut black coat and asked a hairdresser to come to the house so that she would look immaculately groomed in front of all the people who turned up at the church. Maureen did not consider this vanity, she considered that she was carrying out to the letter her mother's last wishes: that Sophie Barry go to her rest mourned publicly by her exquisite and devoted daughter, Maureen, successful businesswoman, person of standing in Dublin.

Her mother would have approved, too, of the drinks and canapés served in the big drawing room and the way that Maureen moved among the guests pale but calm, introducing here and thanking there, and always being able to remember if it was a wreath, a Mass card, or a letter of sympathy that had to be acknowledged.

She had nodded in total agreement to all who told her that her mother was a wonderful woman, because this was only the truth. She nodded that it was better that her mother hadn't had a long illness, she deplored the fact that sixty-eight was too young to die, she was pleased that so many people told her that her mother had been so proud of her only daughter.

"She never talked about anything else."

"She had a scrapbook of all your achievements."

"She said that you were more than a daughter, you were her friend."

Soothing words, gentle touches, graceful gestures. Just as Mother would have liked it. Nobody got drunk and became boisterous but there was the kind of buzz about the whole proceedings that Mother would have thought the mark of a successful gathering. Several times Maureen had found herself planning to talk to her mother about it afterward.

But then people often said that this was the case. Particularly when you had been close. And there were few mothers and daughters as close as Sophie Barry and her only child, Maureen.

Possibly it was because Sophie was a widow and Maureen had been left fatherless for so many years. Possibly because they looked so alike, people read more into their togetherness than there was. Sophie had only become gray late in her fifties, and when she did, it was a steel-dark gray, as shiny and glamorous as had been the raven-black hair. She had been a size twelve up to the last day and said that she would die rather than wear one of those tentlike creations that so many women seem to sink into after a certain age.

Sophie's good looks and harsh standards did not always endear her to the more easygoing in her circle. But she had what she wanted from them, their total admiration all of her days.

And Maureen would make sure that it would continue in terms of whatever needed to be done now. The house would not be sold with unseemly haste, the mortuary cards would be simple and black-edged, with some tasteful prayer that could be sent as a memento to Protestant friends, too. Not something dripping with indulgence-gaining imprecations, no photograph. Mother would say that's what maids did. Maureen would know better than to insult her memory.

Friends had offered to help her go through her mother's things. It can be upsetting, they said, it's often easier if an outsider comes to help. Everything can be divided into categories much less emotionally. But Maureen smiled and thanked them, assuring them that this was something she would like to do herself. She didn't particularly want to go

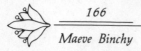

through things alone, but Mother would never have let a stranger look at her private papers in a million years.

Father Hurley, who had known them for years, offered to help. He said it was often a lonely business and he would be happy even to sit with her as company. He had meant well, and Mother had always liked him, she said he was a credit to the Church, nicely spoken, very cultured, knew everyone who was anyone; high praise from Mother. But still, Mother would not have let him become involved in her private papers. A gentle, moving sermon, yes, exactly the right kind of priest for this parish, but he couldn't be involved in anything personal. That would be for Maureen alone.

Walter would want to help, of course, but it was out of the question. Walter had been kept at arm's length during the whole proceedings. Maureen had no intention of marrying him or of being seen to rely on him. Why, then, should he be allowed to be present at all the funeral ceremonies as her right-hand man? This would be giving a false impression to all those old biddies, friends of her mother, women who had nothing left to talk about in their own lives and speculated instead about each other's children. Maureen, unmarried at forty-six, must have given them many good years of chat and supposition, she thought with a grim pleasure.

Kind, courteous Walter, who was thought to be suitable for her because he, too, was unmarried, of a good family, and had a good practice at the bar. Maureen knew that if she wanted to, she could marry Walter. He didn't love her, and she felt nothing even remotely like love for him. But Walter was the kind of man who wouldn't have expected love at this stage in life. Once when he was a younger man, perhaps an unsuitable dalliance or two, maybe even a real affair that didn't work out.

Walter had his male bonding in the law library, he had a busy social life. People always wanted an extra man.

Mother had liked Walter but Mother was far too intelligent to push her toward him. Anyway, Mother would have been the last to use the argument about insuring against a lonely old age. Look at her own years as a woman without a man. Her life had been very full.

Once Maureen had made it clear that she had no thoughts about Walter as a life partner, her mother had never pushed the notion again. There had been no talk of including Walter in a bridge party, a theater outing, or the party made up to go to the Aga Khan Cup at the horse show.

Walter was kind, courteous, and could indeed, after several glasses of good claret, be a little emotional. Sometimes he talked of lonely roads and sacrificing all else on the altar of one's career. But Maureen would laugh at him affectionately and ask him to consider what on earth she and he had sacrificed. They had lovely apartments, good cars, hosts of friends, and the freedom to go where they liked. In Maureen's case, to London and New York buying clothes, in Walter's to the West of Ireland fishing.

In a Dublin which more and more would have accepted such a state, they were not lovers. It had been suggested one evening and rejected, with charm and elegance on each side, and broached once more in case the first refusal had been only a matter of form. But they remained two attractive single people whose eyes often met resignedly over a table, as yet again a hostess had brought them together as an inspired idea for a dinner party.

It was ironic that of all the men who had wandered into Maureen's life, the only one that Mother would have considered suitable was the one who came too late, who came along when Maureen knew she didn't want to change her ways. If

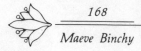

she had met Walter, a young, earnest barrister in his twenties when she had been struggling to establish the shops, she might well have settled for him. So many of her friends had settled for men whom they could not possibly have loved in any real sense. These were not great loves, the wedding ceremonies that Maureen had attended all through the 1960s, they were alliances, refuges, compromises, arrangements. Deirdre O'Hagan, who defied everyone and married her first love in that long summer when they had all been in London, that might have been real love. Maureen was never sure. Even though she had been Deirdre's maid of honor, and they had slept in the same room the night before the wedding, she had not been certain that Deirdre ached for Desmond Doyle and cried out to be with him. As she herself had cried out to be with Frank Quigley.

It was a strange friendship, hers with Deirdre. Their mothers wanted them to be friends so desperately that they gave in at the age of fourteen and agreed to go to the same tennis parties, and later the same hops and rugby-club social evenings on Saturday nights.

By the time they got to UCD they were in fact friends of a sort. And they each knew that their salvation lay with the other. If Maureen said she was going anywhere with Deirdre, then Mother would relax. It was the same in the O'Hagan household; Deirdre could always use Sophie Barry's daughter, Maureen, as an excuse.

That was why they had been able to go off to London together that summer. The summer they should have been at home working for their degrees. The summer they met Desmond Doyle and Frank Quigley on the boat to Holyhead.

Maureen wondered what Frank Quigley would say if he knew that Mother had died. She didn't know how he talked these days, whether his accent had changed, if he spoke as a lot of Irishmen living twenty-five years in London spoke, with two distinct strands in their voices and telltale words of both cultures coming in at the wrong place.

She had read about him; who hadn't read about Frank Quigley? He was profiled always among the Irish who had done well in Britain. Sometimes she saw pictures of him with that sullen-looking young Italian he had married to advance himself still further in the hierarchy of Palazzo.

Of course, Frank might be so suave nowadays that he would write an elegant note of sympathy on a gilt-edged card. He might be so down-to-earth and still such a rough diamond that he would say she should have died a quarter of a century earlier.

One thing Maureen knew was that Frank Quigley would not have forgotten her mother, any more than he would have forgotten Maureen.

This was not arrogance on her part, believing that her first love would remember her with the same intensity as she remembered him, when she allowed him into her mind at all. She knew it was true. Still, it was irrelevant; he might hear about it from Desmond and Deirdre, but it was hard to say whether they all remained friends still.

Admittedly Desmond still worked in Palazzo, but despite Mrs. O'Hagan's great reports of her son-in-law's managerial promotions from time to time, Maureen had the feeling that Desmond had stuck somehow low on a scale and that all the patronage and friendship from his old friend Frank couldn't pull him any higher.

The day of sorting through Mother's things could not be put off forever. Maureen decided to go on the Sunday following the funeral. It would not take long if she put her mind to it and did not allow herself to become emotionally upset by everything she touched.

Already she had wept over her mother's glasses in their spectacle case, which had been given to her in the hospital. Somehow it seemed sadder than anything else to see the sign of Mother's frail, fading eyesight handed to her in a useless little case. Maureen, usually so decisive, hadn't known what to do with them. They were still there, zipped into a side compartment of her handbag. Mother would not have been so softhearted. She would have been cool and practical, as she had been about everything.

They had only fought once, a long time ago, and it had not been about Frank Quigley or about any man. Mother hadn't thought that the clothing business looked all right or sounded respectable enough.

Maureen had blazed her anger. What the hell did it matter how things looked or sounded? It was how they were, what they were about that was important. Mother had smiled a cool, infuriating smile. Maureen had stormed out. Up to the North of Ireland first, where she got a thorough grounding in retail dress sense from two sisters who ran a smart clothes shop and were pleased and flattered to see the dark, handsome young university graduate from Dublin come up to learn all they could teach her. Then she went to London.

It was then that she realized how she had never been really close to Deirdre; they had met rarely while she was there. Deirdre had been tied up with two babies at that stage, and Maureen had been going to trade fairs and exhibitions and learning what to look for. Maureen told Deirdre nothing of her coldness with her mother for fear that it would go straight back to the O'Hagan household, and presumably Deirdre had secrets, worries, and problems that she didn't tell Maureen either.

And anyway, the coldness didn't last. It had never been an out-and-out hostility, there were always postcards and

short letters and brief phone calls. So that Mother could tell
Eileen O'Hagan how well Maureen was doing here, there, and
everywhere. So that appearances could be kept up. Appearances had been very important to Mother. Maureen determined that she would honor this to the very end, far beyond
the grave.

Maureen Barry lived in one of the earlier apartment
houses that had been built in Dublin. She lived ten minutes
by foot and two minutes by car from the big house where she
was born and where her mother had lived all her life. It had
been Mother's home, and Father had married in. For the short
married life that they had. He had died abroad when Maureen
was six, forty years ago this year.

It would be the anniversary of his death shortly, in three
weeks; how strange to think that she would attend the Mass
they always had said for the repose of his soul totally on her
own. Normally she and Mother went together, for as long as
she could remember. Always at eight o'clock in the morning.
Mother had said that it was discourteous to involve others in
your own personal mourning and memorials. But Mother had
always told people afterward that they had been to the Mass.

The living arrangements were yet one more way in which
the relationship between the two women was widely praised.
Many another mother would have clung to her daughter and
kept her in the family home as long as possible, not noticing
or caring about the normal wish of the young to leave the
nest. Many a less dutiful daughter might have wanted to go
away to another city. To London perhaps or even Paris. Maureen was successful in the fashion world. To have two shops
with her own name on them by the time she was forty was no
mean achievement. And such smart shops, too. She moved
from one to the other with ease; each had a good manager
who was allowed freedom to run the day-to-day business. It

had left Maureen free to buy, to choose, to decide to lunch with the fashionable women whose taste she monitored and even formed. She went to London four times a year and to New York once every spring. She had a standing that her mother would never have believed possible in those bad days, the bad time when they had not seen eye to eye. It hadn't lasted long, and every relationship was allowed to have some valley periods, Maureen told herself. Anyway, she didn't want to think about those days now, not so soon after Mother's death.

It had indeed been so sensible to live apart but near. They saw each other almost every day. Never in all the years since she moved into her apartment did Maureen open her front door and find her mother unannounced on her step. Mother wouldn't dream of calling on a young woman who might be entertaining someone and wished to do so privately.

It was different about Maureen going back to her old home. No such strictures applied there. Maureen was welcome to call at any time, but Mother managed to let her know that at the end of a bridge party was a particularly suitable time to drop in for a sherry, because everyone could have the chance to admire both the elegant daughter and the evidence of her consideration and devotion to her mother.

On the Sunday she walked to the house where she would never again see her mother walking lightly down the hall to open the door, viewed through the multicolored stained glass of the hall door panels. It felt strange to go to the empty house, because by now there would be no kind friends and relatives staying around as support. Mother's great friend Mrs. O'Hagan, Deirdre's mother, had been very pressing and begged Maureen to come and see them, to drop in for supper, to use the O'Hagan house just like she had her old home.

It had been kind, but not the right thing. Maureen wasn't

a little girl; she was a middle-aged woman, for heaven's sake. It was not appropriate for Mrs. O'Hagan to invite her up to the house as she had done thirty years ago, when she and Mother had decided that Deirdre and Maureen should be friends.

Mother had always set a lot of store on what Eileen O'Hagan thought about this and that. Eileen and Kevin were her greatest friends. They had always invited Mother to join them at the theater or the races. They had never to Maureen's recollection tried to find a suitable second husband for her. Or perhaps they had. She would not have known.

As she walked through the sunny streets toward her old home Maureen wondered what life would have been like if Mother had married again. Would a stepfather have encouraged her or fought her when she wanted to take up her career in what she had called the fashion industry and her mother had said was common drapery and glorified salesgirl work?

Would Mother have been coquettish with men years ago? After all, Maureen herself did not feel old and past sexual encounters at the age of forty-six, so why should she assume that her mother had? But it was something that never came into their lives.

They talked a lot about Maureen's young men, and how they had all somehow failed to measure up. But they had never talked about any man for Mother.

She let herself into the house and shivered slightly because there was no little fire lit in what Mother had always called the morning room. Maureen plugged in the electric heater and looked around.

Two weeks ago on a Sunday she had come here to find Mother looking white and anxious. She had this pain, possibly indigestion but . . . Maureen had acted quickly, she helped her mother gently to the car and drove calmly to the

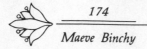

hospital. No point in disturbing the doctor, calling him away from his Sunday breakfast, she had said to Mother, let's go to the emergency room. They were there the whole time in a hospital, they would set her mind at rest.

Mother, looking more and more anxious, agreed with her, and even at this stage Maureen had noticed with sinking heart that her mother's careful speech sounded slurred, her words running together.

They were seen at once, and within an hour Maureen was waiting outside the intensive care unit to be told the news that her mother was having a massive stroke. One that she might very well not recover from.

Mother recovered, but not her faculties of speech; her eyes, bright and burning, seemed to beg for an end to this indignity.

She could press once for yes and twice for no on Maureen's arm. Maureen had spoken to her alone.

"Are you afraid, Mother?"

No.

"You do believe that you'll get better, don't you?"

No.

"I want you to believe that. You must. No, sorry. Of course, you can't answer that. I mean, don't you want to get better?"

No.

"But surely for me, Mother, for all your friends, *we* want you to get better. God, how do I say something that you can answer? Do you know that I love you? Very, very much?"

Yes, and a lessening of the strain in the eyes.

"And do you know that you are the best mother that anyone could have?"

Yes.

Then she had been tired, and not long after that she had slipped into unconsciousness.

They had been right—the friends who had stood in this room, Mother's morning room that got the early light—when they had nodded and said Sophie Barry could not have lived the dependent life of an invalid. It was better that she had been taken quickly away from pain and indignity.

Could it really only have been two weeks since that Sunday morning? It felt like ten years in so many ways.

Maureen unfolded the black plastic sacks. She knew that a great deal of Mother's things could indeed be thrown away, there was no one to gasp and wonder over old mementos of cavalry balls years ago, or programs of long-forgotten concerts signed with some illegible squiggle. No grandchildren to ooh and aah over worlds gone by. And Maureen in her own busy life would not look at them; a lot of things would go.

She sat at the small writing desk: an antique. She might take it for the hallway of her own flat. It was such an impractical thing, dating from a time when ladies penned only little notes or invitation cards. It had nothing to do with today's world. Mrs. O'Hagan had been surprised that Maureen was going to remain in her flat. She was sure that Sophie would have wanted her own home to continue in the family. But Maureen was adamant. She lived a life too full to involve cleaning a house with as many nooks and crannies as this. Her own space was custom-made for her, wall-long closets for her clothes, a study with proper filing cabinets as a mini-office, a big room where she could entertain, its kitchen in full view of the dining table so that she could talk to her guests as she served them their dinner.

No, it would be a backward move to come home to this house. Mother knew that, too.

First she went through the finances. She was surprised

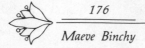

how disorganized Mother had become lately. It was sad to see little notes Mother had written to herself: a reminder here, a query there. It would have been so easy for Maureen to have set up an uncomplicated system like her own; five minutes would have done it, a letter to the bank asking them to pay so much each month to electricity, gas, insurance fund. It would have cut out all these final demands and letters of bewilderment. Mother must have appeared much more in control than she was.

Then there was an endless correspondence with a stockbroker. Like everyone of her generation, Mother had believed that wealth was measured in stocks and shares. Only the broker's letters were to be found: Mother had kept no copies of her own side of the correspondence. It was a sorry tale of confusion and disappointment.

Maureen felt weary and sad as she finished the series of responses to what had obviously been querulous demands for information and explanations why shares that everyone knew were excellent seemed to have vanished into nothingness. Briskly Maureen wrote a letter to the broker, explaining that her mother had died and asking him to send her details of the nature of the portfolio as it stood now. She wished that she had involved herself more, but with Mother there was such a dignity, there was a boundary you didn't cross.

Maureen kept all the letters she had written in her slim briefcase; she would photocopy them later, back at her own apartment. Mr. White, who had been Mother's solicitor, had already congratulated her on her efficiency; he wished that many more young women could be as organized, but then, of course, she hadn't built herself a big business without having a good financial brain and a sense of administration. He had shown her Mother's will, a simple document leaving everything to her beloved daughter, Mary Catherine (Maureen) barry, with gratitude for all her years of devoted love and care. The will had been made in 1962. Just after the reconciliation. After Mother had accepted that Maureen was not going to abandon her idea of how she would live her life. Since the day that Sophie Barry had written down her gratitude for the devoted love and care, twenty-three more years of it had been given. Surely she never would have believed that for over two decades Maureen would remain single and remain her close friend.

It was taking more time than she had thought, and she felt a strange sense of loss, different entirely from the grieving at the funeral. It was as if she had lost her idea of Mother as someone almost perfect. This nest of confusion stuffed into the drawers of a lovely writing desk spoke of a peevish old woman, confused and irritable. Not the calm, beautiful Sophie Barry, who until two weeks ago had sat like a queen in her throne room in this, her morning room, with its tasteful furnishings. Maureen didn't like discovering this side of her mother.

She had made herself a cup of coffee to give her more energy for the task and reached out resolutely for the next big, bulky envelope. She remembered the way Mother used to say, "Maureen my child, if a thing is worth doing, it's worth doing properly." That used to apply to anything from cleansing her face twice a day with Mother's special cream and then splashing it with rosewater to going back and having six more tennis lessons so that she would look that much better at the summer parties. Well, if Mother could see her now, something Maureen doubted, she would certainly agree that the devoted daughter was doing the job properly.

She was totally unprepared for the papers she found in the envelope marked SOLICITOR. She thought it might be some more fussy dealings about shares or pensions, but these were

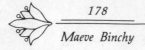

letters from a completely different solicitor, and they were dated forty years ago. There were a series of legal documents, all signed in 1945. And they showed that Maureen's father, Bernard James Barry, had not died of a virus when he was in Northern Rhodesia just after the war. Sophie Barry's husband had deserted her forty years ago. He had left his wife and child and gone to live with another woman in Bulawayo, in what was then Southern Rhodesia.

Maureen realized that, for all she knew, she might have a father still alive, a man of seventy years, living in Bulawayo, Zimbabwe. That she might even have stepbrothers and sisters, men and women not much younger than herself. The woman described as his common-law wife was called Flora Jones and had come from Birmingham in England. Wildly, Maureen thought that Mother would have said that Flora was a maid's name.

She wasn't in the habit of pouring herself a stiff drink in the middle of a Sunday morning. Maureen Barry, disciplined in this as in everything else, realized the perils of drinking alone. She had seen too many of her friends lapse into it, at the end of a long, hard day with no one to relax with. She had learned this from Mother, as she had learned everything. Mother said that widows could slip into tippling if they didn't exercise some control. Widows, what did Mother mean, acting out a lie for forty years? What kind of closeness was it that meant she couldn't tell her only daughter the biggest event of her life? What manner of woman could perpetuate a myth about a man who had to be buried abroad?

With another ripple of shock running through her like the continuous waves after an earthquake, Maureen realized that her mother, who had been a sane woman, had gone out every May and had a Mass said for the repose of the soul of

Bernard James Barry, a man who must have been alive for some, if not all, of the time that she was doing this.

There was whiskey in a decanter. Maureen smelled it; it reminded her of when she had a toothache years and years ago and Mother would put a whiskey-flavored piece of cotton on the gum to numb the pain. Mother had loved her so much.

Maureen poured out a large measure of neat whiskey, drank it, and burst into tears.

It was a measure of the lonely life she led, she realized, that she had no one to tell. There was no bosom pal to ring up, no house where she could run around and share this staggering news. Like her mother, she had kept aloof from intimacies. There was no man she had let close enough to her thoughts to confide in. Her work colleagues knew nothing of her private life. Her mother's friends . . . oh, yes . . . they would be interested. My, my, would she get a hearing at O'Hagans' if she were to turn up with the news.

Flora. Flora Jones. It was like a name from a musical comedy. And now presenting Miss Flora Jones, the Carmen Miranda of our town. There had been letters about divorce, and copies of letters from Mother's solicitor repeating over and over that not only was there no divorce in Ireland, and that his client was a staunch Roman Catholic, but that this was not the matter at issue, the question at issue apparently had been money. Maureen leafed, still unbelieving, through the documents . . . kept meticulously in order—this was a younger, firmer Mother, more in control forty years ago, wounded and enraged and determined that she was going to get the last penny from the man who had betrayed her. A sum had been paid over. A sum which in today's money would have been considered staggering. The solicitor of Bernard James Barry in Bulawayo wrote to the solicitor of Mrs. Sophie Barry in Dublin that his client was willing to realize most of his assets in

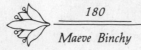

order to provide for his wife and eldest daughter. His client, Mr. Barry, had now, as was already known to Mrs. Barry, a second daughter by Miss Flora Jones, a daughter whose birth he was most anxious to legitimize.

Mother's letter of reply to that had been extraordinary; it was written exactly as Mother spoke. Maureen could hear her voice as she read the words. She could literally hear Mother's voice, slow, measured, articulate, a younger, stronger voice than of late.

". . . while you will understand that there can never be any question of a divorce since it is against the rules of the Church to which we both belong, I cannot legislate for you and your actions in a foreign land. I am writing this letter without the approval of the solicitors but I think you will understand its general drift. I have accepted your settlement for Maureen and myself. I shall pursue you in no court, nor under any jurisdiction. You shall be totally free from me if and only if you never return to Ireland. I shall announce your death. Today is April 15. If you return this letter to me with your promise that you will never come back to Ireland again, then I will say that you died abroad of a virus on May 15.

"If this promise is ever broken, or if you try to get in touch with Maureen in any way even after she is legally an adult, I can assure you that you will be made to regret it to the end of your days. . . ."

It was the way Mother spoke to a tradesman who had offended her in some way or to a handyman who had not done a job to her satisfaction.

He had accepted her terms, the man in Bulawayo, the man Maureen had thought was dead for forty years. He had returned the letter, as ordered to do. Attached to it by a small pearl-topped pin was a postcard. A brown sepia picture of mountains and savanna.

The words on the postcard said, "I died of a virus on May 15, 1945."

Maureen put her head down on her mother's desk and cried as if her heart would break into little pieces.

She didn't feel the time passing. And when she looked at the clock, the way the hands were placed seemed meaningless. It said a quarter past two or ten past three. It was bright, so it must be daytime.

She had come to the house at ten o'clock; she must have been in this semi-trance for over two hours.

She walked around feeling the blood beginning to flow again in her veins. If anyone had looked in the window of the morning room, they would have seen a tall, dark young woman, looking considerably less than her forty-six years, apparently hugging herself around the waist of her smart navy and pink wool dress.

In fact, Maureen was holding in each hand the elbow of the opposite arm, in a physical attempt to hold herself together after this shock.

She felt a rage against her mother, not just because this man had been ordered summarily out of her life and threatened not to contact his own flesh and blood. But she felt a burning anger that if her mother had kept this secret so successfully for so long, why on earth had she not destroyed the evidence?

If Maureen had never found these papers, she would never have known. She would have been happier, more safe and sure in the world she had built for herself.

Why had her mother been so casual and cruel? She must have known that Maureen would find the evidence someday.

But of course, Mother knew that Maureen would not betray her. Maureen would keep up appearances to the end.

Like hell she would.

It came to her suddenly that she could do anything she liked about this whole farce. She had entered into no melodramatic promises about mythical deaths. She had entered into no promise not to contact him for fear of some awful punishment.

By God, she was going to find him, or Flora, or her half sister.

Please, please may they be alive. Please may she find her father from this welter of documents, the latest being from 1950, confirming a final transfer of assets.

Please, God, may he still be alive. Seventy wasn't that old.

She began to work with the kind of controlled, furious energy that she had not known since the night before her first big high-fashion sale when they were up almost all night in the stockrooms marking clothes down, and recataloging and estimating the takings of the following day.

This time she approached her mother's belongings with different categories in mind. She found two boxes, which she filled with early photographs and memorabilia of herself when a child.

If she did find this man, if he was a man with any heart, he would want to know what she looked like at her first communion, in her field hockey outfit, dressed for her first dance.

Items which would have been carefully cut up and destroyed were now filed in boxes and labeled KEEPSAKES.

She sorted and arranged and tidied until she was ready to drop. Then she tied up the bags which were real rubbish, folded the clothes and other items which were to go to the Vincent de Paul Society, and ordered a taxi to take back the boxes of keepsakes to her own flat.

There wasn't a drawer now that hadn't been emptied and dusted out. Much of the ordinary kitchen equipment would go to Mrs. O'Neill, who had come to clean for Mother over the years. Jimmy Hayes, who did the garden, could have the lawn mower and any of the gardening tools he wanted. Maureen also wrote him a letter asking him to take for his own use any plants that he particularly liked and to have them removed quickly. She had decided now that the house would go on the market as soon as possible.

She laid her hand on the small writing desk, the one she had been going to take for the entrance hall of her own apartment. She patted it and said, "No." She didn't want it now. She wanted nothing from here.

The taxi driver helped her in with the boxes. Because he was curious, she told him that she had been clearing away her mother's effects. He was very sympathetic.

"Isn't it a pity now that you didn't have anyone to help you do a job like that?" he said.

That's what people often said to her in different ways, like wasn't it a wonder that a fine girl like herself had never married and settled down?

"Oh, my father would have done everything, but he was away, far away," she said.

She had mentioned her father. She didn't care about the surprised look that the taxi driver gave her, or how odd it was to have a father far away when a mother had died.

She felt that by mentioning him she was making him be alive.

She had a long, long bath and felt better but ravenously hungry. She telephoned Walter.

"I'm being very selfish and literally using you, so feel free to say no, but are there any nice restaurants open on a Sunday night? I'd love to go out for a meal."

Walter said nothing could suit him better, he had been doing a particularly tedious kind of opinion where there

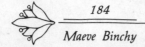

seemed to be no solution or a thousand solutions, and one was as hard as the other. He would love to escape from it.

Together they sat and ordered good food and wine by candlelight.

"You look a little feverish," Walter said with concern.

"I've a lot on my mind."

"I know, it must have been very distressing today," he said.

Her eyes seemed to dance at him across the table. She had never looked more beautiful, he thought.

"I know it's not the time, but then there never is any really good time, but perhaps you might think of . . ."

"Yes?"

"Well, should we go on holiday together, somewhere we would both like? You once said you would like to visit Austria."

"There's no fishing in Austria, Walter." She smiled at him.

"There are probably no fashion trade fairs, either, but we could manage for two weeks, couldn't we?"

"No, Walter, we'd drive each other mad."

"We could leave each other alone."

"Can't we do that better living apart?" She gave him a very bright smile.

"There's something on your mind." He looked hurt and troubled.

"Yes, there is, and I can't tell you now. But please remember tonight and that I wanted to tell you something. I will soon."

"When?"

"I don't know. Soon."

"Is it another man? I know that sounds very corny, but you have that kind of look about you."

"No, it's not another man. Not in that sense. I'll tell you, I've never lied to you, and when I do tell, you'll realize."

"Now I can't wait," he said.

"I know, neither can I. I wish people worked on Sundays, why does the world close down on Sundays?"

"You and I work on Sundays," Walter complained.

"Yes, but offices all over the world don't, damn them."

He knew it wasn't worth asking any more, he would hear nothing. He leaned over and patted her hand.

"I suppose I must love you to let you get away with all of this performance."

"Oh, will you go to hell, Walter. Of course, you don't love me, not even in the slightest, but you're a great friend, and I'm sure, though I don't intend to find out, that you're a smashing lay as well."

The waiter's arrival just at that moment, in time to hear Maureen's extravagant compliment, prevented Walter from saying anything in reply.

She slept a little but not much. She was out of her bed, showered and dressed, by 6:00 A.M. The time difference would be three hours. She would start telephoning International Inquiries and giving the out-of-date numbers, hoping that it would not be too long a haul. She had almost weakened enough to ask Walter if there were international directories of solicitors worldwide that she could study down at the Four Courts, but no, she must give him no details, no hints; later she would tell him. He deserved that. She hadn't decided what she would tell everyone else when she found her father—if she found him.

It was not as difficult as she had feared. It was probably

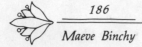

twenty times as expensive in terms of telephone calls, but she didn't care.

The firm no longer existed in Bulawayo, helpful operators got her listings of other solicitors, and finally she found that the original company had moved to South Africa. She found herself talking to people in cities she had never even thought about, even if she had acknowledged their names . . . Bloemfontein, Ladysmith, Kimberley, Queenstown.

She found one of the names that had signed one of the letters in Pretoria. Maureen Barry was crisp.

She explained that her mother had died and that it was her last wish that she, Maureen, should contact her late father. To whom should she now make the inquiries?

It wasn't a file that would have been kept open for forty years, the man told her.

"But you haven't thrown it away. Lawyers don't throw anything away."

"Can't you inquire at your end?"

"I have. They know nothing, the firm has changed, they say, and it's true that all the documents were handed back to my mother at her request. I have to try at your end."

He sounded like a nice man despite his accent and the way he said *rilly* instead of *really* and tried to work out what was the best way to go in the *ind* instead of the *end*.

"I fully realize that this is professional work. To research on my behalf, I am totally prepared to pay a professional fee for your time and expertise," Maureen said. "Would you like me to approach you through solicitors here to put it on a more formal basis?"

"No, it seems to me that you are a person who could be dealt with in her own right."

She could hear him smiling from across the world, a man whom she'd never met in a country she would never visit (nor would any of her friends) on account of its policies. Mother had been heard to say once she felt very sorry for those whites having to give up all their privileges and nice homes. But it hadn't gone down well. Mother hadn't been a fool; she wouldn't go that route again.

He said he would call her shortly.

"I wonder if you have any idea how shortly I hope it's going to be."

"I think so," he said in his curious clipped accent. "If I had just lost one parent and had the hope of finding another, I would know that there was a lot of urgency involved."

She didn't know how she got through Tuesday and Wednesday. He phoned her, the man from Pretoria, on Wednesday at 8:00 A.M. with an address of a solicitor's firm in London.

"Is he dead or alive?" she asked, her hand at her throat, waiting for the reply.

"They didn't tell me. Truly they didn't tell me." He sounded regretful.

"But these people will know?" she begged.

"These people will be able to get a message to whoever is concerned."

"Did they hint?"

"Yes. They hinted."

"What?"

"That he was alive. That you would be talking to the principal involved."

"I'll never be able to thank you," she said.

"You don't know yet whether you have anything to thank me for or not."

"But I'll tell you. I'll ring you back."

"Write to me, you've spent enough on telephone calls. Or better, come out and see me."

"I don't think I'll do that. Would you be of any use to me? What class of an age of a person are you at all?"

"Stop putting on that accent. I am sixty-three, a widower, with a beautiful home in Pretoria."

"God bless you," she said.

"I hope he's alive and good to you," said the stranger from South Africa.

She had to wait an hour and a half before she could talk to the man in the London firm of solicitors.

"I don't know why you're talking to me," he said in a slightly peeved tone.

"I don't know either," Maureen confessed. "But the original agreement was that my father and I should not get in touch during my mother's lifetime. I know it sounds like something from Hans Christian Andersen, but this is the way it happened. Can you listen for two minutes, only two? I can explain it quickly, I'm used to business conversations."

The English solicitor understood. He said he would be in touch.

Maureen began to have far greater faith in the speed of the law than she ever had before. Walter would tell her about delays and adjournments; she knew herself the endless palaver about contracts with suppliers. But suddenly, in the middle of the most important event of her whole life, she had talked with two law firms which seemed to understand her urgency. To sense her impatience and respond to it. On Thursday night she checked the answering machine in her flat, but there was nothing except a kindly invitation from Mother's friend Mrs. O'Hagan to drop in any evening for a sherry just as you did with your own poor mother. And there was a message from Walter, who was going to the West of Ireland over the weekend. There would be lots of lovely walks and gorgeous food, he said, as well as fishing. And there needn't even *be* any fishing if Maureen would care to join him.

She smiled. He was a good friend.

There were two clicks where people had hung up without leaving a message. She felt restless and then annoyed with herself. How could she expect these people to act so swiftly? And suppose her father *was* alive and in England, which was the way it looked now . . . perhaps he didn't want to get in touch, or he did and Flora didn't want him to, or his daughter. She suddenly realized that there might have been other children.

She paced the apartment, walking the length of her long living room, arms hugging each other. She couldn't remember when she had last been like this, unable to settle down to anything.

When it rang, the phone made her jump and the voice was hesitant.

"Maureen Barry. Is that Maureen Barry?"

"Yes." She spoke half words, half breath.

"Maureen, it's Bernie," the voice said. And there was a silence, as if he were waiting desperately to know what she would say.

She was able to say nothing. No words would come out.

"Maureen, they told me you had been trying to get in touch. If that's not so . . ." He was almost ready to ring off.

"Are you my father?" she whispered.

"I'm an old man now, but I was your father," he said.

"Then you still are." She forced a lightness into her voice. It had been the right thing to do; she heard him laugh a little.

"I rang before," he said, "but it was one of those machines. You sounded so formal, I had to ring off without saying anything."

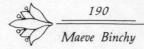

"I know, people should be hanged for that," she said. Again it was right, he was relaxing.

"But I rang again just to hear your voice and think: This is Maureen speaking, actually the sound of her voice."

"And did you like the sound of it?"

"Not as much as now when it's a real conversation. Is it a real conversation?"

"Yes, yes, it is."

There was a silence, but it wasn't a heavy one; it was as if they were both settling into the strange ritual of talking to each other.

"Would you like to meet me?" she asked.

"There's nothing I would like more. But would you be able to come to England to find me? I'm a bit feeble now, I couldn't come to Ireland to see you."

"That's no problem. I'll come as soon as you like."

"It won't be the Bernie you used to know."

She understood he wanted her to call him Bernie, not Father. Mother had always referred to him as poor Bernard.

"I never knew you anyway, Bernie, and you only knew me for a short time. It will be no shock to either of us. I'm freewheeling down to fifty, a middle-aged woman."

"Stop, stop."

"No, it's true. I'm not actually gray, because I have such a regular relationship with a hairdresser . . ." She felt she was burbling on.

"And Sophie . . . she told you . . . before she . . ." He was hesitant.

"She died two weeks ago, Bernie . . . it was a stroke. It was quick and she wouldn't have recovered, it was all for the best. . . ."

"And you . . . ?"

"I'm fine. But what about seeing you, where will I come, and Flora, and your family?"

"Flora is dead. She died shortly after we left Rhodesia."

"I'm sorry."

"Yes, she was a wonderful woman."

"And children?" Maureen felt this was an extraordinary conversation. It sounded so normal, so run-of-the-mill, yet she was talking to her own father, a man she had thought was forty years dead until four days ago.

"There's just Catherine. She's in the States."

Maureen was pleased somehow.

"What's she doing there? Is she working, is she married?"

"No, she's neither. She's gone with this rock musician, she's been with him eight years now. She sort of goes along wherever he is, to make a sort of home for him. She says it's all she ever wanted. She's happy."

"She's lucky then," Maureen said almost without thinking.

"Yes, she is, isn't she? Because she's not hurting anyone. People say she's a loser, but I don't think that. I think she's winning if she has what she wants without hurting anyone else."

"When can I come and see you, Bernie?" she asked.

"Oh, the sooner the better, the soonest the very best," he said.

"Where are you?"

"Would you believe Ascot?" he said.

"I'll come tomorrow," she said.

Before she left, she went through her mail quickly. Hardly anything to do with work came to her apartment; all business mail was addressed to her main shop. There were a couple of

bills, circulars, and a letter that looked like an invitation. It was from Anna Doyle, the eldest of Deirdre O'Hagan's children, a formal invitation to a silver wedding for their parents and a note saying that she apologized for the ludicrously early notice, but she wanted to make sure that the key figures were able to come. Perhaps Maureen could let them know.

Maureen looked at it almost without seeing it. A silver wedding seemed such a small milestone compared with what she was about to embark on herself. She wouldn't think now about whether she would go or not.

It was a very comfortable nursing home. Bernard James Barry had left the Colonies in style, Maureen realized. She had hired a car at Heathrow and driven to the address he had given her.

She had taken the precaution of telephoning the home herself to inquire whether her arrival would not put too much strain on her father, who said he had bad rheumatoid arthritis and was recovering from a mild heart attack.

She had been told that he was in the best of health and was already eager for her to arrive.

He was dressed in a blazer with some colorful crest, he had a carefully tied cravat, he looked the perfect gentleman, lightly tanned, a lot of thick gray hair, a cane and a slow walk, but in every way the kind of man her mother would love to have entertained back in Dublin. He had a smile that would break your heart.

"I have the Egon Ronay guide, Maureen," he said after she had kissed him. "I thought we should go out and have a proper lunch to celebrate."

"You're a man after my own heart, Bernie," she said.

And he *was* a man after her own heart. There were no apologies, no excuses. In life there were only just so many chances for happiness, he didn't regret his daughter Catherine taking hers, he didn't blame Sophie for seeking happiness through status, it was just that he couldn't stick with it himself.

He had known all about Maureen, he had never lost contact, not until Kevin O'Hagan died. He had written to Kevin at his club and asked him for news of his little girl. He showed Maureen a scrapbook he had made, cuttings from the newspapers about Maureen's shops, photographs cut from society magazines about Maureen at this dance or that reception. Photos, too, of Maureen with Deirdre O'Hagan, including one showing her in her maid of honor outfit.

"Would you believe they're having a silver wedding this year?" Maureen winced at the picture of the very inelegant 1960 wedding outfits. How could they have known so little then; had she only developed a clothes sense much later?"

Mr. O'Hagan had written regularly, it was only when his letter was returned from the club with a note that Maureen's father had heard of his friend's death. He had been instructed to leave no evidence of the correspondence in his house; part of the deal had been that Bernard Barry be mourned as a dead man.

They talked easily, old friends with a lot in common, it seemed.

"Did you have any great love that you didn't follow?" he asked as he sipped his brandy. At seventy he felt entitled to a little luxury like this, he said.

"Not really, not a great love." She was uncertain.

"But something that could have been a great love."

"I thought so at the time, but I was wrong. It would never have worked. It would have held us both back, we were too different, it would have been unthinkable in many ways."

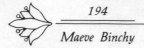

Maureen knew that her voice sounded like her mother's as she said this.

She found it easy to tell this man about Frank Quigley, about how she had loved him so much when she was twenty she thought that her whole body and soul would explode. She found it not at all difficult to use such words, although she had never even articulated them before.

She told how she had done everything but sleep with Frank that summer, and the reason she held back was not the usual fear of pregnancy that had held every other girl back, but simply that she knew that she must not get more involved than she already was, as he would never fit into her life.

"And was this something you believed or was it something Sophie told you?" His voice was gentle, without accusation.

"Oh, I believed it, I believed it utterly. I thought there were two types of people, us and them. And Frank was definitely them. So was Desmond Doyle, but somehow Deirdre O'Hagan managed to get away with it. I remember at the wedding we were all pretending Desmond's people came from some estate in the West instead of a cabin on the side of a hill."

"She didn't get away with it entirely," Maureen's father said.

"You mean, Mr. O'Hagan wrote to you about that?"

"Yes, a bit. I suppose I was someone he could talk to who wasn't involved, who never would be."

Maureen told how Frank Quigley had come to Dublin uninvited, for her graduation. How he had stood at the back of the hall and made whooping sounds and shouted as she went to receive her parchment.

He had called to the house afterward. It had been terrible.

"Did Sophie order him away?"

"No, you know Mother—well, maybe you don't—but she wouldn't do that, she killed him with kindness, she was charm itself . . . 'Oh, and tell me, Frank, would my late husband and I have met your people when we were in Westport?' You know the kind of thing."

"I do." He looked sad.

"And Frank somehow behaved worse and worse. Everything she did seemed to make him more Bolshie and thick and badly behaved. He took out his comb during supper and combed his hair, you know, looking at himself in that bit of mirror in the sideboard. Oh, and he stirred his coffee as if he were going to go through the bottom of the cup. I could have killed him, and I could have killed myself for caring."

"And what did your mother say?"

"Oh, something like 'Have you enough sugar, Frank? Or perhaps you would have preferred tea?' You know, terribly polite, not a hint that anything was out of place unless you knew."

"And afterward?"

"Afterward she just laughed. She said he was very nice and laughed."

There was a silence.

"But I went along with it," Maureen said earnestly. "I can't say she threw him out, she didn't, she never denied him the house, she even inquired about him from time to time with that little laugh. It was as if somehow by mistake we had invited poor Jimmy Hayes, who did the garden, in for supper. And I went along with it because I agreed with her. I went along with her way of thinking."

"And did you regret it?"

"Not at first. He was so foul-mouthed and called me all the snobby bitches under the sky, he almost proved Mother's point, my point. He said he'd show me, that he would be

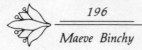

received in the highest houses in the land, and that one day my crabby old mother and I would regret that we hadn't welcomed him to our crummy house. That's the way he spoke."

"Out of hurt." Her father was sympathetic.

"Yes, yes, of course. And of course, he *did* become a merchant prince and Deirdre O'Hagan married his equally ignorant and unacceptable best friend . . . so he was right. His day did come."

"And is he happy?"

"I don't know, I think not. But maybe he's like a lark in the spring. I don't know."

"You're lovely, Maureen," her father said suddenly.

"No, I'm not, I'm very stupid, was very stupid for too long. It wouldn't have hurt anybody to use your phrase, it wouldn't have hurt anybody at all for me to say to Mother when I was twenty-one that I was off with Frank Quigley, pedigree or no pedigree."

"Maybe you didn't want to hurt her. After all, I had abandoned her, and you didn't want it to happen to her twice."

"Ah, but I didn't know you'd abandoned her. I thought you'd gotten an awful virus and died."

"I'm sorry." He looked contrite.

"I'm delighted, you old devil," she said. "Nothing has given me as much happiness in my whole life."

"Come on out of that! An old man ready for a wheelchair!"

"Will you come and live with me in Dublin?" she asked.

"No, no, my dearest Maureen, I won't."

"You don't need to be in a home, you're as fit as a fiddle. I can see that you're well looked after. Not in Mother's house, we'll get something together. Some place bigger than my flat."

"No, I promised Sophie."

"But she's dead now. You kept your promise while she was alive."

His eyes were sad.

"No, there is a kind of honor about a thing like this, they'd reassess her, you know, they'd go over everything she said, it would be degrading her afterward. You know what I mean."

"I do, but you're being too honorable in a sense. She didn't give you the chance to stay in contact with your own daughter, she didn't give me that chance, she didn't play really fair with us. I thought you were dead until a few days ago."

"But at least she told you in the end," said Bernard Barry, his face happy.

"What?"

"Well, at least she told you that she wanted you to find me. I heard that from the solicitors. When she knew she was dying, she wanted you to have the chance to meet me again."

Maureen bit her lip. Yes, that was what she had said at the outset, when she was making those early inquiries to Bulawayo.

She looked closely at her father's face.

"I must say I was touched and pleased at that. I thought she was implacable. Kevin O'Hagan told me that there was an anniversary Mass for me every year."

"I know," Maureen agreed. "It's coming up again shortly."

"So she did something she needn't have done, I owe it to her not to go back and disturb her memory. Anyway, child, I don't know anyone there anymore, not since Kevin died, and I'd only be an object of curiosity to them all. No, I'll stay here. I like it, and you'll come and see me from time to time, and

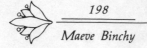

your sister Catherine and her young man will come. I'll be in clover."

Her eyes filled with tears. She would never tell him that Mother hadn't sent her to find him, she would let him think something good as he sat at sunset thinking he was in clover.

"I'll find lots of excuses to come and see you then. Maybe I'll open a shop in Ascot here or in Windsor. I mean it."

"Of course you do, and won't you be coming over for Kevin's daughter's silver wedding? Won't that be another excuse?"

"I mightn't go to that. Frank Quigley was the best man, you know. It's meant to be a kind of a reunion of everyone who was there, dredging up all the past memories and everything."

"Isn't that all the more reason to go?" asked Bernie Barry, the man with the tan and the twinkle in his eye who fell in love on a business trip forty years ago and had the courage to follow his star.

7

Frank

He never knew why everyone made such a fuss about traveling. Frank loved to get into his car and head off a hundred miles or more along highways and past signposts. He felt free and as if there were a sense of adventure about it all. Even if it was only a catering exhibition that he had been to a dozen times before, he enjoyed it. And why wouldn't he? As he often reminded himself, not everyone else on the highways

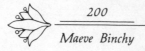

had a Rover, this year's model, with fitted stereo and radio filling the sleek, comfortable world with music. Or whenever he wanted it, with *Italian for Businessmen.* Nobody in Palazzo Foods knew that Frank Quigley could understand every single word of Italian spoken in his presence. He never let a flicker of the eye acknowledge that he had understood what might be being said. Even when it was about him. Particularly when it was about him.

Sometimes Frank thought that his father-in-law, Carlo Palazzo, might have a suspicion, but if he had, he kept it to himself. And he would have admired Frank all the more for it. He had let Frank know a long time ago that they had been watching him and grooming him, and that he would never have gotten to first base with the boss's daughter unless Carlo Palazzo and his brother had wanted it that way.

Frank had known this already; it came as no surprise that a wealthy girl like Renata would be heavily protected by her father and uncle from fortune hunters. He knew that he was suitable because he didn't need to marry the Palazzo princess to rise in the company. He didn't even need Palazzo. Frank Quigley would have been able to walk into any business in Britain. He had no initials after his name, he had never finished his formal schooling. He didn't need any of it. He had the flair and the ability to work long, hard days and nights. They had known all that fifteen years ago when they let him take Renata out to dinner. They knew he would lay no untoward hand on the dark, shy heiress to the Palazzo fortunes until they were wed. And the Palazzos knew that if ever he were to be the teeniest little bit unfaithful to his wife, it would be something anonymous and discreet and far from home. There would be no hint of scandal.

Frank sighed about the unwritten rules. He had sailed a little near the wind on one or two occasions but nothing he couldn't handle. Until now. Now the situation was very different, and he needed every moment alone that he could seize in order to work out what to do. If it were business, if it were only business . . . ah, then he would know exactly what to do. But Joy East was not business. Not when she was in her yellow T-shirt and nothing else, walking confidently around her house, proud and sure of herself. And sure of him as he lay there admiringly, afternoon after long sunny afternoon, smiling at her mane of streaked brown-and-gold hair, her perfect teeth, her long, tanned legs.

Joy East, the designer who had gotten Palazzo into the smart magazines, who had raised their image from the tatty to the stylish, as Frank Quigley had raised their sales and their progress from the mass of small so-called supermarkets to the very front rank. Joy East, who had told him the first night they had looked at each other with non-professional eyes that they would be the ideal match. Neither wanted to change life-styles, neither was in any position to force the other to do so. Joy wanted her independence and freedom, Frank wanted to remain in his marriage with the boss's daughter. Who better to suit each other than two people with everything to lose by being silly and everything to gain by enjoying each other's company discreetly? She had told him this partly in words, partly by her look, and partly by the way she had leaned across the restaurant table and kissed him full on the lips.

"I checked first," she had said, laughing. "There's nobody in the place except tourists."

It had been exciting then, and it had continued to be exciting. Frank had rarely met women like Joy. The finer and indeed the main points of the women's movement had passed him by; this new independence seemed to him very exotic. Joy East was proud of her single state; she had almost married, she told him, a very lucky escape when she was twenty-three,

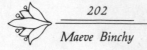

but she had called it off days before the wedding. Her father had been furious and they still had to pay a huge whack of the wedding reception cost, and the cake, and the limousines. Not to mention all the talk and the fuss. Everyone would have preferred her to get married just to save all the embarrassment. And the man? Oh, lucky escape for him, too, Joy thought, laughing and thinking about him not at all.

She lived in a small house on the corner of a road which had been not at all fashionable when she found it but which day by day was seeing the moving vans of ever smarter neighbors. Her white-walled garden was private and had vines on the walls. Her long, comfortable living room could fit sixty comfortably at one of her parties. Joy gave wonderful parties and often said that it was terribly easy to flatter and please people by asking them for two hours of drinks and canapés at your house.

And they loved her in Palazzo for doing it. So generous of Miss East, the board always said, above and beyond what Miss East needed to do for them. It bought her further good-will. Their admiration was unstinting. Joy East could invite clients, press people, foreign contacts, and local dignitaries into her house with such ease. She hired caterers and then contracted cleaners afterward. Joy told Frank that it was no trouble; in fact, it was positively useful. She had her house cleaned once a month professionally, she had a freezer full of hors d'oeuvres. She always cleared away her ornaments and valuables before any gathering. You never knew if strangers might be light-fingered, much better to leave out forty big blue glass bowls as ashtrays. They had cost one pound each in some warehouse. She had another forty in a cardboard box in the garage on a high shelf over the small sports car.

Frank Quigley, the handsome Managing Director of Palazzo, and Joy East, the Design Consultant who had been in charge of Palazzo's image, from its Art Deco building to its smart carrier bags, had been having an affair for three years and they both could say with certainty that nobody knew about it. They were not fooling themselves like so many other lovers in the world who believed that they were invisible. They knew that nobody else had the slightest suspicion. Because they had been very careful and they had lived by a set of rules.

They never telephoned each other except on legitimate business for the company. And Joy made no telephone calls to the Quigley apartment about anything at all. Once the affair had gotten under way, Renata was never brought to Joy East's house, whatever the social occasion. Frank Quigley felt that it would be undignified for his wife to be entertained in a house where he himself had been entertained so many afternoons a week in a very different sense of the word. Frank would not let his wife lay her fur coat across the wide bed where he and Joy had spent so many hours. Even though he swore to himself that Renata would never learn of the relationship, he still felt that he owed it to her not to betray her by pretending to be an equal guest in a house which was in reality so much his home. He didn't think about any other kind of betrayal, because Frank had always believed that his strongest quality was an ability to compartmentalize his life. He had always been able to do this. He never thought of his violent, drunken father and his weak, forgiving mother . . . not since he had left them to live in London. But when he had returned to visit them and his brothers and sisters, who had never left the small town in the West of Ireland, he brought no tales and even no thoughts of his London life back with him. He had managed to come back if not exactly shabby then at least unkempt. None of them would have guessed at his life-style in the business world and the social life of retailing. He had

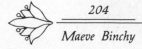

bought Renata a shapeless tweed coat for her one duty visit there and had told her they should play down the comfort they enjoyed back in Wembley. Renata had understood very quickly; she had gone almost wordlessly to help in the kitchen with the women while Frank had talked to his brothers and offered a little investment here and buying into something there . . . all of them polite ways of giving money without being seen to do so. During the four days he had spent in the place where he had grown up, his leather briefcase and handmade shoes were locked in the trunk of the hired car with Renata's silk scarves and jewelry box.

Frank had said that you diminished everything by trailing one life and one set of memories with you. Better far to live whatever life you were living at the moment to the full with no connecting links.

So a wife could not be brought unawares to the house of a mistress.

Similarly, when the Quigleys entertained, as they always did at Christmas, Miss East would be said to be out of town. They met on common ground, all right, like at his father-in-law's, but the conversation was always about work. Frank was literally able to divorce himself from the other side of their life together and talk guiltlessly about plans and projects. He got none of the sense of illicit excitement that he knew others felt about an extramarital affair. He knew that Joy felt the same. She must have felt the same. After all, it was she who had laid down the ground rules.

Joy had been direct in saying they would have no sense of overresponsibility to each other. She was not going to suffer the agonies of the typical Other Woman, she had assured him. There would be no image of poor Joy sitting alone with a sandwich on Christmas Day listening to "Jingle Bells" on the radio. No, she'd been thirty when she'd met him, and she had lived ten years more or less alone. She had a hundred places to go for Christmas and would spend no time feeling abandoned. They would take the time they could have without destroying either their careers or their plans for the future. She was free as the air to go where she pleased without consulting him. If a trip to the States came up, she would take it, and he could find other ways of filling those afternoon hours until she returned.

It had been idyllic . . . yes, a real afternoon idyll over three years. In summertime they often sat and drank cold white wine and peeled each other pears and peaches in the warm walled garden. In winter, they sat on the thick rich carpet beside the fire and watched pictures in the flames. At no time did they ever say what a pity that they couldn't get away together for a week, for a holiday, or for a lifetime. Renata's name was never mentioned between them. Nor was David, the name of the man in the advertising agency who had great hopes about the lovely Joy East and sent her large bouquets of flowers. Sometimes she went out with him on weekends, but so great was the sense of independence between Frank and Joy that Frank never asked whether they slept together or if David's attentions were in any way a threat to his own position. He assumed that David had been kept at arm's length with a convincing story about work and not wishing to get involved.

Frank had listened to the stories of colleagues, men who had had, as they put it, a little fun, played around a bit, thought they had a good thing going. Always and in every case there had been some disastrous turnabout of events. And it was invariably obvious and predictable to the outsider but never to the man involved. Frank examined his own relationship with Joy as minutely as he would have examined a contract or a proposition put to him in his office. If there were any flaws, then he couldn't see them. Not until the Christmas

party at Palazzo last year, which was when the trouble had begun. And even then it had been small and insignificant. At first.

It was all very clearly etched on his mind. Supermarkets found it hard to have Christmas parties like other firms did, since they were literally serving the public at all hours. But Frank was ever mindful of the importance of some kind of ceremony and group loyalty, particularly at a festive time.

Frank had persuaded Carlo to have the party on the Sunday before Christmas each year. It would be a lunchtime party, with Carlo as Santa Claus for the kiddies. Wives and children all came, there were small gifts for everyone and paper hats, and because it was a family day out, the usual office party nonsense didn't happen, with young secretaries being sick behind the filing cabinets and older managers making fools of themselves doing a striptease.

Renata had always loved it and was very good with the children, organizing games, and decorating with paper streamers. Every year for as long as he could remember, Frank's father-in-law had looked fondly at his daughter and said that she was so wonderful with the bambinos, wasn't it a pity that there were no bambinos of their own. Every year Frank had shrugged and said that the ways of the Lord were strange.

"It's not for lack of loving," he would say regularly, and Carlo would nod gravely and suggest that perhaps Frank should eat more steaks; a lot of red meat never did a man any harm. Every year, with patience and a smile fixed easily on his face. It was a small price to pay, it was not intended as humiliation, it wasn't received as such. Frank took it as an old man's affectionate and perhaps tactlessly expressed regret. It was one of the few areas where he humored Carlo Palazzo. In business they spoke as equals, always.

But last Christmas the party had been different. Joy East was usually in charge of decorating the big warehouse where they had the festivities. Not the actual work of pinning crepe up on the walls and laying out the trestles with the sausage rolls and mince pies, of course, but with organizing a color scheme, providing huge paper ornaments or giant sunflowers, as she had done one year. Arranging for someone to make mighty bells out of silver paper. Seeing to it that a big green baize-covered table full of gifts be arranged for Santa Claus Carlo and that the photographer from the local and sometimes even national papers be present. Together Frank and Joy had organized a huge Christmas calendar that would have the name of every employee on it. It cost practically nothing to print, and yet everyone who worked in Palazzo took it home proudly to keep for the next year. It sometimes changed their mind if they were thinking of leaving. It was hard to leave a place where you were so highly thought of as family that they put your name among the names of board members and senior managers on the calendar.

Last Christmas Joy said she was going to be away in the time before the party. There was this packaging fair she really had to go to. It was important; she needed new ideas.

"But that's on every year at this time and you don't go," Frank had complained.

"Are you telling me what I can do and can't do?" Her voice had been steely.

"Of course not. It's just that it's become such a tradition . . . your ideas for the Christmas party . . . always. Long before you and I . . . always."

"And you thought that it would always be so . . . long after you and I?"

"What is this, Joy? If you're trying to say something, say it." He had been brusque to cover his shock.

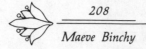

"Oh, I'm never trying to say anything, I assure you. I really assure you of that. Either I say it or I don't say it. There's no question of trying to say anything."

He had looked at her sharply; her voice had sounded slurred when she was repeating the word *assure.* It was unthinkable that Joy East had been drinking, drinking in the middle of the day. He put the suspicion out of his mind.

"That's good then," he had said with false joviality, "because I'm the same. If I want to say something, I say it. We're two of a kind, Joy."

She had smiled at him oddly, he thought.

When she returned from the packaging fair, they met as had been arranged at her house. One of the many things that made it all so safe was that Joy really did work from home in a small, bright studio filled with light, and Frank did have legitimate reason to call on her. But even better, her house was very near the offices of the firm of accountants they used as tax advisers. Frank had even more legitimate reason to visit them regularly. If his car was ever seen in the area, he was well covered.

Joy said she hadn't done much at the packaging fair. It was Mickey Mouse stuff.

"Then why did you go?" Frank had asked, irritated.

He had been responsible for finding other people to take over Joy's work in preparing the hall for the party, and nobody had anything like her flair.

"For a change, for a rest, for some time off," she had said, considering her words.

"Jesus, I never think a trade fair is a rest," he had said.

"It is if you hardly leave your room in the hotel."

"And what did you do in your room in the hotel that was so important?" His voice was cold.

"I never said it was important, now did I?"

"No."

"It wasn't at all important what I did in my room. I read the catalogs, I had room service, I had a lot of nice cold white wine. Oh, and I had a nice Scotsman, head of a stationery firm. But nothing at all important."

Frank's face had gone white, but he was still in control. "Is this meant to hurt me?" he asked.

"But how could it? We're two of a kind, you've often said it. You have your life with your wife, I have my life with the odd ship that passes in the night. Nothing hurtful there."

They were lying in her bed. Frank reached out for a cigarette from the slim case on the bedside table.

"I usually prefer you not to smoke here. It does sort of linger in the curtains," Joy said.

"I usually don't need to smoke here, but the things you're saying sort of linger in my mind and make me anxious," he said, lighting up.

"Ah, it is all a game, isn't it?" Joy said perfectly amicably. "I thought about this a long time while I was away. What you and I have is not love, not one of those great passions that make people do foolish things . . . it's just a game. Like tennis, one person serves, the other returns it."

"It's much more than a game . . ." he began.

"Or like chess." Joy was dreamy now. "One person makes a crafty move, and then the other responds to it with something even craftier."

"You know very well what we have. There's no point in finding fancy words for it. We love each other . . . but we have set limits to this love, you and I. And we admire each other and we're happy together."

"It's a game," she repeated.

"Well, people who go out to play a game of golf or squash or chess together are friends, Joy. For God's sake, you

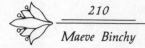
don't decide to spend a day with someone you don't like. Use this example if it gives you pleasure, keep saying *game, game, game.* But it doesn't mean anything. It doesn't change anything. We're just the same, you and I."

"Oh, you *are* playing it well." She laughed admiringly. "Trying to diffuse it all, asking no questions about whether there really was a Scotsman or not. I think you'd be a very dangerous adversary in a game."

He put out his cigarette and reached for her again. He held her close to him and spoke into her long, shiny hair with its stripes of gold among the brown and its smell of lemony shampoo.

"Well, so would you . . . a terrifying adversary. Isn't it just as well that we're the best of friends and the best of lovers and not enemies at all?"

But he had spoken more cheerfully than he felt, and her body had not been responsive to him. She had a half-smile that was disturbing and had nothing at all to do with any pleasure which she might or might not have been feeling.

At the party Joy was dressed in a dazzling navy and white dress. The gleaming white collar was cut low into her cleavage, revealing a lot of breast and an expensive lace-trimmed brassiere. Her hair seemed to shine like gold and copper. She looked ten years younger than thirty-three, she looked like a young beautiful girl on the prowl. Frank watched her with alarm as she moved through the crowds of Palazzo employees. This time there was no doubt about it; she had been drinking. And well before she arrived at the party.

Frank felt a cold knot of nervousness in his stomach. Joy sober he could cope with easily, but she was an unknown-quantity drunk. His father's terrible and unpredictable rages flashed before him suddenly. He remembered the time that the entire dinner had been thrown into the fire in a fit of temper . . . nearly forty years ago but as clear as yesterday. And what had always stuck in Frank's mind was that his father had not intended to do it; he had wanted to eat his dinner, as he told them over and over all night. It had given Frank a fear of drunks; he drank very little himself and he scanned his managers and sales force for signs of the bottle. It was the feeling that you couldn't rely on someone who was so dangerous. They would probably be all right, but you couldn't be sure. He looked at Joy East's flashing smile and low neckline as she cruised around the room, ever refilling her glass at the trestle tables, and he felt not at all sure that the day would end all right.

Her first target was Carlo, struggling offstage into his Santa outfit.

"Wonderful, Mr. Palazzo," she said. "Wonderful, you go out and knock them dead, tell them what Santa will put in their pay envelopes if they're good little girls and boys and work like good little ants."

Carlo looked puzzled. Frank acted quickly to draw her away.

"Joy, where are the tubs for the children? Please?" His voice was urgent.

She came up close to him and he saw that her eyes were not focusing properly.

"Where are the tubs?" she asked. "The tubs are being presided over by your wife. The saintly Renata. Santa Renata." Her face broke into a big smile. "That would be a nice song . . . Santa Renata . . ." She sang it to the tune of "Santa Lucia" and seemed pleased with it, so she sang it a little louder. Frank moved slightly away. He had to get her out. Soon.

At that very moment Renata appeared to explain that the pink wrapping paper was on the gifts for girls and the blue for

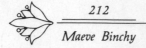

boys. One year her father had given the girls horrible monsters and spiders and the boys comb-and-mirror sets. This time they were taking no chances.

"That's right, Renata, take no chances," Joy said.

Renata looked at her, startled. Never had she seen Joy East looking like this.

"You look . . . very smart . . . very elegant," Renata said.

"Thank you, Renata, *grazie, grazie mille,*" Joy said, bowing flamboyantly.

"I have not seen you wear clothes like this and look so full of life before." Renata spoke quietly but with a little awe in her voice. She fingered the edge of her expensive but very muted woolen jacket. It had probably cost four times as much as the striking garment that Joy was wearing, but Renata looked like a bird of little plumage, dark hair, sallow skin, and designer suit in lilac and pink colors with a braid of lilac-colored suede at the edge of the jacket, nothing to catch the eye. Nothing at all.

Joy looked at Renata steadily.

"I'll tell you why I look so different. I have a man. A man in my life. That's what makes all the difference."

Joy smiled around her, delighted with the attention from Nico Palazzo, who was Carlo's brother, and from Desmond Doyle and a group of senior management who were all in the circle. Renata smiled, too, but uncertainly. She didn't know quite what response she was meant to make, and her eyes raked the group as if to find Frank, who would know what to say.

Frank stood with the feeling that the ice in his stomach had broken and he was now awash with icy water. There was nothing he could do. It was the sense of powerlessness that made him feel almost faint.

"Was I telling you about this man, Frank?" Joy asked roguishly. "You see me only as a career woman . . . but there's room for love and passion as well."

"I'm sure there is."

Frank spoke as if he were patting down a mad dog. Even if he had no connection with Joy, they would have expected him to be like this. Soothing, distant, and eventually making his escape. They must all see now what condition she was in; they must have noticed. Was it only because he knew her so intimately, had traced every feature of her face and body for three years with his hands, that he realized she was out of control? Everyone around seemed to be treating it all as normal Christmas high spirits. If he could stop her just now, before she said anything else, then all might not be lost.

Joy was aware she had an audience and was enjoying it. She put on a little-girl voice that he had never heard her use before. She looked very silly, he thought quite dispassionately. In her sober state she would be the first to criticize any other woman with an assumed, lisping voice.

"But it's forbidden in this company to love anyone except Palazzo. Isn't that right? We all love Palazzo, we must have no other love."

They laughed, even Nico laughed, they were taking it as good-natured banter.

"Oh, yes, first love the company, then other loves," Nico said.

"It's infidelity to love anyone else better," Desmond Doyle said, laughing.

Frank flashed him a grateful look; poor Desmond, his old pal from those long-ago days in Ireland, was helping him inadvertently, he was taking the heat off. Maybe he could be encouraged to say more.

"Well, you've never been unfaithful, Desmond," Frank

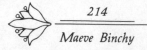

said, loosening his collar. "You're certainly a long and loyal Palazzo man." He felt sick to his stomach after he said it, remembering suddenly the time that Desmond had been allowed to go after the rationalization and how he had to fight hard to get him reinstated. But Desmond didn't seem to see the irony. Desmond was about to answer with something cheerful when the voice of Joy East cut in again.

"No one should be married except to the company. When you join Palazzo, you must marry the place, marry Palazzo. Very hard to do. Very hard. Except for you, Frank. You managed it all right, didn't you? You really *did* marry a Palazzo!"

Even Nico, who was very slow, must have realized by now that something was wrong. Frank had to move quickly. But he must not appear to be rattled. He must take it indulgently as anyone would take the public idiocy of a normally exemplary colleague.

"Yes, you're right, and I'm glad you reminded me, because my father-in-law will be down on us all like a ton of bricks if we don't get the presents going soon. Renata, should we get the children to line up now . . . or does somebody make an announcement? Or what?"

In other years Joy East had arranged everything like clockwork. Renata had a look of relief all over her face. She had thought that there had been an insult, a jibe, but obviously since Frank didn't see one, she had been wrong.

"I think we should tell Papa that the time has come," she said, and moved away toward her father.

"I think we should tell Papa that the time has come," Joy said to nobody in particular.

Desmond Doyle and Nico Palazzo exchanged puzzled looks.

"Joy, you must be tired after all that busy time at the packaging conference," Frank Quigley said loudly. "If you like, I can run you home now before it all gets too exhausting here."

He saw the relief on a few faces around him. Mr. Quigley was always the one to cope with the situation, any situation.

His smile was hard and distant as he looked at Joy. It said in very definite terms that this was her one chance to get out of what she had walked them into. There wouldn't be any other chances. His smile said that he was not afraid.

Joy looked at him for a few seconds.

"All right," she said. "Let's say I'm tired after the packaging conference, tired and very, very emotional, and that I need to be taken home."

"Let's say that then," Frank said easily. "Tell Renata to save me a nice boy present from Santa Claus," he called out. "I'll be right back to collect it."

They looked at him in admiration as he led Miss East, who was behaving most oddly, out of the big hall and toward the parking lot.

There was complete silence in the car, not one word spoken between them. At her door she handed him her small handbag and he took out the key. On the low glass table was a bottle of vodka with one third of it gone and some orange juice. A heap of unopened Christmas cards and a small, smart suitcase, as if she were going on or had come back from a journey. With a shock he realized that she must not have unpacked her case after her trip to that conference.

"Coffee?" he asked. It was the first word spoken.

"No thanks."

"Mineral water?"

"If you insist."

"I don't insist. I couldn't care less what you drink, but I wouldn't give a dog any more alcohol than you've had already."

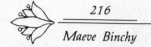

His voice was icy cold.

Joy looked up at him from the chair where she had sat down immediately.

"You hate drink because your father was such a drunk," she said.

"You're telling me what I told you. Have you any further insights or shall I go back to the party?"

"You'd like to hit me, but you can't, because you saw your father beating your mother," she said, a crooked smile on her face.

"Very good, Joy, well done." His hand was clenched, and he would have liked to have struck something, a chair, even a wall to get rid of the tension he felt.

"I said nothing that wasn't true. Nothing at all."

"No, indeed, and you said it beautifully. I'm going now."

"You are not going, Frank. You are going to sit down and listen to me."

"Now that's where you're wrong. Since I did have a drunk for a father, I am only too used to listening to drunks. It's a useless exercise. They don't remember anything the next day. Try telephoning the time. Tell it all to them, they love a good sob story from people with enough drink in them to float a navy."

"You have to listen, Frank, you have to know."

"Another time, a time when you can pronounce my name without stumbling over it."

"About the conference. I wasn't there."

"So you said, you told me. A Scotsman . . . well, well. Don't tell me it's preying on your mind?"

"I wasn't anywhere near it. I didn't leave London."

Her voice was odd; she seemed to have sobered up a bit.

"So?" He was still poised to go.

"I went to a nursing home." She paused. "To have an abortion."

He put his car keys in his pocket and came back into the room.

"I'm sorry," he said, "Very sorry."

"You needn't be." She didn't look at him.

"But why, how . . . ?"

"The pill didn't suit me. I changed the type several times, but still . . ."

"You should have told me." He was gentle now. Forgiving.

"No, it was my decision."

"I know, I know. But still . . ."

"And so I went to this place . . . very nice place, actually, it's a real nursing home for other things, too, not just terminations, as they call them." Her voice shook a little.

He laid his hand over hers, the coldness was forgotten. "And was it very bad, was it awful?" His eyes were full of concern.

"No." Her face was bright, and she smiled at him, a smile only a little lopsided. "No, it wasn't awful at all. Because when I went in there and went to my room, I sat and thought for a while, and I thought, Why am I doing this? Why am I getting rid of a human being? I would *like* another human being around me. I would like a son or a daughter. So I changed my mind. I told them I had decided not to go through with the termination. And I went to a hotel instead, for a couple of days, then I came back here."

He looked at her, stricken.

"This can't be true."

"Oh, yes, it's true. So now you see why you couldn't just toddle off back to the party. You had to know. It was only fair that you should know. And know everything."

If he lived to be an old man, something that his doctor said was highly unlikely, Frank Quigley would never forget that moment. The day he learned he was going to be a father, but not the father of Renata's child, not the father who would be congratulated and embraced by the Palazzo tribe. A father who would be ostracized and cut off from the life he had built for himself for a quarter of a century. He would never forget her face as she told him, knowing that for the first time in their very equal relationship she held all the cards. Knowing that drunk and upset and having broken all their rules, she was still the one in charge. Because of biology, which said that the women bore the children, she was winning, and that was the only reason. Frank Quigley would not have been beaten by anything except the human reproductive system.

He had played it just right, of course, at the time. He had telephoned back to base and said that Joy needed a bit of attention. He had sat down and talked to her, but his mind was in overdrive. His words were soothing and supportive; his real thoughts were taking a journey into the future.

He allowed his real reactions only a moment's indulgence while he relished the thought that he had fathered a child. If Carlo knew, there would be a lot less of the chat about eating more red meat. If Carlo knew. Carlo must never know. And Renata would be hurt beyond repair. Not only at the infidelity, the knowledge that an affair had been going on under her very nose for years, but at the fact that this woman had produced a child, the one thing that Renata had failed to do.

As he stroked Joy's fevered forehead and assured her of loyalty and his great pleasure at the news and the way that things had turned out, Frank was working out logically and coldly what he must do next, what avenues were open to him.

As he urged cups of weak tea and thinly sliced bread and butter on the weeping Joy, he listed the possibilities that lay ahead and the disadvantages of each one. When he found the one that had the least dangerous mine field attached to it, that was where he would head.

Joy could have the child, and he would acknowledge that it was his. He would say that he did not intend to leave his marriage but felt in fairness that the son or daughter should grow up knowing the care of a father. He considered this for seconds, only to dismiss it.

In a more liberated society this would work. But not with the Palazzos. Not for one minute.

Suppose Joy were to say that she was having the child and that the identity of the father was to remain unknown, undiscussed? Again not something beyond the imaginings in the 1980s for a liberated woman. But again this was the world of Palazzo. It would be frowned upon, it would be speculated about, and worst of all, if Joy were ever to hit the bottle again, it would all be revealed.

Suppose he were to deny paternity. Literally say that Joy was lying? He wondered why he had even considered this route. Joy was a woman he had intended to spend a great amount of time with; he didn't love her only for the good sex they had, he loved her mind and her reactions to things. Frank asked himself why this possibility had crossed his mind. He had never thought of stabbing Carlo in the back and taking over the company. He had not decided to woo and win Renata only for her money and position. He was not that kind of bastard. So why even entertain the idea of turning his back on the woman who had been his lover for three years, the woman who was going to bear his child? He looked at her, slack-jawed and awkward in the chair. He realized with a shudder how much he feared drink and the effects of it. He

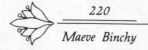

knew that whatever happened now, he would never be able to trust Joy or trust himself to her again.

Suppose he were to persuade her to have the termination, for everyone's sake? There were still two weeks in which it would be safe. Perhaps he could persuade her.

But if he couldn't, then he risked a hysterical response. And if she were to go ahead and have the child, knowing that he wanted it aborted, then things would be about as bad as they could ever be.

Suppose he were to ask her to go away, to start a new life with a set of glowing references. Joy move away from London? Joy start life afresh with a small baby just to please Frank? It was unthinkable.

Suppose he were to ask her to give the child to him. Suppose that he and Renata were to adopt this baby. The child would inherit the Palazzo millions. Everyone would be pleased. Frank and Renata had done the rounds of the adoption societies; at forty-six he was too old to be an adoptive father. Not a real father as it turned out, but then nature was never known to be a great supporter of bureaucracy.

But Joy had deliberately decided to have the child because she wanted another human being around her. She would not consider it. Or not now, at any rate. Don't dismiss it utterly. She might, later on in the pregnancy. It was unlikely yet not impossible.

And then it would be adopting his own child. That would be very satisfying. In honesty he would have to tell Renata, but they need not tell her family.

Frank stroked the forehead, administered the cups of tea, and thought his own thoughts as he consoled Joy East with murmurs and sounds that would never constitute any kind of promise or contract in the unlikely event of their being recalled.

The weeks had passed somehow. The bad behavior at the Christmas party was hardly commented upon, Frank was as usual congratulated for having as usual averted any little silliness. Joy was back at work, head held high in the new year, plans and ideas tripping out of her. There were no recurrences of drinking. Also, there were no lazy afternoons by her fireside.

They met for lunch early in the new year. Frank had said in front of several of the managers that the place was lacking in anything new. What it needed in these days after Christmas was some pizzazz. He would take Joy East out to lunch and have a brainstorming session, he said. Women always loved a business lunch, and he wouldn't mind one himself. They went to the best restaurant, where they were bound to be seen.

She sipped her diet tonic water, and he drained his tomato juice.

"An expense-account lunch is wasted on us." Joy smiled at him.

"As you told me that time, I'm a drunk's son. I'm afraid of drink," he said.

"Did I say that? I don't really remember all the things I said that day. Is that why you don't come to me in the afternoons?"

"No, it's not that," he said.

"Well, why not? I mean, there's no need for any precautions now, it would be like bolting the stable after the horse had fled . . . we should get value . . ." Her smile was warm and welcoming. Like the old Joy.

"It might be bad for you. They say it's not good at this stage of the pregnancy," he said.

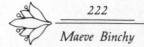

She smiled, pleased that he was caring. "But you could come and talk to me anyway, couldn't you? I've waited a lot of afternoons."

That was true, she had kept her word about not contacting him. Ever.

"We do have to talk," he said.

"So why are we trying to talk in a restaurant where everyone sees us? Those women over there, they're in-laws of Nico Palazzo. They haven't had their eyes off us since we came in."

"We will be seen in public for the rest of our lives. This is exactly where we must discuss how our lives will continue. If we go to your house, we slip into the old ways, we're back in the days when we only had ourselves to consider." His voice was calm. But she seemed to sense his anxiety.

"You mean, you wanted a get-away car and witnesses if I'm going to tell you anything unpalatable. Is that it?"

"Don't be silly, Joy."

"No, I'm not being silly, you're trying to get out of it, aren't you? You're actually scared to death."

"That's not so, and stop smiling that smile that isn't a real smile. It's a paper-thin smile you put on for customers and contacts. It's not genuine."

"And what was ever genuine about *your* smile, Frank? Did you not know your smile never reached your eyes, never? It stopped always around the mouth."

"Why are we talking like this?" he asked.

"Because you are full of fear, I can smell it," she said.

"What's turned you against me, did I say anything?" He spread his hand out in wonder.

"You don't need to make those Italian gestures at me, I'm not a Palazzo. What did you say? I'll tell you what you said. You said we should sit down in a public place and make decisions about the rest of our lives. You forget that I know you, Frank, you forget that you and I know when you meet an adversary, the first rule is to meet him on common ground, not your territory or his. You're doing that. We both know that if there's a danger of a row, the rule is: Make sure the meeting is held in a public place. It stops people from making scenes."

"Are you feeling all right, Joy? Seriously?"

"It won't necessarily work, you know, drunk or sober. At home or out I could make a scene if I wanted to." She looked mulish.

"Of course you could, what *is* this? We're friends, you and I, where's the hostility?"

"We are not friends, we are fencing with each other, we are playing games, looking for the advantage . . ."

"Well, then, if that's all we are, what on earth are we having a child together for?"

"We're not having a child together," Joy East said. *"I* am having a child."

There was a look of triumph on her face like he had seen only when she had beaten a rival, won an award, or somehow gotten her way against all the odds.

It was then he knew that she intended him to dangle there, forever watching his step, forever in her power. It was her child and her decision, but only for as long as it suited her. She was never going to promise him either secrecy or involvement. Her plan was that he should never know. That he would be forever tied to her.

Frank Quigley had come across schemes like this before, the supplier who had bought up the market but hadn't told you. He would want you to advertise the produce and then suddenly could raise the price because you were committed. Frank had dealt with that one in his time. Someone had tried

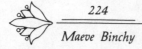

it on him, but only once. Frank had smiled and said there was no way he was going to pay more than the agreed price for the product. But wouldn't they look foolish, the man had said, having spent all that money advertising it and then having to admit they didn't have it? No, not at all. Frank had smiled back with easy charm. They would just take out another advertisement apologizing that the suppliers had proved unreliable. Everyone would think well of Palazzo for its honesty, the suppliers would be ruined. It had been so simple. But then it had only involved fruit, it hadn't involved a child.

He had brought into play every available ounce of charm that he possessed, and limp as a wet rag at the end of the lunch, he congratulated himself that they were at least speaking normally on the surface.

They talked about the company. Twice he made her laugh, real laughter, head thrown back and pealing with mirth. The two women who she had said were Nico's in-laws looked over with interest. But there was nothing for them to take home with them as gossip, this was the most innocent lunch in the history of the world. Otherwise it would not have been here and in full view of everyone.

He had told her about his Christmas, and then she told him about hers. She had gone to stay with friends in Sussex. In a big family home where she had been before, full of children, she said.

"Did you tell them?" he asked. He felt the conversation must not be allowed to wander too far from what they were both thinking about lest he be labeled callous.

"Tell them what?" she asked.

"About the baby?"

"Whose baby?"

"Your baby. Our baby if you like, but basically, as you said, your baby."

Joy gave a little purr of satisfaction. It was almost as if she were saying, "That's better. That's more like it."

"No," she said. "I'm not telling anyone until I've decided what to do."

And then there was no more. They spoke as they always had about plans and schemes and the inadvisability of letting Nico know anything at all that was taking place. The wisdom of Palazzo's buying the new site in that area which was meant to be coming up—Joy was afraid it was coming up too fast. The big houses were changing hands for a lot of money and then even more money needed to be spent on them to make them smart. That kind of people would shop in fancy delicatessens or even go into Harrods, she felt, Palazzo's would be wiser to aim for somewhere less ambitious, somewhere where you could get a huge parking lot. That's the way things were going now.

"We could even try to make a feature out of the parking lot," Joy had said excitedly. "You know how gloomy they look at best, and how they look like places you're going to be murdered in at worst. Perhaps it could all be brightly painted and there could be a covered terrace around it, a type of cloister effect, we could rent space to market stalls, give the place more life . . ."

She had been talking in terms of staying on, Frank had noted.

Joy East, if she were planning anything at all, planned to take three months' maternity leave and return to work once her child was born. Frank was not going to be informed about his role. That was the way she was going to play the game.

He had left that lunch white with fury, far angrier and even more determined to regain control than he had been before Christmas. He would not be left suspended like this.

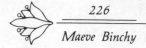
If she would not reveal her intentions like any normal person, then he was not going to respond normally.

Two could play a game of cat and mouse.

Long before Joy mentioned her pregnancy to anyone else, Frank had made his contingency plan.

Based entirely on Joy's own projections about the need not to go too far upmarket for their customers, Frank Quigley commissioned surveys.

He had explained to the young men and women in the market-research bureau that they wanted confirmation of their belief that they should expand into less well-off areas. The survey was to be done nationwide but on a very small sample. It was the kind of survey which if Frank had seen cold he would have dismissed on the ground that its findings could not possibly be conclusive. But this time he wanted to let the board see from an outside agency that the way forward was to expand and to leave North London far behind. To open up on a trial basis in the Midlands, in the North of England even. The key to it would be design and image. Palazzo was to be presented as stylish and desirable. Joy East was the one to create that image.

It would be promotion, it would be a seat on the board for Joy. He would see her once a month at board meetings, true, but he would not see her every day.

And she would not see his father-in-law every day.

And she would not be in danger of meeting his wife.

He had few weapons, he had to outwit her by cunning.

She had to think that the promotion, the move, and the change were against his wishes.

The survey, which Carlo Palazzo fondly believed he had commissioned himself, was complete by March, when Joy East broke her news with maximum drama. She announced it

under the heading of Any Other Business at the weekly management meeting.

Her eyes had been suspiciously bright. Frank knew what
was coming.

"Well, I suppose this *is* other business in a way. I bring it
up in case you should hear it elsewhere and wonder why I
had said nothing of it to my colleagues. I will be seeking three
months' maternity leave in July. . . . Obviously I'll work
around it to make sure that any promotions are well covered,
but I felt you should know that it was upcoming." She smiled
around sweetly, meeting the eyes of the fifteen men in the
room.

Carlo was at a total loss. "Well, heavens, good Lord, I did
not even know you were thinking of getting married . . . my
congratulations."

"Oh, no, nothing as settled as that, I'm afraid." A tinkly
laugh. "Just a child. We don't want too much of a shock to the
system like getting married as well."

Nico's jaw dropped, the others shuffled their praise and
pleasure, but looking sideways at Carlo and Frank to try to
gauge the mood of the meeting.

Frank Quigley looked pleasantly surprised and admiringly amused.

"This is very exciting news, Joy," he said evenly. "Everyone is delighted for you. I don't know what we'll do without
you for three months, but will you be able to come back to us
after that?"

The inquiry was warm and courteous; nobody could have
seen the way their eyes locked hard across the table.

"Oh, yes, indeed. I've been busy making arrangements.
These things aren't done lightly, you know."

"No, indeed," he said soothingly.

By this stage Carlo had recovered enough control to be

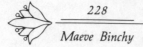
able to murmur a few pleasantries, but he called Frank to his office.

"What are we going to do?" he asked.

"Carlo, it's 1985, it's not the Middle Ages. She can have thirty children if she wants to. You're not shocked, are you?"

"Yes, of course I am. Who is the father, do you think? Is it anybody at Palazzo?"

Frank felt he was acting a part in a play. "Why should it be? Joy has a full life of her own outside here."

"But why, why on earth?"

"Perhaps she felt she is in her thirties, she is alone, she might just *want* to."

"It's a very inconsiderate thing to do," Carlo grumbled. "And inconvenient, too. Look at the way it will upset our plans for the north."

Frank spoke very carefully. "When were you hoping to get that operational, not until the new year? Its planning stages will only be coming on stream in autumn when she comes back to work . . ."

"Yes, but . . ."

"But doesn't it suit you down to the ground, not that you should *say* that to her, of course? You were already worried that she might not want the move. Now that she's having a child, it might be just what she'd need: new environment, fresh start, more space and room up there, away from London . . ."

"Yes . . ." Carlo was doubtful. "I think this has thrown a big wrench in the works."

"Then if that's where you want her, you should make it sound very, very attractive for her. Put it to her in a way that it seems just the right step for her to take . . ."

"Perhaps *you* should explain it to her."

"No, Carlo." For the second time Frank felt that he was

actually acting out a part onstage. "No, because you see, in a way I don't want to lose her from the London side of things, even though I think in my heart you're right. It's best for the company that she should go up north and get Palazzo into a different league, a national league."

"That's what I thought," Carlo said, believing it.

"So I'm the wrong one to persuade her."

"Suppose she thinks I am banishing her away?"

"She can't think that, Carlo. Haven't you all the documentation and surveys and inquiries to prove you were thinking of it ages back?"

Carlo nodded. He had, of course.

Frank let the breath out slowly between his teeth. Nowhere in that whole paperwork did Frank Quigley's name appear; in fact, in the files there were several letters dissenting slightly and wondering whether Miss East would be better kept in London. He couldn't be faulted now.

Frank did not have long to wait. Joy burst into his office, eyes blazing and clutching a piece of paper in her hand.

"Is this your doing?" she asked.

"I have no idea what you're talking about." He was bland, unruffled.

"Like hell you don't. You're sending me away. By God, you're not going to get away with this, Frank. I'm not going to be shunted out of your sight when things get too hot to handle."

"Sit down," he said.

"Don't tell me what to do."

He walked past her and called out to his secretary in the next room. "Diana, can we have a big pot of coffee? Miss East and I are about to have a row and we need fuel."

"Don't think I'm bowled over by that kind of witticism," Joy said.

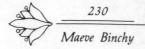

"It wasn't a witticism, it was the plain, unvarnished truth. Now what *is* this about? Is this Carlo's plan to put you on the board and give you responsibility for the expansion?"

"Carlo's plan, don't give me Carlo's plan. It's your plan to get rid of me."

His eyes were cold. "Don't let's add paranoia to everything else."

"To what else, what else are you talking about?"

His voice was low and hard. "I'll tell you what else. You and I loved each other, I still love you. We agreed to make love, you were the one looking after contraception. When it no longer worked for you to look after it, it would have been fair to tell me and let me be in charge of that side. Yes, Joy, that would have been the fair thing. It was not fair to allow me to let you conceive a child by accident."

"I would have thought you'd be glad to prove you were able to," she snapped.

"No. You would have thought wrong. Then to continue your unfairness, you will not let me know what your plans are for the child we conceived. I have agreed that it's your responsibility if that's what you want. You said you would let me know. You have not let me know. You have played some kind of game with me throughout. I don't know any more than I knew at Christmastime."

She was silent.

"And now you come screaming in here with some cock-and-bull story that I'm banishing you off to the provinces, whereas the truth is that I did everything in my power to get you to stay here. You can believe this or not as you wish, but that is the case."

There was a knock on the door, and Diana came in with the coffee. She laid it on the desk between them.

"Is the row over?" she asked.

"No, it's just getting to the peak." Frank smiled.

"I don't believe you," Joy said when Diana had left. "Carlo never had a thought of his own."

Frank went to a file and showed her a letter. In black and white it said that it might be a waste of Joy East's capabilities to have her tied up away from the nerve center of the business. He told her that there were more. He could find them if she needed proof.

"Then it's Carlo, he can't bear the shameless unmarried mother bit . . . it's he who's sending me away."

"Joy, I warned you about the danger of paranoia. If you look through these files, that survey was commissioned back in January. Months before you made your announcement."

"That bloody survey. Who are they anyway? They seem like a Mickey Mouse outfit to me," she grumbled.

Frank had a moment's regret. She was so sharp, no complaint, and bright; her thinking was exactly on the same line as his own. What a pity that it had to end in this acrimony and game-playing.

"Well, however they are, Carlo believes everything they say, and they may have a point, you know. You said a lot of it yourself already, long ago, before all this."

"I know." She had to admit that this was true.

"So what will you do?"

"I'll make up my own mind without any patronizing pats on the head from you," she said.

"As you wish, Joy, but may I remind you, this is *my* office and it was *you* who came to see me. It's not unreasonable that I should ask, since you seem determined to involve me."

"When I've decided what I'm going to do, I'll let you know," she said.

"You said that before."

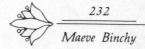

"But that was only about *my* child. This is about *your* company. You have a right to know."

He sat for a long time staring ahead of him after she left, her cup of coffee undrunk. He thought she had looked frightened and a little uncertain. But perhaps he was only imagining it.

She was a clever woman, and she knew that she could make him sweat it out, not knowing what she was going to say next and where she was going to say it.

He thought about it again that evening in their apartment. Renata sat on one side of their big marble fireplace looking into the flames, and he sat on the other. There were often long, companionable silences between them. But that night he said nothing at all.

Renata eventually spoke.

"Is it boring sometimes being with me in the evenings?" There was no complaint in her voice. She was asking as she might have asked the time or whether they should turn on the news on television.

"No, it's not boring," Frank said truthfully. "It's restful, actually."

"That is good," Renata said, pleased. "You are a very good husband to me, and sometimes I wish I had more fire and light and sparkle."

"Oh, Jesus, I get enough of that at work. It's like a Guy Fawkes bonfire. No, you're fine the way you are."

And he nodded to himself, as if agreeing with what he had just said. He didn't want to change her for a different model, a brighter, shinier brand.

The weeks passed with no further word from Joy; the plans for the expansion continued. Carlo said that Joy East was certainly giving it a lot of attention; whether she intended to go or not was anyone's guess.

"Don't force her," Frank advised. "She'll go, but not before she's ready."

He hoped he had read it right. Because she was succeeding in unsettling him.

He got an ornate invitation to a silver wedding celebration for Desmond and Deirdre Doyle. He looked at it grimly. In ten years, possibly, he and Renata might be sending out something similar. But he wondered if it was likely.

He wondered also what Desmond had to celebrate, a wedding that everyone had assumed was shotgun even though it turned out not to have been the case. A lifetime of being snubbed by the awful O'Hagan family back in Dublin. A life's work getting nowhere fast in Palazzo. Difficult children. The eldest shacked up with some out-of-work actor, apparently, the boy hightailing it back to Mayo, of all places, and Helen. A nun, a very odd, disturbed girl. Frank didn't like to think about Helen Doyle, who had appeared twice in his life, both times trailing disaster behind her and around her.

No, the Doyles had little to celebrate, which was probably why they were having this party.

An unlikely outing it was going to be.

But not as unlikely as the outing that Renata told him about when he came home from work.

"Joy East has invited us to dinner, just you and me and her, she says."

"Did she say why?"

"I did ask her, and she said she would like to have a talk with us."

"Is it at her house?"

"No, she said that you always say when something has to be said it should be said on neutral ground." Renata sounded puzzled.

Frank's stomach churned with fear.

"I don't know what she means by that," he managed to say.

"Well, she said she's booking a table in this restaurant . . . and that she checked with Diana that you are free, so she telephoned me to see if I were free."

"Yes. Well."

"Do you not want to go?" Renata sounded disappointed.

"She's been very odd lately. This pregnancy has unhinged her a bit, I think, that and the move . . . not that she's said yes or no to that, by the way. Can we get out of it, do you think?"

"Not without being very rude. But I thought you liked her?" Renata looked confused.

"I do, I did, it's not that. She's a bit unbalanced. Leave it with me."

"She said to ring her tonight." Renata seemed withdrawn.

"Yeah, I will. I have to go out again anyway. I'll ring her while I'm out."

He got into his car and drove to Joy's house. He rang the doorbell and knocked, but there was no reply.

He went to a public telephone and called her. She answered immediately.

"Why didn't you let me in?"

"I didn't want to."

"You *told* me to call."

"I told you to telephone, it's a different thing."

"Joy, don't do this, don't have a scene in front of Renata, it's not fair on her, she's done nothing to deserve it, nothing. It's cruel."

"Are you begging, do I hear you begging?"

"You can hear what you goddamn like, but just think, what harm has she ever done you?"

"Does this mean yes or no to my invitation?" Joy asked in a cool voice.

"Listen to me . . ."

"No, I am not going to listen anymore. Yes or no?" There was a threat in the question.

"Yes."

"I thought so," said Joy East, and hung up.

It was the same restaurant where they had had lunch last January. When Joy's stomach had been flat and when Nico's in-laws had seen them laughing. Now it was different.

Joy, still on mineral water to Frank's enormous relief, was gracious and anxious that they should be well seated and choose wisely from the menu. She did most of the talking, as Frank was edgy and Renata very reserved.

"You know the way in films they say: 'You must be wondering why I asked you to come here tonight . . .' " She tinkled.

"You said you had something to talk about." Renata was polite.

"I do. I have come to some decisions finally after a lot of thought, and I think it's fair that I should tell you about them. Frank because of work . . . and Renata, you because of Frank."

He felt the floodgates begin to open. God damn her to the pit of hell. It wasn't even a woman scorned, it wasn't that kind of fury. He would have played straight with her. Or sort of straight anyway.

"Yes?" Renata's voice was anxious. Frank hadn't trusted himself to speak.

"Well, about this baby . . ." She looked from one to the

other. And waited. It seemed like an age, but it was probably three seconds.

Joy continued: "I think it is going to change my life much more than I imagined. For a month or two I wondered if I'd done the right thing. Perhaps even at this late stage, I should give the child away, give it to some couple who would have a loving, secure home. I might not turn out to be such a great mother figure, all on my own."

She waited for one of them to deny this politely. Neither of them did.

"But then I thought no. I went into this knowing what it was about, so I must go through with it." She smiled happily.

"Yes, but what has this to do with us exactly?" Renata asked. Her face was fearful.

"It has this to do with you. If I were going to give the child to anyone, I would most certainly have offered you the chance. You would be such good parents, this I know. But since I'm not, and since you might have harbored some hopes . . ."

"Never . . . I never thought of it." Renata gasped.

"Hadn't you? I'm sure *you* did, Frank. After all, you haven't been able to get any joy out of the adoption societies, Carlo tells me."

"My father has no right to speak of such things," Renata said, her face a dark red.

"No, perhaps not. But he does, of course. Anyway, it was to make these matters clear that I asked you here, and to tell you that I will be going north soon, much sooner than anyone expected. I've sold my house here and bought a really lovely old Georgian farmhouse in need of repair, but magnificently proportioned, small and beautiful, and a perfect place for a child to grow up. If he or she is only going to have me around, then the poor love had better have a pony and somewhere to play as well!" Her smile was all-embracing.

Renata took a deep breath. "And will the child's father be involved at all?"

"Not at all. The father is someone I met casually at a packaging conference, a ship that passed in the night."

Renata's hand flew to her mouth in an involuntary gesture.

"Is that so shocking?" Joy asked. "I wanted to have a child, and he was as good a person as anyone else."

"I know, I mean, it was just that I thought . . ." Her voice trailed away, and she looked at Frank, whose face was stony.

"What did you just think, Renata?" Joy was like honey now.

"I know this is silly." Renata looked from one to the other. "I suppose I was afraid that the child might have been . . . Frank's child. And that this is why you even contemplated offering it to us . . . please, I don't know what I am doing talking like this . . . please." There were tears in her eyes.

Frank was frozen. He *still* didn't know which way Joy would jump. He couldn't put out his hand to comfort his wife.

Joy spoke deliberately and slowly: "Oh, Renata, surely you couldn't have thought that. Frank and I? We're too alike to be a number, to be the Grand Affair of the century. Oh, no. And anyway, Frank a father, that's not very likely, that wouldn't have been in the cards, would it?"

"What . . . what do you mean . . . ?"

"Oh, Carlo told me about his problems . . . I'm afraid your father is very indiscreet sometimes, but only when he knows it won't go further. Please don't say back to him that I

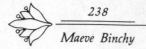
ever mentioned it. But he was always so sad that Frank did not give him the grandson . . ."

Frank spoke for the first time in a long while. He thought he had managed to take the shake out of his voice.

"And your child? Shall you tell him it was a one-night stand in a hotel room?"

"No, no, of course not, something much more romantic and sad. An untraceable, wonderful person, long dead. A poet maybe. Something sad and beautiful."

Somehow they finished the meal; somehow they found other things to talk about. The hurt went a little from Renata's eyes, and the lines of tension from Frank's face. And the serenity and bloom of pregnancy settled ever more on Joy East. She paid the bill confidently with her credit card, and when Renata went to the ladies' room, she sat and looked calmly across the table at Frank.

"Well, you won," he said.

"No, you won."

"How did I win, tell me? You frightened me to death and now you're denying me any part in the child's life. How is that winning?".

"You got what you wanted. You got me out."

"You're not starting that again?"

"I don't need to. I investigated the market-research bureau. They told me you hired them, they even had the date, it was just after we had lunch in this restaurant. As usual, it turned out the way you wanted it to. I'm out of your hair. The coast is clear for the next project. I do wonder who she'll be. But I'll never know. Any more than you'll know what it's like to play with a two-year-old, your two-year-old. Because you're not capable of fathering one. That's both your alibi and my excuse for cutting you out."

"You never told me why. Why all this hate?"

"It's not hate, it's determination. And why? I suppose because you have cold, cold eyes, Frank. I didn't see that until lately."

Renata was coming back across the room. They stood up; it was time to go.

"You'll be back for the meetings . . . and everything?" Frank said.

"Not all of them. I think if this operation is to be a success, we mustn't let anyone involved think that we keep running to London all the time. Major decisions should be made in the place itself. Otherwise they'll just think they're a little outpost instead of important on their own terms."

She was right, of course, as she had been so often.

He held the door of the taxi open for her. She said she was too big to fit into her little sports car anymore.

For a brief moment their eyes met.

"We both won," she said softly. "You could put it like that."

"Or neither of us won," he said sadly. "That's another way of putting it."

And he put his arm around his wife's shoulder as they went to where the Rover was parked.

Nothing would ever be the same between them after tonight. But the world had only cracked a little for them. It hadn't blown apart as it might have. And in a way that was winning.

8

Deirdre

The article said that anyone could be truly beautiful if she would give twenty minutes a day. Deirdre settled herself with a happy little wriggle into her chair and pulled the packet of biscuits toward her. Of course she could give twenty minutes a day. Who couldn't? Lord, weren't we all up and awake for sixteen hours, for heaven's sake? Twenty minutes was nothing.

She repeated the words *truly beautiful.* She could hear them being said about her when the day came. Doesn't Deirdre look truly beautiful? Who would think she was married for twenty-five years? Imagine that she's the mother of three grown children.

She sighed with pleasure and began to read. Let's see, what would she have to do? It would be her own little secret, investing this amount of time. The reward would be sensational.

First it said you must assess yourself and list your good points and weak areas. Deirdre took the little silver pen with a tassel on it from her handbag. This was fun, great fun. What a pity she had to do it on her own. Her eldest daughter, Anna, would say that she was fine as she was, no need to list figure flaws and dry patches in her skin. Her second daughter, Helen, would say it was ludicrous to be a victim and to think that looks were important; with all the suffering in the world women couldn't afford to take time analyzing their blemishes and deciding whether their eyes were deep-set or too close together.

Her son, Brendan, far away from her now, living in Ireland on a remote hillside in his father's part of the country . . . what would Brendan say? She found it almost impossible to imagine how Brendan would react anymore. She had wept night after night when he had first left home with few explanations and fewer apologies. Only when he had asked her straight out on the telephone . . . when he had cut across her tears to ask, "If you had your choice, if you had the power to choose my life, what would you have me do that would be so good and so important for us all?" she hadn't been able to answer him. Because to say that she wished things were different was no answer. You couldn't wish a circle to be square or black to be white.

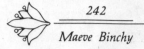

But according to this beauty article, there were things you could wish to be different and make them different. Like the shape of your face, a little judicious use of the blusher and the lightener could do wonders. Deirdre looked at the diagrams happily, she *would* learn to do it right. There was nothing worse than people who attempted it and got it wrong, they looked like Coco the Clown.

That was something that she could imagine Maureen Barry saying in the old days. She and Maureen used to have so much fun at one time. Deirdre's mother had been bosom pals with Mrs. Barry, and so the girls had carte blanche to do anything they liked as long as they were with each other. Deirdre thought back on those holidays in Salthill years ago. She had called the house in Rosemary Drive "Salthill" as a reminder, but she saw the name on the gate so often that it didn't really suggest the sea and sunshine and total freedom of their teens.

Maureen had been so entertaining those times, there was nothing that they felt they couldn't tell each other. Not until the summer they came to London, the summer that everything changed for both of them.

Deirdre wondered about the girls they had been to university with in Dublin. Did they often wonder what had happened to blond Deirdre O'Hagan? They would all know, of course, that she married young; maybe she would even put an announcement of her silver wedding in the *Irish Times.* Rub their noses in it, the uppity ones who had gone on to be barristers or to marry barristers. The types who thought that Dublin was the center of the universe and had only heard of Harrods as a place to shop and Chelsea as a place to live. Pinner? They used to say Pinner? as if it were Kiltimagh or somewhere like that. Oh, in *north* London. I see. It was their ignorance that they weren't traveled. But still, she would put in an announcement. Or maybe it was something that the children should do . . . a little message wishing them well on the twenty-fifth anniversary. She would check the papers and see how people did things these days.

What a pity there wasn't still that closeness with Maureen Barry. If only the years could be rolled back, she could pick up the phone and ask her. Straight out. And talk to her, too, about face-shaping, and how to shadow the jawline. But she would never ask Maureen anything like that these days. Things had changed completely as the years went by.

There were no friends around here who could share the fun of all this self-improvement. No, indeed, her neighbors would think it frivolous and silly. A lot of the women went out to work, they either knew such things, anyway, or else they hadn't time for it. Anyway, Deirdre would never dream of letting them into her business, letting them know that this was a big thing in her life, that it was her one chance to prove that a quarter of a century had added up to something. Deirdre intended to impress her neighbors rather than let them share in the fun. They weren't really important, not like people back in Dublin, but still, it was good to let them see that the Doyles were people of importance, of worth.

What would Desmond say if he saw her studying this article so intently? Would he say something flowery like that she was truly beautiful already? Or might he just say, That's nice, in the curious, flat way he often said things were nice without engaging in them at all? Or might he sit down and say to her that there was really no need for all this fuss and preparation? Desmond often told her not to fuss. She hated that, she didn't fuss, she just saw to it that things were done right. If somebody hadn't lit a fire under Desmond all these years, where would they be now? she would like to know.

Deirdre would not share her beauty secrets with her hus-

band. Long, long ago in that strange summer when it all began, Desmond would lie on a narrow bed and admire her as
she brushed her long, fair curls, he would say that he never
knew that peaches and cream was anything except a line in a
song until he saw Deirdre's lovely face. He would reach over
for her and ask if he could help her rub more of that nice cold
cream in, maybe down her throat a little, maybe around her
neck and arms. Maybe . . . maybe. It was so hard to remember Desmond being like that. But the article in the magazine
said that she could recapture all that fresh glow, it was only a
matter of proper skin care.

Deirdre would follow every single step, all those upward
and circular movements when massaging in the throat cream,
all that avoiding the delicate tissue around the eyes. She was
going to look right on this day if it killed her. She was going
to show them that they had been wrong to pity her twenty-
five years ago when she had married Desmond Doyle, a
counterman in a grocery shop, a boy from a poor family in the
back of beyond in Mayo. A family that nobody had ever
heard of.

This day would be her silvery revenge.

They had all said yes, every single person who had been expected to come. There were some, of course, who had been
asked but knew that they were not meant to come. Like Desmond's odd brother, Vincent, the man who never left his
mountains and his sheep in that lonely place where Brendan
had chosen to spend his life. There had been a message from
her son that his uncle very much regretted but it was a bad
time to get away. That was the way it should have been done.
Deirdre had nodded, pleased at the correct response.

And of course, the Palazzos, who ran the huge company

where Desmond had worked for so long. Unfortunately they couldn't come, a sweet letter from Carlo and Maria, signed personally, wishing them all kinds of happiness and full of regrets that it would coincide with their annual visit to Italy. There would be a gift and flowers. But it was right that they didn't come. They were too high up, they would cramp everyone else's style. And Deirdre's mother, who felt able to talk to everyone, might discuss with them too closely Desmond's career in the company. She might discover that Desmond had never risen high and had at one stage been let go. This would be at odds with the glowing picture Deirdre always painted.

Frank Quigley and his wife, Renata Palazzo, said they would love to come. Deirdre thought grimly that Frank, for all his vast success and his unfair advancement up the ladder even before he married the heiress to the Palazzo fortunes, was still a good man to have at a function. He always seemed to know the right thing to say, and said it. She remembered back to their wedding day, Frank had been the best man then, he had been well able to handle anything that had turned up. Including Deirdre's mother and father, with their faces like early Christian martyrs throughout the ceremony and the so-called festivities.

And Father Hurley was coming; he said it would be a marvelous chance to visit a couple whose marriage had worked out so well. Deirdre knew she could rely on kind Father Hurley to say the right thing all evening.

And of course, the Irish contingent would arrive. The date had been long fixed in their minds. There had been a possibility that her brother, Gerard, might not be able to make it, but Deirdre had telephoned with such surprise and hurt and bewilderment that somehow his plans had changed. She had told him straight out on the telephone that there was no point in *having* a silver wedding if the family couldn't be there.

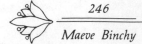
"Will Desmond's family be there?" Gerard had asked.

"That's not the point," Deirdre had said.

Mother was coming, of course, and Barbara; they were going to make a long weekend out of it all, come on the Thursday, do a few shows, take in a lot of shopping. Barbara's husband, Jack, would combine it with a business trip, of course. That's what he was always able to do.

And when they arrived, they would have drinks on the lawn in Rosemary Drive in the late afternoon. Then they would all go to a special Mass where the priest would refer to blessings of the sacrament of matrimony in general and specific reference to Desmond and Deirdre in particular. Father Hurley would be called on as the priest who had married them to say a few words. . . . Then, after photographs outside the church and everything, they would gather back at Rosemary Drive, and champagne would be opened.

There had been no champagne back in 1960, but Deirdre would not let her brow furrow about that. If she were to be truly beautiful, she must keep worry lines away from her face.

She told herself that there really was no need to have worry lines. Everything would go perfectly.

And even if . . . no, no, smooth out the temples, don't screw up the eyes.

The beauty plan had suggested you do a countdown and a chart. Nothing pleased Deirdre more, she loved making out plans and schedules like this. Anyway, she already had her own countdown to the silver wedding in terms of things to be organized.

Desmond had shaken his head sadly, but men didn't understand the way things were done. Or maybe, Deirdre thought crossly, *some* men did, and those were the ones who got on. Men like Desmond who had never risen in Palazzo, who were leaving and going into partnership in a corner shop. Those men didn't understand.

And because Deirdre was so plugged into her countdown, she knew she had exactly one hundred ten days to go when the telephone rang and it was her mother at the other end of the line.

Mother rang only every second weekend, on Sunday evenings. Deirdre had instituted that practice years ago; they rang each other on alternate Sundays. Sometimes she felt that Mother had little to say, but that couldn't be possible. Mother wasn't good at writing letters, so these conversations were Deirdre's lifeline. She remembered everything that was said, and even kept a little spiral notebook by the phone to jot down names of Mother's bridge friends, or of the party that Barbara and Jack had been to, or the concert that Gerard had taken Mother to. Sometimes Mrs. O'Hagan would exclaim that Deirdre had the most extraordinary memory for little things. But Deirdre thought it was only natural that you should want to recall important moments in your family's life. She was always mildly put out that Mother hardly ever remembered any of her friends and never inquired about Palazzo or about any of the outings that Deirdre had described.

It was unexpected to hear from Mother in the middle of the week, in the middle of the day.

"Is anything wrong?" Deirdre said at once.

"No, Deirdre. Lord above, you sound just like your grandmother." Kevin's mother always began every greeting by asking if anything was wrong.

"I meant it's not your usual time to call."

Mother softened. "No, I know, I know. But I'm in London and I thought I'd try and see could I catch you at home."

"You're in *London!*" Deirdre cried, her hand flying to her

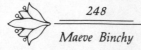
throat. She looked around the living room, untidy and covered with Desmond's papers, plans and projections, notes that he had been discussing with the Patels, the family who ran the shop that he insisted was far more his life's dream than the great Palazzo company. Deirdre herself was dressed in a faded apron, the place was a mess. She looked out the window fearfully, as if her mother were about to come straight in the door.

"Yes, I just got in from the airport. The underground is marvelous, isn't it? Just whizzes you in, door-to-door almost."

"What are you doing in London?" Deirdre's voice was almost a whisper. Had Mother come three months too early for the silver wedding? Was there a crisis?

"Oh, just passing through . . . you see, the tour leaves from London."

"The tour? What tour?"

"Deirdre, I told you all about it . . . didn't I? I must have. I've told everyone else."

"You mentioned no tour to me." Deirdre was mutinous.

"Oh, I must have. Maybe I wasn't talking to you."

"We talk every Sunday night of our lives. I was talking to you four days ago."

"Deirdre, is anything wrong, dear? You sound so strange. Like as if you're fighting with me or something."

"I didn't know of any tour. Where are you going?"

"Down to Italy first, and then by ship. We pick up the ship in Ancona and head off from there . . ."

"Where do you head off to?"

"Oh, a variety of places . . . Corfu, Athens, Rhodes, Cyprus, and someplace in Turkey."

"A cruise, Mother, you're going on a cruise!"

"I think that's a very grand name for it."

"It sounds like a very grand outing."

"Yes, well, let's hope it won't be too hot out in all those places. I think it's probably not the right time of year to head off . . ."

"Then why are you?"

"Because it came up. Anyway, enough of this. Are we going to meet?"

"Meet? You're going to come here? Now?"

Mother laughed. "Well, thanks a lot, Deirdre, that sounds like a great welcome, but actually I hadn't intended on going out to darkest Pinner . . . I thought you might come in and join me for a spot of lunch or coffee or whatever."

Deirdre hated Anna calling it "darkest Pinner." It was such an insult, as if the place were off the beaten track. And here was her own mother, who was from Dublin, for heaven's sake, who didn't know where anywhere was and whether it was on or off any track, saying the same thing.

"Where are you staying?" she asked, trying not to let the irritation show.

Mother was in a central hotel, very central, she said; it had only taken her two minutes to leave the Piccadilly line and be in her foyer. Simply remarkable. It would be easy for Deirdre to find, too.

"I know how to get there." Deirdre was white-faced.

"So shall we say the bar here at one-thirty? Will that give you time . . . ?"

Deirdre left a note to Desmond on the table. These days she never knew whether he was going to come back or not during the day. His arrangements with Palazzo seemed to be fluid. Frank Quigley had said there would be proper arrangements made; for a manager like Desmond, setting up on his own, it wasn't a question of severance pay, redundancy, compensation, golden handshakes. . . . It was all defined as

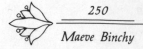

proper arrangements. Deirdre hoped it would be finalized by the time of the silver wedding.

Grimly Deirdre went upstairs and put on her best suit. Her hair was limp and greasy-looking. She had planned to wash it later in the day, now there wasn't time. Her good handbag was being mended, the catch had worked loose. There was a grubby-looking bandage on her wrist where she had burned herself on the oven. She didn't like to open it all up and apply a fresh one; they had told her that it should be done at the hospital.

In low spirits and filled with a vague apprehension, Deirdre Doyle set out to meet her mother. She felt drab and unattractive. She looked what she was, she decided, catching a reflection of herself in the window of the train that took her into Baker Street. She looked like the middle-aged housewife from the suburbs, married to a not very successful man, no job to exercise her mind, not enough money to dress herself properly. Suffering badly from the empty-nest syndrome. Perhaps more than most: one daughter trying to be accepted in a convent where they wouldn't let her take her vows; another daughter who sometimes didn't come to see her parents more than once in a fortnight; and her son, her beloved son, gone, fled to live at the other side of another country.

She was sure that she and Mother would fight. There had been something in the tone of the phone call that she hadn't liked. Mother had been impatient with her and patting her down as if *she* were the difficult one.

It was extremely irritating, but Deirdre would not lose her temper. Years of being reasonable and refusing to raise her voice had meant that there were few arguments in Rosemary Drive.

Deirdre had always prided herself on that. It was something to show for all those years and all that had happened.

Mother was sitting in a corner of the big oak-paneled bar as if she were a regular. She looked very good; she wore a fawn linen jacket and skirt with a cream-colored blouse beneath. Her hair had been freshly done; in fact, she must have spent the hour that her daughter used to struggle in to central London sitting peacefully in a hairdressing salon. She looked relaxed and at her ease. She was reading a newspaper, and unless she was putting on an elaborate act, she seemed to be reading it without the aid of glasses.

A woman of sixty-seven and she looked somehow younger and fresher than her own daughter.

Eileen O'Hagan's eyes looked up just at that moment, and she smiled broadly. Deirdre felt her movements somehow stiffen as she walked across to meet her mother. They kissed, and Mother, who was already on friendly terms with the waiter, called him over.

"Just a glass of wine and soda," Deirdre said.

"Nothing stronger to celebrate your old mother coming to town?"

"You can't be this lady's mother. Seesters, yes . . ." the waiter said on cue. But it had a ring that was altogether too truthful for Deirdre.

"Just wine and soda," she snapped.

"Let me look at you . . ." her mother said.

"Don't, Mother, I look bad. I wish you'd told me. . . ."

"But if I had, then you'd have gone to an immense amount of fuss and worn yourself out . . ." her mother said.

"Then you admit you didn't tell me, that it didn't just slip your mind."

"It was out of kindness, Deirdre. You were always one to go to such efforts, that's why I didn't tell you."

Deirdre felt the tears sting in her eyes. She fought to keep the hurt tone out of her voice.

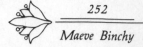

"Well, all I can say is that it's a pity. Desmond would have loved to have had you to the house, and the girls will be very sorry they've missed their grannie."

"Nonsense, Deirdre, Anna's at work. Helen's at prayer, Desmond is up to his eyes. Why create a great fuss?"

There it was again, that hated word, *fuss.* Deirdre clenched her fists and saw her mother glance at her whitened knuckles. This was very bad; she had vowed that there would be no argument. She must keep to that.

"Right, well, here we are anyway," Deirdre said in a voice that sounded to her own ears curiously tinny. "And, Mother, you do look remarkably well."

Her mother brightened up. "This suit has been a godsend, you know I bought it three years ago in Maureen's shop. Maureen always had great taste. I used to wonder why some of her clothes were so expensive, but her mother always said you paid for the cut and that they never really went out of fashion. . . ."

Mother patted the skirt of her outfit with pleasure.

"It should be just the thing for a cruise." Deirdre tried to sound enthusiastic.

"Well, yes, I didn't think there was any point in getting all those floral silks . . . leisurewear, cruisewear they actually call them nowadays. Better to bring something suitable, something familiar, and I have a few cotton dresses for sightseeing." She looked animated and excited.

"And what possessed you to take off on something like this?" Even as she spoke, Deirdre knew that hers sounded like the voice of an older woman remonstrating with a difficult daughter rather than the enthusiasm that there should have been for a self-sufficient parent capable of enjoying herself on her own.

"As I told you, it came up, and I have a friend who was also free at this time, so it seemed only sensible . . ."

"Oh, good, someone's going with you." Deirdre was pleased. Two old ladies on board ship would at least have each other to talk to at the time and be able to share the memory afterward. She tried to remember which one of her mother's bridge cronies would be likely to accompany her.

"Yes, and I thought I'd seize the chance of letting you meet each other, not for lunch, we'll have that on our own, but Tony said he'd pop down and say hello . . . Ah, there he is . . . what timing!"

And as Deirdre felt the base of her stomach fill with lead, she realized that her mother was waving at a florid-looking man with a blazer and a red face who was coming across the room, rubbing his hands delightedly. Mother was going on a cruise with a man.

"This is nice," Tony said, crushing Deirdre's hot hand in his own and telling the waiter that he'd like a large G and T, Cork and Schweppes, ice and slice.

The waiter was puzzled. Mother said affectionately that Irish gin drinkers were fanatically partisan and only drank the home brew as far as gin was concerned.

"But we're very democratic, we drink the English tonic," Tony said, beaming around him. "Well, Deirdre, what do you think of all this caper?"

"I've only just heard about it this moment," she said, hardly able to find the words.

"It should be a great old jaunt altogether," he said. "No decisions about whether to go and see places, they come to see you instead. Perfect for the lazy man. And lazy woman." He actually patted Mother's hand.

"Were you afraid to tell me this, too, in case I'd fuss?" Deirdre asked, and could have bitten off her tongue.

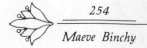

Tony weighed in before Mother could answer.

"Oh, there you are, Eileen. She's as jealous as the others. Barbara nearly went mad when she heard that her mother was taking me instead of her, and Gerard said that in all decency your mother should take her son instead of a toy boy like myself." He threw back his head and laughed heartily, and Mother laughed with him.

Deirdre thought, he knows Barbara and Gerard. Why had neither of them said anything about this to her? How dare they keep quiet about something as big as this? And was he serious about Mother taking him? Mother could not possibly be paying for this loud, vulgar man. Or was this a joke, too?

Mother seemed to read her face. "Don't worry about a thing, Deirdre, my love, it's only his way of going on. Tony's not after the deeds of the house."

"Fat chance I'd have if I *were* after them," he boomed. "Your mother will live forever. I'll croak one of these days. I hope not on the cruise, though a burial at sea would be something to remember, wouldn't it?"

Deirdre felt a genuine sense of nausea. This man, who must be almost the same age as her mother, was a serious part of her life. And until this minute nobody had been able to tell her.

She forced the smile back onto her face and saw her mother's approving glance. She found her mouth dry and bitter as she searched for some suitable words.

But Tony was not a man who would allow silences. He had had her glass refilled, he had commandeered a dish of olives and a bowl of chips on the ground that one had to have all the trappings. He had assured her that he would take great care of her mother on the cruise, squeezed her hand hard again, and said he would leave the key at reception. The key. The man wasn't even pretending that they had separate rooms. Deirdre felt a sense of unreality wash over her, and she hardly noticed that he had kissed her mother good-bye on the cheek.

Mother had booked a nearby restaurant. It was small and French and expensive. The napkins were thick, the silver was heavy, and the flowers on the table were real and plentiful.

In her twenty-five years living in London, Deirdre had never eaten in a place like this, and here was her mother, her mother from a small country, a small city compared with this one, ordering as if she were used to it.

She was glad that Mother was making decisions. Not only could she not understand the menu, but she would not have been able to order, so confused and upset did she feel.

"Why didn't you tell me anything about . . . er . . . Tony?" she asked eventually.

"Well, there wasn't all that much to tell until we decided to go on this cruise together, and then, as soon as we set off on that, I *did* tell you." Mother spread out her hands as if it were the simplest thing in the world.

"And Gerard and Barbara . . . do they . . . did they . . . ?"

"Well, they know Tony's a friend of mine, and naturally I told them our holiday plans."

"And were they . . . did they . . . ?"

"Gerard drove us to the airport this morning. Tony's right, he's green with envy, he keeps saying it's just what he needs. He works too hard, he *should* take time off, and he can well afford it. Maybe this is the spur."

"But did he say . . . what did he think . . . ?"

"He didn't say that he'd take a holiday, and you know Gerard, he probably is thinking about it."

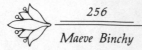

Could Mother really misunderstand her or was this deliberate? Deirdre was not going to be brushed aside.

"What about Barbara and Jack? What do they think of you going away with a man?"

"Dearest Deirdre, I'm not going away with a man in that sense. I am going away on a holiday certainly, and I am going with Tony, and yes, indeed, he is a man. What do you mean, what do they think? They don't think at all, I am perfectly sure."

"But Jack's family . . ."

As long as Deirdre could remember, Jack's family had been spoken of with some kind of awe. His father was a high court judge, his uncle was an ambassador. Barbara had done what the O'Hagan family had wanted by marrying such style, instead of what she, Deirdre, the eldest, had done—marrying a nobody and doing it in a great hurry.

But Mother looked totally bewildered.

"Jack's family?" she repeated, as if Deirdre had somehow begun to speak in a foreign language. "What on earth connection could they have with anything?"

"You know . . ."

"I don't think they ever met Tony. No, I'm sure they didn't. Why do you ask?"

Deirdre looked hard at her mother. Mother knew bloody well why she asked. She asked because the high and mighty Jack's family were always mentioned. They had been mentioned since Deirdre's young sister, Barbara, had started going out with a son of the well-connected tribe. Deirdre remembered the huge wedding given for Barbara, with the marquee, the witty speeches, the politicians, and the photographers. It had been very different from her own wedding day. And now suddenly Jack's almighty clan didn't seem important anymore.

Feeling a flush darken her cheek, she spoke directly to her mother.

"And do you and . . . Tony . . . have any further plans . . . like after the cruise, do you think you might get married or anything?"

"Do try to keep the surprise out of your voice," her mother said. "Stranger things have happened, you know. But the answer is no. No plans like that."

"Oh?"

"And anyway, enough about me and my trip. Tell me about all your doings." Mother smiled in anticipation.

Deirdre looked dour. "None of them are anything nearly as interesting as your plans."

"Come, come, Desmond's setting up on his own, *and* you're going to have this whole silver wedding shindig . . ."

It was such a Tony word, *shindig.* Mother hadn't spoken like that before.

"Where did you meet him?" Deirdre asked abruptly.

"Desmond?" Now Mother was being playful. "When you brought him home, of course, and told us about the wedding. But you know that."

"I didn't mean Desmond, and you know that." Deirdre was cross. "I meant Tony. How did you become involved with him?"

"We met at the golf club."

"Tony's a member of the golf club?" The surprise and disbelief were clear in her voice.

"Yes, he plays off twelve," Mother said proudly.

"But how did he become a member?" Years ago someone flashy like Tony could not have been proposed, it would have been as simple as that. Had her Desmond known how to play golf, which he did not, he would not have been acceptable. How could someone like Tony get in?

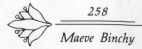

"I've no idea. I suppose the way we all became members." Mother was vague.

"And do all your other friends know him? Did Mrs. Barry know him, for example?" Deirdre had chosen Maureen Barry's mother, the great social barometer of their Dublin. Surely Tony had not been welcomed in her set?

"Sophie? Yes, of course, poor Sophie met him from time to time. Sophie Barry didn't play golf, remember, so she wouldn't have known him in that context."

"Don't tell me Tony plays bridge?"

"No, he's frightfully dismissive of old pussycats, as he calls us, spending hour after cheery hour, day after day, dealing cards."

Mother laughed merrily, and suddenly her life seemed much more fun than Deirdre's own. Desperate not to let her mother change the subject again, Deirdre tried once more.

"And, Mother, please, what does Gerard think? What does he say? No, not about taking holidays himself. What does he say about you and Tony?"

"I've no idea."

"You must know."

"No, I mean, how would I know? I only know what he says to me, I've no idea what he says to anyone else. He has a rather nice girlfriend at the moment, he may talk about it with her, but I imagine not." Mother looked supremely unconcerned.

"But he must . . . surely . . ."

"Listen, Deirdre. Everyone has their own life to lead, Gerard is probably much more worried about his career at the bar, should he become a section council, should he stop playing the field with these little bimbos and settle down? He probably worries about his health, he's nearly forty, he may think a lot about cholesterol and polyunsaturated fats. He might wonder whether to sell his flat and buy a house. What time on earth is there for him to spend thinking about his mother? I ask you!"

"But if you're doing something . . . if you're getting into something . . ."

"I'm sure he thinks I'm old enough to look after myself."

"We all have to look after each other," Deirdre said a trifle unctuously.

"That's where you are totally wrong. We all have to make very sure we don't interfere in people's lives. That's the great sin."

The unfairness of it stung Deirdre like the lash of a whip. How *dare* Mother come out with this preachy nonsense about not interfering in people's lives. For a quarter of a century Deirdre had been trying to live up to some kind of image, some expectations for her. She was the daughter for whom there had been such hopes. The eldest of the family, very bright at university, an honor student, she might have gone into the Department of External Affairs, as it was called then; she might have been on the way to being an ambassador or marrying one. She might have done the bar, as her brother had done. She might have made the brilliant match that her sister, Barbara, had done.

Instead she had fallen in love one long hot summer and trapped herself into a strange prison. Where since nothing was good enough for the O'Hagans and their hopes back home, then everything must be made to look as if it were.

Deirdre had lived her entire life on this premise, to please the mother who was now sitting opposite her, justifying her pitiable relationship with a common, flashy man by saying that the main rule of living was not to interfere! It was not possible.

Deirdre spoke very slowly. "I know what you're saying,

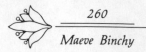

but I think it's important too not to be entirely self-centered and to take the wishes of others into account as well. I mean, did I or did I not spend all my teenage years hearing about people who were suitable and people who were not suitable?"

"Not from me you didn't."

"But you were always wanting to know what people's fathers did and where they lived?"

"Out of interest." Mother was airy about it. "It's always nice to know who people are in case you knew them years ago or something. That's all it was about."

"No, it wasn't, Mother. You and Mrs. Barry—"

"Oh, Deirdre, Sophie Barry had nothing in her whole life except some kind of nonsensical pecking order. Nobody who knew her took any notice of it."

"Maureen did."

"Well, more fool Maureen, and anyway, I don't think you're right, Maureen lived her own life, made her own way despite all poor Sophie's rubbishing on about being in trade."

"You mean to tell me that you and Daddy were perfectly happy that I married Desmond? Don't try to tell me that. I won't believe it."

There were tears in Deirdre's eyes, tears of rage, hurt, and confusion. Suddenly the screen was falling away, the mask was being dropped, she knew she was on dangerous ground here. The polite pretense of years was being swept away.

The woman in the fawn linen suit and the cream blouse looked at her with concern. She began to speak and then stopped.

"Now, you can't deny it!" Deirdre was triumphant.

"Child, you're talking about a lifetime ago," her mother said.

"But what I say is true, you did care, you did care that Desmond wasn't top drawer enough for us."

"What do you mean for us? We weren't marrying him, you were, he was your choice, the words *top drawer* weren't even mentioned."

"Not aloud maybe."

"Not at all. I assure you, your father and I thought you were too young, of course we did, you hadn't taken your degree, we were afraid you would never get any qualification. In that I suppose we wished you would wait, that was all."

Deirdre took a deep breath. "You knew we couldn't wait."

"I knew you wouldn't wait, that's all I knew. You were very determined. I wasn't going to oppose you."

"You knew why."

"I knew you loved him or thought you did. Now that you've stayed with him and are dead set on having all this palaver in the autumn, then you were probably right, you did love him, and he loved you."

To Mother it seemed too simple: If you lived together for twenty-five years and were prepared to acknowledge it, you loved each other. Deirdre was thoughtful.

"Well, isn't that what happened?" Mother was waiting for a yes or a no or an 'I told you so.'

"More or less, but no thanks to anyone at home." Deirdre was still mulish.

"I don't know what exactly it is you're trying to say, Deirdre. Of all my children I thought you were the most contented. You went for what you wanted, you got it. Nobody forced you to do anything, you had your freedom, you went to university, you could have worked for a living, but you never did. Sophie and I used to say that you got everything on a plate. Now it seems there's some grievance."

Mother was interested but not distressed; she was con-

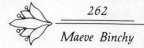

cerned but not unduly curious. She tossed a salad expertly and waited for an explanation.

"Why did you let me marry Desmond if you thought I was too young?"

"I only thought, let's cause the least grief possible in the world. That's what I always think. Your father did think you might be pregnant, but I knew you weren't."

"How did you know that?" Deirdre's voice was a whisper.

"Because nobody, not even in the far back year of 1960, would have got married to someone just for that reason if she didn't want to. And you weren't. Anna wasn't born until months and months later, quite wiped poor Sophie's eye, I think. I have a feeling she had the same thoughts as your father."

"Yes."

"So, Deirdre, what's the federal case, as they say? What am I supposed to have done? We gave our permission. Was that bad? No. We came to the wedding, that's what you wanted. You said you didn't want a huge, showy number and you wanted it in England, we went along with that. We took Barbara and Gerard out of school for the ceremony.

"The house is there for you and Desmond to come over and see us, but you never do. You came once, and you were so touchy we didn't know what to say to you, everything upset you. We came to see you a few times, and we're all heading over to see you again for your silver wedding, something, it may be said, that isn't at all what we're used to, and somehow still, in spite of all this, I am the worst in the world, and by implication your father was, and your sister and brother are."

Eileen O'Hagan mopped up the dressing of her salad with a piece of French bread and looked at her daughter for an explanation.

Deirdre looked at her wordlessly.

The waiter came and took away their plates and discussed at length an apple tart and a burnt cream. Deirdre's mother went into the option with animation; it gave Deirdre a chance to gather her thoughts.

"I ordered one of each. I hate to be directive, but I thought it best."

"That's fine, Mother."

"And what were we talking about before? Oh, I know, Daddy and I were supposed to have hated Desmond or something, isn't that it?"

"Not exactly."

"Well, not just not exactly, not at all. We both thought he was very nice, bullied within an inch of his life by you, of course, but then you'd be bound to be bossy, you get it from me." Eileen O'Hagan was pleased to have passed on such sterling qualities.

"What did you say about him to each other?" Deirdre's voice was small.

"Daddy and I? Hardly anything. He was providing for you all right, that was what we worried about, I suppose, in those days, so it was good that this side of it wasn't a problem. I think we were upset that you didn't have a career."

"I had three children in rapid succession." Deirdre was defensive.

"Yes, but afterward. Anyway, I suppose we thought that maybe it was a bit hierarchical in that setup with the Italians, the Palladians—"

"The Palazzos, Mother."

"Yes, well, that's about the only negative thought we ever had about Desmond, so you can stop doing your outraged lioness bit about him."

Mother laughed affectionately.

Deirdre looked at her as if she were someone never seen before.

"And Mrs. Barry, was she not questioning you about us?"

"No, sweetheart. To be very honest, there wasn't all that much interest at all. Nobody had. You know that yourself about Dublin, out of sight out of people's minds and immediate conversation and interest."

"But not for you, surely you couldn't have forgotten me, your eldest daughter." Her lip was trembling.

"Of course, I don't forget you, silly thing, but not all the little bitty things that you think were never off our lips, this promotion, that remark that the Palladians passed about Desmond, the time that Anna was at the same reception as Princess Di."

"It was Princess Michael of Kent."

"Well, you know what I mean, Deirdre, it's not some kind of score card, you know, points for this, minus points for that."

There was a silence. A long silence.

"I'm not criticizing you, you do know that?"

"Yes, Mother."

"And even if Kevin and I hadn't liked Desmond, which was not the case—whatever we were allowed to get to know of him we liked very much—but suppose we hadn't . . . what would have been the point of saying it or letting it be thought? We weren't going to live your lives for you."

"I see."

"When I was married to Kevin, my parents were delighted, they crowed and brayed and made me very, very uneasy."

"You should have been pleased."

"No, I was suspicious. I thought that they wanted me off

their hands, and I also thought they equated money with some kind of happiness or success. Your father didn't give me much of either."

"I don't believe you!" Deirdre's mouth was wide open.

"Why shouldn't I tell you this? You and I are middle-aged women, we're talking about life and love. Your father was what they call now a chauvinist pig; in those days we called it a man's man and were meant to be grateful that he wasn't chasing the ladies. He stayed at his clubs every evening until late, you remember that growing up, don't you? I bet Desmond was at home to get to know his children."

"He wasn't a member of any clubs." Deirdre sounded wistful.

"And weren't you the better for it? Anyway, I always thought I would neither encourage nor discourage any of my children, let them choose for themselves and go along with it."

"Barbara's wedding . . ." Deirdre began.

"Nearly put us in the poorhouse. What a bloody shower, Jack's family. They gave us a wedding list of their guests from their side of the family as long as your arm . . . we decided to do it the way the young couple wanted it. Though Barbara has often said to me she wished they had had less of a send-off, nothing ever lived up to it."

"Barbara said that?"

"She says it every time she has a glass of sherry, it's hardly breaking a confidence to tell you. She says it in the golf club, and she tried to say it the night she was in the audience at the *Late Late Show,* but apparently they didn't get a mike to her."

For the first time Deirdre laughed a genuine laugh, and the waiter was so pleased he came running with a plate of bonbons and a refill of coffee.

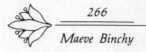

"And I know you think I should be happy with my six grandchildren, your three and Barbara's three. But I never see yours. They grew up without us, and when we did meet them, they were like white mice they were so afraid of us. And I was sick to death of Barbara's three when they were at the poisonous stage, we were unpaid, unthanked baby-sitters, and now that they're nice and interesting I don't see hide nor hair of them. And I don't think that Gerard is going to give us any news in that direction, but that's his business. I don't want to send him out to mate just so that I can have more people to call me Grannie."

She looked lively and eager, she did not look like someone who wanted more people to call her Grannie, let alone someone who had grown-ups who did.

"And suppose you and . . . er, Tony . . . get on well on this cruise, why don't you think there might be a chance of . . . well, something more permanent?"

Deirdre somehow felt that if he were accepted by Mother's cronies at home and by her sister and brother, he couldn't be quite as common and unsuitable as she had thought at first.

"No, that's not on the cards."

"As you said earlier, it's not such a barbarous idea."

"Well, it is really, Deirdre. Or his wife would think so anyway."

"He's married. Mother, I don't believe it."

"Oh, but you must, I assure you."

"Does anyone know, is his wife sort of around, are people aware of her?" Deirdre's voice was very concerned.

Her mother was silent for the first time. She looked at Deirdre with a strange expression. It was hard to read her look. It was partly sad and partly as if she had known that things would be like this. There was a little frisson of impatience in the disappointment.

She didn't answer Deirdre's question, she never answered it. She called for the bill, and they walked together back to her hotel.

She said she had a little more shopping to do, and she sent her love to Anna and to Helen. There was no point in sending love to Brendan, they both knew that he was only rarely in touch. No rapport of weekly phone chats had been established between Deirdre and her son on Sunday nights as there were between Deirdre and her mother.

Eileen O'Hagan said she wished Desmond well and thought that he was quite right to have left the Palladians or the Palazzos or whatever they were called. A man had to do what a man had to do. And so had a woman.

She said she would send a postcard from somewhere that looked nice and exotic.

She said since Deirdre hadn't offered that she would be sure to give Deirdre's warm wishes to Tony and tell him that Deirdre had said bon voyage.

And as she left her daughter, who would get the tube back to the station where the Metropolitan line would take her back to Pinner and the table full of preparations for a party one hundred ten days away, Eileen O'Hagan reached out her hand and stroked Deirdre's cheek.

"I'm sorry," she said.

"What for, Mother? Why are you sorry? You gave me a lovely lunch. It was really good to see you." And Deirdre meant it.

"No, I'm sorry that I didn't give you more."

"You gave me everything, I was only being silly, you said yourself that I was the most contented of your children. I never knew that."

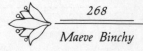

Her mother opened her mouth as if to speak but closed it again, and when Deirdre turned to wave, she saw that Eileen O'Hagan's lips were moving. She thought she was just mouthing good-bye.

She was too far away to hear her mother saying, "I'm sorry that I gave you no notion of happiness. Only how to pretend you are happy and that's no gift at all. It's a burden for your back."

Deirdre waved again just before she went down the steps to the tube station, and she hoped her mother would stop mouthing at her. After all, here in Piccadilly Circus the whole world could be passing by, and there could be anyone, just anyone, who might see them. Someone from Pinner or someone from Dublin. The world was getting smaller, and you should always behave as if you were under some kind of observation, because when it came down to it, that's what we all were most of the time. Under observation.

9

Silver Wedding

They had set the electric teamaker for seven o'clock.

Desmond had grumbled that it was too early, they would both be worn out by the time the thing began. But Deirdre said it was better far to be ahead of themselves instead of running after themselves all day. Be up and organized before the caterers came.

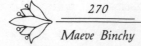

"They're not coming until three o'clock," Desmond had said.

"Everything has to be cleared away for them."

"God Almighty, Deirdre, we're not going to spend eight hours clearing the kitchen worktops. And isn't it all done already anyway?"

She took no notice of him, she poured him out a cup of tea.

For years, since they had moved into separate beds, in fact, they had this morning ritual of the electric teamaker on the table between them. It somehow soothed them into the day, took the little edges off the slight sense of morning disappointment that they each seemed to feel.

"Happy anniversary," he said, and reached out for her hand.

"And to you," she said, smiling. "Will we give our presents now or later?"

"Whatever you like."

"Maybe later." She sipped her tea and ticked off in her mind all the things to be done. She had an appointment at the hairdresser and a manicure as a special treat. Her new outfit was hanging on the wardrobe under its cellophane wrapping. She hoped it was a good choice, the woman in the shop had been very pushy, kept calling her Madam and speaking to her as if she weren't there. Madam would look very well in pale colors, Madam doesn't want to grow old before her time. Madam could do with a little detail on the shoulder if Madam really insists that she won't wear shoulder pads.

Deirdre would like to have worn pads, almost everyone did nowadays, like the women in *Dynasty* and *Dallas*, but she remembered that time years ago when she had bought a very upholstered-looking jacket and Maureen Barry had laughed at it and called it Deirdre's Marshal Bulganin outfit. She daren't risk that again. Or risk even the memory of it.

She knew that whatever Maureen wore today it would be stunning, it would take all the attention away from her, away from Deirdre, whose party it was. The woman in the shop said she couldn't believe that Madam was really celebrating a silver wedding, but that was in the shop. The woman was anxious to flatter her and make a sale.

The woman hadn't seen Maureen.

She would take the limelight today, as she had taken it twenty-five years ago. When the bride had looked pink and frightened and flustered, and the maid of honor had looked dark and cool and elegant in a plain pink linen dress and a big pink flower in her hair. And Frank Quigley had never taken his eyes off her. From one end of the day to the other.

Would it be the same today? Would the great Frank Quigley remember his passion for Maureen Barry with regret as the one thing he didn't win in his life? If she knew Frank, he would probably have turned it into a success rather than a failure. Look at the bigger and better prize he had won. Married to the entire Palazzo fortune. He wouldn't have had that if Maureen had accepted him all those years ago.

But she wouldn't think destructive thoughts. Not today. Today was her day more than her wedding day had ever been. She had worked hard for it, put in long hours, long years. Deirdre Doyle would have today.

Desmond looked at his face in the bathroom mirror. It looked back at him, younger, he thought, than it had done a while ago. Or maybe he just imagined that because he felt better. He didn't have that constant pain in the base of his stomach that he used to have going in to Palazzo. He enjoyed leaving the house now. Mornings were so much easier.

He had suggested that he and Suresh Patel start a news-

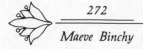

paper delivery service in the area. People would like to have a paper to read in their homes if it arrived before seven. And it was a great success. It was run by the owlish boy, who kept the accounts meticulously and also delivered the papers before heading off to school. He dropped the *Daily Mail* into Rosemary Drive for Desmond, too, and it meant that he could read it and leave it for Deirdre.

He was annoyed with her that she had not wanted Suresh Patel and his wife to come to the silver wedding.

"It's only for people who were at the ceremony," she had complained.

"John and Jean West weren't there," he had countered.

"Don't be silly, Desmond, they're our next-door neighbors."

"Well, Suresh is my partner, isn't he?"

"Only very recently, and anyway, he won't know anyone."

"Half of them won't know anyone."

"Be reasonable, can't you, his wife doesn't even speak English. What am I to say to people, 'This is Mrs. Patel, Desmond's partner's wife, who can only nod and smile'?"

He had left it. But it rankled. He felt sure that if Suresh Patel was having some ceremony in his house, the Doyles would have been invited. But it wasn't worth a major row; if he had won, then he would have had to look after the Patels all evening. And there were so many other things to concentrate on. Like his son who was coming back . . . of his own free will to be there for the celebrations. Perhaps now that he too had been able to escape from a world that had frightened him they might have more in common. Perhaps the old prickliness would have softened, if not gone altogether.

And he would be glad to see Father Hurley again; he was a kind man. Even in those bad far-off days when priests were

meant to be disapproving of sin and anticipating the sacrament of matrimony and everything. There had been no con-
demnation when he had gone and asked Father Hurley if he
could arrange to marry them as quickly as possible. Even
quicker.

"Are you sure?" Father Hurley had asked.

"Oh, yes, the tests were positive," Desmond had said,
fighting the panic.

"No, I meant, are you both sure this is what you want to
do? It's for life."

It had been an odd question at that time. Desmond had
paid little heed to it. The only important thing had been could
the priest get them married in three weeks, so that their child
would not be impossibly premature. The child that was never
born. The child that miscarried on Christmas Eve.

He wondered if Father Hurley had ever thought about it,
whether the priest, who had after all baptized Anna, realized
that she was born a full fourteen months after the shotgun
wedding. And that a sister or brother had been lost before
that.

Desmond sighed. Father Hurley probably had enough to
think about in an Ireland which was rapidly catching up with
the rest of the world in terms of godlessness. He would be
unlikely to spend time speculating about what had happened
in marriages made a quarter of a century ago.

Anna woke around seven in her flat in Shepherd's Bush, she
went straight to the window to see what kind of day it was.
Good, a bright, crisp autumn day. London was lovely in autumn. The parks were at their best. She had been walking last
night with her friend Judy, and they had seen possibly a
dozen different shades of gold and orange on the trees. Judy

said that in America, up in New England, they had special tours and holidays for leaf peekers, for people who came to peek at the leaves changing color. You could organize that in London, too.

Anna was going to work for the morning. She would only be in the way in Rosemary Drive, things would be up to high do there, the fewer people there were about the better. She would go there around three, the same time as the caterers, just to keep Mother out of their hair and from driving them up the walls. She had begged Helen not to turn up until five, the official time that the celebrations began. The thought of letting her sister, Helen, loose on any house where professional caterers were preparing a meal was enough to frighten anyone.

Helen was in very poor form at the moment, there had been some problem yet again in the convent. Apparently the rest of the community didn't want Helen to take her vows and be a permanent member of the house. This was what Anna was reading between the lines. Helen, of course, was reading nothing of the sort, seeing only a series of petty irritations, confusions, and obstacles.

Anna sighed. If she was in a religious community, which was possibly the last place on earth she would want to end up, then the very, very last person on earth she would like with her was Helen. There was something very unsettling about Helen's very presence. On the few occasions she had come to see Anna in the bookshop it had been a matter of trying to hold on to big piles of books in displays—no other customer knocked them over, but Helen would. As she had actually swept the credit-card machine off the cash desk, breaking the glass on a display cabinet. As her coat always caught somebody's cup of coffee. Not a restful presence anywhere. She hoped that Helen wouldn't say the wrong thing too often this evening.

What could she say that would be terrible? Well, something about Brendan, along the lines of wasn't it great we forced him to come back . . . Which wasn't the case, but Father would think it was. Or about Father having left Palazzo and working with a terribly nice Paki. Helen was the only person Anna knew who actually used words like *Paki* and *Eyetie.* Yes, she could refer to Renata Quigley as an Eyetie.

Anna padded off in bare feet to make herself a cup of instant coffee. Another pleasure and advantage of not living anymore with Joe Ashe. It had to be real, the coffee, it had to be freshly ground in a machine that would split your head apart. She would not like to live forever on her own, but she was daily finding more and more positive things about not living with Joe Ashe.

He had left as good-naturedly and easily as he had arrived. He had kissed her on the cheek and said that she was being very heavy over nothing. He had said he'd miss her, and he had taken quite a few of her records and a very expensive rug she had bought for their bed. She had watched him fold it and had said nothing.

"You did give me this as a present, I think." He had smiled lightly.

"Sure, Joe," she had said. She would not be heavy over a bedspread. Only about another woman in her bed.

Judy had been very good over the breakup.

"I'm always here, ring me if you feel a bit bleak. I'll listen. Don't ring him out of loneliness, only ring him if you could take him back."

Friends were great, Anna thought, real pure gold. Friends understood when you got infatuated with people, and didn't

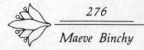

mind you going mad for a while; they were still there when the infatuation was over. As it nearly was. Very, very nearly.

And she wasn't going to embark on anything again for a long while. Ken Green understood that; he had said that he wanted the smell of Joe Ashe's rather sickly aftershave well gone from the place before he came around in earnest. Ken was very droll. He got on very well with her father, too, which was odd, and persuaded Dad and Mr. Patel to take a small selection of his paperbacks to display with the magazines, just in case there was a market, he had said . . . and of course, there had been. Father and Mr. Patel were going to expand. There was an opening for a bookshop in the area. Ken had even suggested that Anna might think of opening one herself, in conjunction with them.

"Too near home," she had said.

"Maybe you're right." Ken was agreeable but not in the way Joe Ashe agreed with people. Joe agreed for an easy life, Ken because he had thought it out. She half wished she had asked him to the silver wedding do, but it was far too public a commitment, Mother's friends would whisper, and Grandmother O'Hagan would be bound to want to know everything even though there was nothing to know.

Brendan had arrived in London early, off the boat train in Euston. It coincided with the morning rush hour. He stood watching for a quarter of an hour while the commuter population of that part of London buzzed and scuttled and darted up ramps and down stairs, down to taxi lines, in to grab a quick breakfast standing at a counter, leaping onto escalators. They looked so self-important, he thought, as if whatever petty job they were racing to were important, as if they were people of substance. And this is what his father and mother would like him to be doing, racing down from Rosemary Drive to catch a train to Baker Street, and another tube to somewhere like here. It was a preposterous way to live, and all to be able to *say* to someone that this was success.

Brendan knew he must not spoil his gesture in coming to the celebration by voicing these thoughts.

And he also remembered that Vincent had warned him to buy some proper clothes to wear for the occasion.

"You'll always be able to use a good suit, lad," his uncle had said.

"Aw, no, Vincent, not a suit, I'd never wear a suit, for God's sake."

"Well, that's what we wore in my day. But then a jacket and trousers?"

"A parka maybe?" Brendan had brightened.

"Not a parka, you idiot, not for a big party in their house, a smart dark jacket, navy maybe, and light blue trousers. Sure you'll have them hanging on to you at the next dance you go to here."

His uncle had given him folding money. It was a sacred trust to buy something smart to wear. He had written to Anna, telling her how much he had to spend. He had hoped she wouldn't make fun of him, but he had wronged her even to suspect she might do such a thing.

Her letter was enthusiastic and grateful. She told him that Marks or C and A or any High Street store would have a bewildering selection and that she was touched and pleased that he was going to so much trouble. She wrote that she herself was going to wear a dress and jacket in navy and white with awful bits of lace trimming on both, because she thought it would please Mother; it looked what Mother called dressy and Anna called yucky, but it was Mother's day. Anna wrote how she had told Helen that since Vatican Two nobody ex-

pected nuns to arrive in places dressed in sackcloth and ashes, but of course, Helen would suit herself, as always.

Maureen Barry came out of Selfridge's and thought she saw Desmond and Deirdre's son, Brendan, walking down Oxford Street with a huge Marks and Spencer's bag as if he had bought half the shop.

But she decided that this was ridiculous. There were twelve million people in London, why should she see a member of the family she was thinking about?

And for all she knew, the boy might still be in the West of Ireland, there had been some kind of coldness. Her mother had told her that not long before she died. She said that Eileen O'Hagan had said that there had been some great cover-up, but the facts were that the son of Deirdre and Desmond had run away, and run of all places back to the very townland his father managed to escape from. The same place that Frank had run from. Maureen told herself to be reasonable. Even if the boy was in London, he would surely be out in Pinner, helping to set up tables for the function. She must stop being fanciful and thinking she had this town down to size as she did Dublin. Only that morning at the hotel she had thought she saw Deirdre's mother, in the distance across the dining room; in fact, it had been so like her she was nearly going across to say hello, but the woman had been joined by a flashy-looking man wearing a blazer with a big crest of some sort. Perhaps it was the sign that she needed glasses. She smiled, remembering how they had all told each other years ago when coming to work in London that they should get false teeth and eyeglasses on the National Health, it had seemed a scream to need either.

It was good to be back in London again, Maureen

thought, she had a spring in her step and three credit cards in her wallet. She was merely going on a recce, as the film people called it, a little prowl examining the style in other people's boutiques and in the big fashion stores. And if she wanted to, she could stop and buy herself any treat she wanted. She walked in a cloud of the expensive perfume she had just bought in Selfridge's, she had bought her father a jaunty cravat there, too. He would look well in that, and he would like the fact that she had thought him a cravat man.

Helen Doyle sat in the kitchen of St. Martin's with both her hands around the mug of coffee as if to get some warmth from it. It was not a cold morning, but not even the bright shafts of sunlight coming in the window seemed to warm her. Across the table sat Sister Brigid, the others had gone. They must have known that the confrontation was coming, they had either gone back to their rooms or gone about their business.

A yellow cat with a broken paw looked trustingly up at Helen. She had found it and made a sort of splint which helped it to walk. The others said she should take it to the cats' home, but this would be curtains for the yellow cat, Helen said. It wouldn't eat much, they could mind it surely.

It was just one more sign of Helen around the house, and another chore. It would be impossible to expect Helen to feed or clean up after the cat *all* the time. The cat began a very loud purring and arched its back to be stroked. Tenderly Sister Brigid lifted it up and carried it out to the garden. She came back and sat beside Helen. She looked straight into the troubled eyes and spoke.

"You have so much love and goodness to give," she began. "But this is not the place."

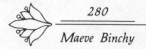

She saw the lip, the lower lip that Helen had been biting nervously, begin to tremble. And the big eyes fill with tears.

"You're sending me away," Helen began.

"We could sit here all morning, Helen, you could call it one thing, I could call it another. I could say that you must find yourself and what you are looking for in some other surroundings, you will say that I am throwing you out, turning you away from St. Martin's."

"What did I do this time?" Helen looked piteous. "Was it the cat?"

"Of course, it wasn't the cat, Helen, there's no one thing, one incident. Please know that . . . could you *try* to understand that it's not a punishment, not an exam where you pass or fail? It's a choice and this house is our life, we chose it and we have to choose how it will be shared."

"You don't want me, you've all decided at a meeting, is that it?"

"No, it's not it, there was no court passing sentence on you. When you came here in the first place, it was on the understanding that—"

Helen interrupted hotly. "In the old days nuns couldn't pick and choose who they had with them, if you didn't like another member of the community, that was hard luck, you had to offer it up, it was part of the sacrifice—"

"Nobody dislikes you . . ." Sister Brigid began.

"But even if they did, in the old days it wouldn't have been a matter of a popularity contest like it is now."

"If there were a popularity contest, there are many ways you'd come out on top. And anyway, when we look back on the old days, they were bad old days, in the very old days girls could be thrown into convents literally if they were wild or disappointed in love or something. That was a fine way to build a community." Brigid was firm.

"That didn't happen to me, nobody forced me; in fact, they tried to keep me back with them."

"That's why I'm speaking to you today." Brigid was gentle. "Today no false optimism about when you will take your vows. Because you won't, Helen, not here with us. It would be unfair for me as head of this house to let you go to a family celebration in the belief that you were well on the way toward being a nun in our order. One day you will thank me from the bottom of your heart. Today I wanted you to look at your family with different eyes, look at the other options. . . ."

"You mean I'm out today. I can't come back here tonight!" Helen was stricken.

"Don't be so dramatic. . . ."

"But when? If you're giving me notice, when do you want my room?" Helen was hurt and bitter.

"I thought that if you could think for a while, don't do any more work, just think, take stock of yourself, and what you might want to do . . ."

"When?" Helen repeated.

"Christmas seems a good time." Brigid was firm. "Say two or three months. You should know by Christmas."

Frank and Renata Quigley planned the day ahead.

"Will I dress up or down?" Renata asked.

"Up as high as you can go." He smiled.

"But that wouldn't be considered . . . I don't know . . . showing off a bit?" Renata was doubtful.

"Oh, you couldn't please Desmond's wife. If you're too casual, you didn't make the effort, if you do make the effort, you're overdressed. . . ."

"So?"

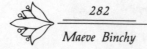

"So let her have something she'll be glad to have in the photographs. The woman's a monster for snapping this and that. Every time someone farts it's recorded in that place."

"Frank, really!"

"No, you don't know what they're like. Seriously, though, their place is coming down with framed photographs. I remember a wall full of them at least."

"That's nice in a way."

"Yes, it would be if there was anything to remember. Anything to celebrate."

"But you were friends, why do you talk like this?"

"I was friends with Desmond, never with Deirdre, anyway. She resented me being free, she was afraid—rightly, I think—that poor old Desmond would feel tied down by comparison. Still, we'll dress ourselves up to the nines and dazzle their eyes out."

She smiled back at him. Frank was so cheerful these days, since they had come to so many decisions. There was the expansion of the business. It was going ahead up north, and it did not mean, as Renata had feared, that Frank would be away a lot. No, he hardly ever traveled there, her father and uncle did, and of course, Mrs. East had been very much part of it. Even with the baby boy, she seemed to thrive on work. Some women were able to do everything, Renata thought sadly.

Still, things were good nowadays, and this morning she was going to get injections and vaccinations, shots needed for the journey. Frank would go to work, as he did almost every Saturday; he said it was so quiet in the big Palazzo building that he could dictate peacefully and get more done in an hour than he normally did in a week of ordinary days. She reminded him to get a haircut. He was looking a bit shaggy around the neck.

Frank didn't need to be reminded, he would go to Larry and have hot towels as well as a trim. He would wear his best suit and the new shirt. If Maureen Barry was going to look at him, she would admire what she saw. That was why he had asked his wife to dress up, too. When Renata had the full works, she looked very good. Maureen Barry would not be able to say that the man she rejected had to marry a colorless mouse with money.

Father Hurley had a great place to stay when he came to London; he always described it as a cross between a luxury hotel and a gentlemen's club. It was, in fact, a religious house, a simple place now where they rented most of their high-ceilinged rooms as office space. Once these had been parlors with polished tables holding copies of *Missionary Annals.* It was an oasis to come back to after a day in such a big, noisy city. Father Hurley found the morning a little overtiring, it was good to know that he could come back to this house and have a rest.

His friend Daniel Hayes was principal, a soft-spoken man who seemed to understand a great deal without having to have things explained in words. He had known last night when he asked after Father Hurley's nephew that this was not an avenue to travel any farther. Diplomatically and with the polished ease of years Father Hayes slipped to another topic. Father Hayes also seemed to know that his old friend James Hurley was somehow uneasy about the silver wedding he was going to attend.

"I can tell you, Daniel, you don't know them from a hole in the ground, a nice young pair, she a real product of upper-class Dublin . . . though we didn't know the phrase then. He was a bit of a rough diamond from the West of Ireland

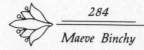

without a penny to bless himself. Anyway, the usual story, and she was well and truly pregnant, and I knew the family— *her* family, that is—and could I marry them in a flash?"

"And you did?" Father Hayes prompted.

"Well, I did, of course, what else did we do in those days? Cover the shame, hide the sin, get the thing regularized as soon as possible. . . ."

"And did it not work out . . . they are still together?"

"I know, Daniel, it's just that there's something odd there. Firstly they didn't have a child."

"What?"

"Oh, they did later, three of them. But not at the time. They sort of played at being married, pretended it . . . as if they were taking parts in a play. . . . Right, Desmond will play the husband and Deirdre will play the wife."

"I expect a lot of people do that."

"Yes, I expect they do, and there're ways in which we're playing at being priests. But do you know what I mean? As if the whole thing didn't ring true. Like Deirdre sending me a picture of them all on a picnic or somewhere, blinking into the light, as if she had to prove it to people."

"Prove what?"

"Lord, I don't know, that they were a normal family or something."

"They might be just very unhappy," Daniel Hayes said. "A lot of people are, seriously. They go into these marriages with such ridiculous expectations. I never thought that all the celibacy bit seemed too much of a hardship to me. . . ."

"Me neither," Father Hurley agreed. His face was sad.

"Of course, when it does work, it must be the greatest thing in the world, a friendship so real and true you'd trust the other with your life. . . . We never had that, James."

"No, indeed." Father Hurley still seemed down.

"But your sister had it, didn't she? I remember your telling me that you thought she had a totally good relationship, that they seemed to know each what the other was about to say and then smiled when they said it."

"True, but their life hasn't been easy—"

Father Hayes interrupted him. "Of course not, but it's only that kind of relationship we're talking about. . . . It would surely buoy them up when things were bleak. You don't see anything like that in this wedding you're going to in Pinner."

Father Hurley had been successfully diverted. "No, it's going to be a lot of empty phrases, like it was a quarter of a century ago."

"Ah, that's what we're here for, James." His friend laughed. "If the priests can't put a bit of conviction into meaningless, comforting phrases, then I ask you . . . who can?"

The caterers arrived at three o'clock. It had all been arranged weeks ago. But Philippa of Philippa's Catering knew a fusser when she saw one, and Mrs. Doyle had all the characteristics of someone who could raise a class-A fuss. There were to be canapés and drinks for an hour or so; then the party would proceed to a Roman Catholic church, where there would be a Mass, and the Doyles would say aloud that they renewed their marriage vows. Then, pink and triumphant, they would return to Rosemary Drive, it would now be heading for seven, there would be more drinks, and the guests would be asked to help themselves to a cold buffet—salmon and cold chicken in a curry mayonnaise. There would be warm herb bread with it. Philippa, having seen the size of the house and the smallness of the oven, had advised against hot food, she had convinced

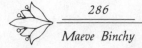
Mrs. Doyle that people would most certainly think it was a *real* meal even if it was cold and there were no potatoes.

As Philippa unloaded crates from her van and set up her center of operations in the Doyles' small kitchen, she hoped that someone might have been detailed to distract this woman with the freshly done hair and the obviously new manicure who held her hands awkwardly as if the varnish would chip.

Mercifully a daughter arrived, a sensible-looking girl, dark and intelligent. She was carrying her own outfit on a hanger. Through the kitchen window Philippa had seen her thanking a man who had driven her. The girl had leaned back into the car and kissed him. Philippa liked to see something like that, it made a change in the highly tense homes she often found herself working in.

Still, if it weren't for the weddings, the bar mitzvahs, the silver weddings, the retirement parties, where would her business be? She thought that Mrs. Doyle and her husband must both be barking mad to go back into a church and say publicly that they were still married. As if it weren't obvious. As if anyone else would have either of them! However, question it not, just keep unpacking, get the table decoration started, and maybe send in a tray of tea to the bedroom so that the mother and daughter could be kept up there.

"You look absolutely beautiful, Mother," Anna said. "You haven't a line on your face, did you know that? You're like a young girl."

Deirdre was pleased. "Oh, stop it now, you're going too far."

"I mean it. And isn't your hair great! Very elegant in all those swoops."

Deirdre looked at her daughter's short, dark, shiny head of hair.

"Of course, if *you* went to the hairdresser a bit . . . just now and then for a nice set . . . you'd look very much better. I know it's smart nowadays to wash your hair every day in the shower. . . ." Deirdre was trying to be helpful.

"I know, Mother. . . . Oh, look, isn't this marvelous, a pot of tea . . . brought to us on a tray! *This* is the life, isn't it?"

Deirdre frowned. "I wish your father was back, he's going to be running late. I don't know what he had to go down to Patel's for. . . ."

"It's not Patel's, it's the Rosemary Central Stores, Mother, *and* Dad is the joint owner, *and* Saturday is very busy, so obviously he's going to help Suresh *and* he'll be back in plenty of time. You know Dad."

"What time's Brendan coming?"

"He should be here anytime. He was looking around a bit, he said he didn't want to come too early and be in the way."

"Lord, wouldn't you think he'd come . . ."

"And of course, he'll be here tomorrow and the next day and the next."

"And why he couldn't stay in his own home . . ."

"Mother, Brendan's back now, isn't that what we all hoped? He's staying with me because it's easier, handier. He's going to be here every day seeing you."

"His father could easily have moved all those boxes and files from his room."

"It's not *his* room anymore, no more than *my* room is mine, it'd be pointless having them waiting for us, much better letting them be offices and for filing and everything."

"Helen's room is still there, and she's off in a convent."

"It's always wise to give Helen somewhere to lay her head, you never know when she'll need it." Anna sounded resigned.

"Will I change now, do you think?"

"Why don't you wait a little bit longer, Mother? We'll get hot and sweaty if we get into our finery too soon."

"I hope it's going to be all right."

"It's going to be magnificent. Everyone you want is coming to it . . . we don't have to raise a finger . . . they'll all be as impressed as hell."

"Not that we're trying to impress anyone," Deirdre said firmly to her daughter.

"No, indeed, what would be the point?" Anna asked, wondering if her mother could be serious. What was this about if it wasn't to wipe eyes around the place, show Grandmother O'Hagan what style they lived in, let Maureen Barry know that life in Pinner was full of sociability, point out to Frank Quigley that though Desmond hadn't married the boss's daughter, he had still done well for himself. Show Father Hurley what a good, strong Catholic way of life went on in what he probably thought of as Heathen England. Let the neighbors see what a team they could field, thirty people, and caterers, and speeches and a good non-vintage champagne for the toasts. What was all that if it wasn't intended to impress?

When they heard the commotion downstairs of someone beating on the side door and voices being raised, they knew Helen had arrived. She didn't want to come in the front door to inconvenience people, so she had been trying to push open the side door, and because boxes of wine were against it, she had been having difficulties. She was handed a cup of tea very briskly by Philippa of Philippa's Caterers and pointed upstairs.

Helen came into the room. They knew by the droop of her shoulders that something was wrong. Anna hoped that they might get away without discussing it.

"Doesn't Mother look terrific, Helen?" she cried.

"Great," Helen said dutifully and absently.

"And Brendan's going to be here any moment."

"Is he staying here?" Helen asked.

"No, we . . . er . . . thought it would be . . . more suitable if he stayed at my place. He's there now changing, I left the key for him under a plant pot. More suitable, more central, closer to things."

"What things?" asked Helen.

"Any things." Anna gritted her teeth.

"So he's not sleeping here tonight?"

"No, he wouldn't even consider . . ." Deirdre was beginning.

"Anyway, his room is an office for Dad now, so . . ."

"Is my room an office for Dad?" Helen asked.

"No, of course not. Why do you ask?"

"I thought I might sleep here tonight," Helen said. "If it's no trouble, that is."

Anna held her breath. She didn't trust herself to speak. So Helen had decided to leave her convent. And she chose now to tell everyone. *Now,* one hour before Mother's and Father's silver wedding party. Anna fixed her eyes on the two dressing gowns that hung on the back of the door. Father's had a long cord. Perhaps Anna could take this and strangle Helen, or would that in the long run mean further disruption? It was hard to know.

She was saved from having to work it out because Brendan had arrived. He ran lightly up the stairs, and his mother and sisters ran to meet him. He looked tanned and well, they thought, and handsome, too, in a smart navy jacket, a sparklingly white shirt, and a tie with a discreet design on it.

"I got silver colors in the tie, I thought it would be suitable," he said.

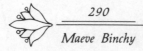

Deirdre Doyle looked at her only son with pride. There would be no need to apologize for Brendan today nor explain him away. Whatever kind of life he was leading in that backwoods, at least he had dressed up today, when it mattered. And he was going to be pleasant to people, not hanging back and muttering. She would not have dared to hope for this much.

Desmond came back in plenty of time to wash and change, and at five minutes before the official starting time Philippa was able to pronounce that they all looked magnificent and that everything was under control.

More and more in her business she felt it was a matter of calming down the hostess and family just as much as preparing a good menu and serving it well.

They stood in their sitting room. The doors to the garden were open, they were ready. With as little comment as possible Anna had found an outfit to suit Helen among their mother's clothes. It was a simple green skirt and a long creamcolored overblouse. It was simple enough to have been the nunnish kind of clothes she wore . . . if she wanted it to be. But also it was perfectly adequate as lay clothes, too, if that was the route she chose.

Any moment now the guests would arrive. The Doyles had refused a drink from Philippa, saying that they would need to keep their heads clear.

Philippa noticed that there were no private moments between them. They didn't squeeze each other's hands and say: "Fancy, a silver wedding!" They didn't seem excited in themselves over the event, only that it was being marked.

The first to arrive was Grandmother O'Hagan. Deirdre's eyes raked the taxi to see if she would be followed by Tony. But mercifully Mother had decided to come unaccompanied. And just as she was being ushered in, Frank and Renata's car pulled up. The florist's van arrived with a huge floral arrangement from Carlo and Maria with many, many regrets and warmest wishes on a wonderful family occasion. It had been arranged the previous day by Frank Quigley's secretary, who had also left a message with Carlo Palazzo's office noting that it had been done.

And when the Wests next door had peered out and seen the place filling up, they arrived, and they were followed by Father Hurley, who had been driven there by his friend Father Hayes.

"Won't Father Hayes come in, too, and have a drink?" Deirdre Doyle had said. You couldn't have too many priests at something like this.

Father Hayes was tempted just to a sherry, he said it was wonderful in this world where so many people took marriage so lightly to find a couple whose love had survived for so long.

"Well, yes." Deirdre had been pleased by the compliment, if somewhat startled by the way it was expressed.

At that moment Maureen Barry arrived.

She must have left her taxi at the corner of Rosemary Drive, she walked easily through the gate and up the little path to the door. The guests were both in and outside the house, it was one of those warm autumn evenings that made it not totally ridiculous to be in the open air.

Maureen seemed to expect all eyes to be on her, yet there was nothing vain or coquettish about the way she came in.

She wore a lemon-colored silk suit, with a lemon and black scarf. She was slim and tall, and her black hair shone as if it were an advertisement for shampoo. Her smile was bright and confident, as she turned with excitement from one to another.

She said all the right things and few of the things that

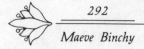

were in her mind. Yes, that was Brendan she had seen this morning struggling with a big green Marks and Spencer's bag. Obviously the outfit he was wearing now. Perfectly adequate, but think what a big, handsome boy could look like if he had been dressed by a tailor.

Yes, amazingly it *had* been Deirdre's mother that she had seen that morning at breakfast with the rather over-obvious-looking man. Was it possible that the great and esteemed Eileen O'Hagan was having a relationship? How her father would enjoy hearing of that, when she went to Ascot to see him tomorrow.

She kissed her friend Deirdre and exclaimed with pleasure over the wonderful dress. In her heart she wondered how Deirdre could have fallen for the obvious-looking lilac, the matronly garment with the self-color embroidery at the shoulder. It was a pastel Mother of the Bride outfit. Deirdre deserved better, she could have looked so good. *And* the dress had probably cost a fortune as well.

The Doyle girls didn't look smart either. Helen seemed to be wearing a blouse and skirt, perhaps that was the nearest that the order could come to letting her wear home clothes. Anna, who was quite striking if she had just left herself alone, was wearing a very tarty-looking navy and white outfit: everywhere there could be a white frill there was one, at the neck, on the hem, at the wrists. It was like a child's party frock.

And Frank.

"How well you look, Frank, it must be years and years," she said.

"But it's impossible that for you time has stood still," he said, mocking her tones by imitating her, very slightly.

Her eyes hardened.

"Renata, this is Maureen Barry, she and I played maid of

honor and best man at the great occasion twenty-five years ago. Maureen, this is Renata, my wife."

"I'm delighted to meet you."

The two women took in each other's clothes at a glance.

Maureen saw a girl with a nondescript face and well-cut designer garments, carefully made up and wearing discreet jewelry. If that gold chain was what she thought it was, Renata Quigley was wearing the price of several houses in Rosemary Drive around her neck.

"Frank tells me you are a very successful businesswoman, and you have high-fashion shops." Renata spoke as if she had learned a little speech. Her accent was attractive.

"He's building me up a bit too much, Renata, two small outlets, but I am thinking of opening up over here. Not in London, more out Berkshire way."

"I was sorry to hear that your mother died," Frank said. He lowered his voice suitably.

"Yes, it was sad, she was very lively and opinionated always, she could have had many more years. Like Mrs. O'Hagan over there." Maureen nodded in the direction of Deirdre's mother, who was holding forth in a corner.

Renata had moved slightly away to talk to Desmond and Father Hurley.

"Of course she hated me," Frank said, not letting his eyes leave Maureen's.

"Who? I beg your pardon?"

"Your mother. She hated me. You know that, Maureen." His eyes were hard now. As hers had been.

"No, I think you're quite wrong, she never hated you. She spoke very well of you always, she said you were very nice, that one time she met you. I remember her standing in the morning room at home and saying, 'He's a very nice boy, Maureen.' " As Maureen spoke, she re-created her mother's

little laugh, the unkind dismissal, the sense of amused wonder.

It was the most cruel thing she could have done.

But he was asking for it, arrogant, handsome, and powerful, playing with people's lives and planning what they would buy and where they would buy it.

"You didn't marry?" he asked. "There wasn't anyone you could marry?"

"Not anyone I did marry, no."

"But you were tempted, perhaps a little here and there . . ." His eyes still held hers. They hadn't faltered under her sarcasm, her reproducing her mother's deadly voice.

"Oh, Frank, of course, I've been tempted here and there, like all businesspeople are. That has nothing to do with being married. I'm quite sure you have found the same in your life. I'd be *very* surprised if you didn't. But to marry and settle down, there has to be a reason for that."

"Love maybe, or attraction even?"

"Not enough, I think. Something more prosaic like—" She looked around and her glance fell on Deirdre. "Like being pregnant maybe, or else—" She looked around the room again and stopped when she was looking at Renata.

But she wasn't quick enough. Frank said it first.

"Like money?" he said blandly.

"Exactly," she said.

"Not very good reasons, either of them."

"Well, certainly not the pregnancy one. Even more especially when it turns out not to have been a real one."

"Did you ever find out what happened?" Frank asked.

Maureen shrugged. "Lord, I wasn't even told that there was any question of it in the first place, so I wouldn't be told that the danger had passed or whatever."

"I think she had a miscarriage," Frank said.

"Did Desmond tell you that?" She was surprised.

"Not a bit of it, but it was their first Christmas in London, and I was in a bit of a bad way, a bit letdown and feeling very lost. I asked could I spend Christmas with them. The excuse was Deirdre wasn't well. She looked bad, too. I think that's what it was."

He sounded much more human, her eyes had softened, and she felt his had, too.

"What bad luck to tie themselves into all this, for nothing, over a false alarm," she said.

"They may like it, the children could be some consolation," Frank argued.

They were talking like friends now, old friends who hadn't seen each other for a while.

Philippa was relieved when the party began to decamp toward the church. She had no idea and didn't even want to imagine what went on there, but she knew it was some kind of important landmark for them. Not just to serve food and drink but go back to the same kind of church where the whole thing had begun. She shrugged cheerfully as she organized the collection of glasses, the airing of the room. At least this bizarre kind of two-tier arrangement gave them a chance to clear up the hors d'oeuvres part of things and let them lay out the salads without interruption.

The church was at a nice easy walking distance; that was why it had been thought a feasible plan. If they had all to get lifts and taxis and sort out who went with whom, it would have taken forever.

They all knelt in a little group, the thirty people who formed the silver wedding party.

It was a perfectly normal Mass, many of them congratulated themselves that they didn't need to go tomorrow since a

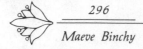

Saturday-evening attendance was sufficient in these liberated days.

Some like Anna who didn't go anyway did not see the great incidental advantage.

Brendan always found Mass a social event back home with Vincent. He didn't think his uncle believed in any kind of God, but he went to Mass on a Sunday as regularly as he would go to get gasoline or to the markets to buy sheep. It was part of the life they lived.

Helen prayed hard at the Mass so that God would tell her what was right. If Sister Brigid said that she was running away, what was it from and which was the right direction if the convent was the wrong one? If she could have some kind of sign. It wasn't much to ask.

Father Hurley asked himself why he felt that this was all some kind of charade, almost a television version of renewal of vows. Any moment now someone would say, "Cut. Can we take that again from the top?" He didn't feel this about any other aspect of his ministry. There was just something he didn't like about a public reiteration of something that was said and meant a long time ago. Yet the faithful were always being asked to renew their baptismal vows, so why did he feel uneasy in this instance?

Frank looked at Maureen in the church and thought what a fine-looking woman she was, full of spirit, so like Joy East in many ways. He thought briefly of Joy and of his son, who was called Alexander. The son he would never get to know.

It had been thought inappropriate to take pictures at the church. It wasn't as if it were a real wedding, they would look a little ancient to be photographed, Deirdre tittered, hoping that someone would disagree with her.

Maureen did, strongly.

"Come on now, Deirdre, I still have to take the plunge,

and when I do, I'll want banks of photographers outside," she said.

"And after all, people get married at *any* age, any age at all," Deirdre's mother said, which caused Deirdre's heart to lurch a little.

"And with the way the Church is going, maybe even the clergy will get married, Mother, and Father Hurley will be coming down the aisle in a morning suit," Helen said.

They laughed at that, particularly Father Hurley, who was rueful and said that even if he was forty years younger, he wouldn't be able to take on such an undertaking.

And soon they were back in Salthill, 26 Rosemary Drive. The neighbors who had not been invited waved and called out greetings, the lights were on, and soon the supper was under way.

"There's a lot of conversation, like at a real party," Deirdre said to Desmond almost in disbelief.

Her face was flushed and anxious, her hair had fallen from its hard lacquered layers and seemed softer somehow. There were beads of perspiration on her forehead and upper lip.

He felt strangely touched by her anxiety.

"Well, it *is* a real party," he said, and he touched her face gently with his hand.

It was an unfamiliar gesture, but she didn't draw back, she smiled at him.

"I suppose it is," she agreed.

"And your mother is getting on well with everyone," he said encouragingly.

"Yes, yes, she is."

"Brendan's looking in fine shape, isn't he? He said he'd be very interested in coming down to the Rosemary Central Stores tomorrow morning to see how it operates."

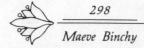
She was surprised. "He's going to come the whole way across from Shepherd's Bush early in the morning when he could have stayed here in his own room?" She was still peeved that he wouldn't stay.

"It's not his own room, Deirdre, it's the office."

"There'd have been room for him," she said.

"Yes, and he will stay sometime. But as a visitor."

"As part of the family," she corrected him.

"As a visiting part of the family," he corrected her back.

It was gentle. But the Desmond Doyle of a few months back would not have done it. He would have been too anxious, too willing to play the parlor game of lies, backing up whatever story Deirdre told her mother and Maureen Barry about his mythical prowess at Palazzo, trying all the while to engineer these conversations out of the hearing of Frank or Renata, who would know them to be untrue.

How restful it was at last for Desmond Doyle to have his own position, his own place. To be for the first time his own person, not Palazzo's person. It gave him by a grim irony the kind of confidence which his wife had always wanted to see in him, but which would have forever escaped him in Palazzo land.

"Mother is actually talking normally to Dad," Brendan whispered to Anna at the other side of the room. "Does this happen often?"

"Never saw it happen before," she said. "I don't want to take away from your sense of well-being, but I do think that you have captured a very rare sighting, make the most of it."

And indeed, as they looked, the little tableau broke up. One of the caterers was speaking to Mother, there was a slight problem in the kitchen.

"It's bound to be Helen," Anna said sadly. And it was.

Helen was all for putting candles on the gateau, she had

bought twenty-five of them and had rooted through the bottom of the cupboard to find old cake tins holding the plastic candle holders. She could find only fourteen. She could not think why.

"Probably because that would be the age at which normal people wouldn't really want any more," Anna said crisply. "All right, Mother, go back to the guests. I'll cope with it."

"It's not a question of coping with it." Helen was hurt and angry now. "I was just making a little gesture so that we could be festive."

Philippa of Philippa's Caterers said that the written agreement had been a gateau, with toasted almonds to be applied at the last moment to the cream topping, the toasted almonds to read: "Desmond and Deirdre October 1960."

"I think it *is* better like that, Helen, don't you?" Anna spoke as she might have spoken to a dog that was foaming at the mouth or a four-year old who was severely retarded. Ken Green said he spent a lot of his life speaking to people like this; it got you a reputation for being very patient, slightly thick, and a person who could be relied on in any crisis. Anna remembered that Ken always said that the more enraged he was, the more slowly he spoke.

"Don't you think we should leave the caterers to it, Helen?" Anna said, enunciating every word very clearly and slowly.

"Oh, piss off, Anna, you're a pain in the arse," Helen said.

Anna decided that they were definitely coming to the end of Helen's term of life in a religious order.

Helen had flounced out into the garden.

"Shall I go after her?" asked Philippa, the caterer.

"No, she's probably safer out there, there's no one she

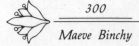

can insult beyond reprieve, and not too much she can break." Anna thought that Ken would be proud of her and wondered why she was thinking of him so much anyway.

Helen sat and hugged her knees in the garden where she had sat, misunderstood and thinking herself unloved, all the years of her childhood. She heard footsteps behind her. Anna no doubt asking her to come in and not to make a scene, Mother telling her not to sit on damp stone, Grandmother O'Hagan about to ask when she was ever going to be professed. She looked up. It was Frank Quigley.

A terror seized her throat, and she felt a momentary light-headedness. It was of course impossible that he was going to touch her, molest her in her parents' home.

But he looked so menacing in the dark.

"I heard from your father that you're thinking of leaving St. Martin's," he said.

"Yes. They want me to go, they threw me out."

"I'm sure that's not true."

"Sister Brigid says the others don't want me." She realized as she spoke that she sounded like a child of five years of age with her thumb in her mouth.

"Sister Brigid is far too fond of you to think that, let alone say it."

"How do you know? You saw her only that night, that awful night." Helen's eyes had become as big as dinner plates. The memory of the time she had tried to steal a baby for Frank and Renata Quigley, the night that had turned out so badly, and when the real descent had begun in St. Martin's.

"No, Helen, I've met Sister Brigid many times since then," Frank said. "We didn't speak of you much, we had other things to talk about. . . . She was giving me advice. She gave me very good helpful advice, I have you to thank for that."

"I meant well that night, I really thought it would have suited everyone."

"It might have, you know, but we couldn't do it that way, always running, always hiding, always pretending. That's not the way to live."

"That's the way I've always lived." Helen sounded rebellious and defensive.

"No, no, it isn't."

"In this house we always pretended, we still are tonight."

"Shush," he said soothingly.

"How did you learn to be so upright and not to have to act like the rest of us?"

"I'm not upright. You of all people should know that." Frank spoke seriously. "I have done things I am ashamed of, one of them with you. I am very, very ashamed of that."

For the first time since that day in his apartment Helen Doyle looked Frank Quigley in the eyes. For the first time for many years in any encounter she said absolutely nothing.

"I was always hoping that you would meet somebody nice and somebody young and tender, someone who would put that strange sad day into some kind of perspective for you. Show you that while it was important in one way, in many others it was not important at all."

Still, Helen said nothing.

"So I supposed I was sorry when you went into St. Martin's, because I always thought then that what happened might appear magnified."

"I never thought about it again," Helen said. She looked at him as she told him the lie, her eyes confident and her head held high.

He knew she was lying, but it was important that she didn't realize.

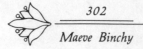
"That is so much the right way to be, and it certainly puts me in my place."

He smiled at her. Ruefully, admiringly. He got it just right. And he could see she was beginning to feel better.

"So what will you do when you do leave, if you're going to?"

"I'll leave. I don't know yet. Maybe I need time to think."

"Is this the place to do your thinking?" He looked uncertainly up at Salthill, 26 Rosemary Drive.

"Maybe not."

"Maybe you should go away, right away from London. You're good with children, Brigid tells me, very good."

"Yes, I like them. Certainly. They don't get as upset as adults."

"Could you mind one? For a year or two while you're thinking?"

"Do you know one?"

They seemed to talk as equals, her fear of him fell away.

"I do, his name is Alexander. I don't know him, but I know his mother. However, she and I had a fight, and she doesn't like me; if I suggested you, she would say no. If she were to advertise and, say, if you were to apply . . ."

"Wouldn't it be too much of a coincidence?"

"No, we can do it through Carlo. She asks Carlo about a nanny. Carlo says the daughter of one of his ex-managers, she knew your father."

"Is it Miss East?"

"Yes."

"What did you fight about?"

"This and that."

"Is Alexander nice?"

"I don't know, Helen."

"But you'd like to know?" She seemed to have grown up in minutes.

"I'd love to know."

"Fine," said Helen Doyle. "I have to do my thinking somewhere, it might as well be with Alexander East."

The cake was produced and cut. And when everybody had a slice of rich gateau on a plate, Desmond tapped on a glass and said that Frank Quigley, who had done the honors so well a quarter of a century ago, was going to say a few words.

Frank stood forward, he said that it was a great happiness and a great honor to be asked to speak. He made it seem both. Those who listened felt for a moment that he was lucky to have been invited.

He said that he remembered the day when Deirdre, looking roughly the same as she did tonight, had made this commitment; she was young and beautiful, she had her life ahead of her, there were many decisions to make, many paths to choose. She had chosen Desmond Doyle. Smoothly he brought them from the marriage through the early days of Palazzo, to the joys of children, to their luck in each and all of these children, a daughter rising high in the book trade— Palazzo had tried to poach her, but with no success. Another daughter giving her entire life to looking after people, and a son with a love of the land. These were three rich rewards for Deirdre and Desmond to look at and see their hopes realized.

He himself had not been so fortunate in the early days, he hadn't met anyone he loved until later on in life. His gaze passed gently over Maureen, standing cool and admiring in her lemon silk dress. But then he, too, had known the happiness of married life, though unfortunately, unlike Desmond, he had not been given the joy of fathering three fine children. But his heart was happy tonight and in no sense tinged with

the envy that it might have held over the years. At the weekend he and Renata were going to Brazil, where a legal adoption had been arranged and where they were going to take home with them and give a home to a girl called Paulette. She was eight months old. Nuns had arranged the papers. She would be very much younger than his friend Desmond's children, but he hoped that the friendship would be there always, as his had been. A lifelong friendship, he said. Some things never change.

It had been masterly, there were a few tears brushed away, and the champagne glasses were raised.

Everyone was touched by Frank. Every person in the room.

Even Maureen Barry.

"My God, you are one performer," she said to him admiringly.

"Thank you, Maureen." He was gallant and suave.

"No, I mean it. You always were. You didn't have to try so hard, just to prove my mother wrong, to prove me wrong."

"But your mother loved me, she said I was a very nice young man." He put on her mother's voice. It was a good imitation.

"I'm glad about the child," she said.

"Yes, so are we."

"And will I see you all when I open my shop in England?"

"It will be a time before Paulette will be old enough for your clothes."

"Oddly enough, I'm having a children's boutique, too."

"Well then." His smile was warm. But not warm enough.

Maureen thought she would discuss it with her father. The old rascal was full of advice. She wasn't going to let drop a prize like this again.

Father Hurley said he wanted to use the phone, but there appeared to be a line. Anna was speaking to someone.

"Sure, come around," she was saying. "Listen to me, Ken Green, this is 1985, we are all free to make our own choices. My choice is that if you choose to be here, that would be great." There was a pause.

"And I love you, too," she said, hanging up, surprised with herself.

Deirdre's mother was on the phone next.

"Yes, Tony, perfectly satisfactory, no opportunity. No, no, not reneging on anything, but you know the whole art of life is knowing the right time to say things. Yes, yes. Nothing changed. Absolutely. Me, too. Lots."

Father Hurley picked up the telephone to tell Father Hayes that he was getting a mini-cab back, he would be sharing it with several others, a large car had been ordered.

Yes, he said, it had been delightful, he just felt he mustn't take up the phone, other people might be telephoning people to say they loved them.

No, he said testily to Father Hayes. He wasn't even remotely drunk, he had just been sitting listening to a woman and her granddaughter talking on the telephone. That was all.

The move to go was general now. But there was a sense of something not quite completed.

Deirdre found the camera. She had new film in it all ready for the occasion, she ran into the kitchen where Philippa's team were busy putting plastic wrap over the leftovers and storing them in the fridge. There would even be things for the freezer.

Deirdre explained how the camera worked, and Philippa listened patiently. It was a characteristic of this kind of woman that she thought her camera was complicated.

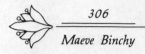

They gathered around the couple in a semicircle. They smiled. The camera flashed and flashed again.

Among the pictures in the roll of twenty-four there would be one which was bound to look good when enlarged, would look just right. There would be the picture of The Silver Wedding on the wall, for everyone to see. Everyone who came to Rosemary Drive from now on.